Simona
TAYLOR

May
Summer
Never End

ARABESQUE®

MAY SUMMER NEVER END

An Arabesque novel

ISBN 1-58314-633-4

www.kimanipress.com

Printed in U.S.A.

For my daughter, Megan Rachel, born on June 13, 2005. My beautiful, dark-eyed angel, may you dream greater dreams than I ever would, soar to greater heights than I ever could and may your life be filled with more breathtaking romance than even I could possibly imagine.

How To Get By in Europe on Just Pennies a Day

The 5:25 local from Montpellier to Perpignan was quiet for a weekday, but even so, Rissa hadn't expected to have an entire carriage all to herself. With two facing *banquettes,* and space on the sides of the seats and in the overhead storage, there was ample room for six people and all their luggage. She didn't need to use that space either, since all she was carrying with her since those wayward college girls had made off with all her valuables was her handbag, a small backpack and her laptop computer. As for the computer, it had probably been spared only because it was a few years out of date, and hardly worth stealing anyway.

Rissa didn't mind the solitude. She was, by nature, a loner. It gave her the opportunity to stare out the window and soak in as much as she could of the scenery flitting by. In spite of her worries, the South of France was, after all, the South of France, and the chance to experience it didn't just come along too often in your lifetime, especially not for people like her.

Although the train was traveling at high speed, there was much to see. The gorgeous Vermillion Coast stretched out for at least a hundred miles, alternating between sharp, rocky cliffs that plunged into the deep blue Mediterranean, vineyards set out in neat, ordered rows, small towns and villages and, occasionally, marinas and holiday campsites hugged by sandy beaches. Once in a while, the train would stop at one of the larger towns, and she would have the added excitement of watching commuters to-ing and fro-ing along the station platforms. It was the height of summer, and apart from the usual business activity, the stations teemed with holiday-travelers, from families hauling vacation gear and harried parents herding wayward children to young backpackers who, like herself, carried all they owned on their shoulders.

The solitude, unfortunately, also gave her plenty of time to ponder upon her present situation. She propped her chin on her hand as the problem that had been nagging her for the past week popped back into her head.

Money.

It was funny how nonchalant you could be when credit cards, travelers' checks and cash were within easy reach, but when you got up one morning and found everything gone except for the handful of euros you had in the back pocket of your jeans, money suddenly became an issue—really fast. And in spite of what the TV commercials claimed, replacing travelers' checks and credit cards wasn't all that easy, especially when things like your passport and driver's license had also been taken. Getting back on her feet would take time, and Rissa was confident enough in the system to know that things would eventually work out…but in the meanwhile, she needed to eat.

Money, money, money. She released her frustration in a gusty sigh.

The door to her carriage burst open and a head poked inside. A young, brown-skinned girl, who looked to be in her mid-teens, asked her something in rapid-fire French. Rissa, whose foreign language skills did not extend much further than ordering a cup of coffee at a *café-terrasse,* or inquiring as to the whereabouts of the nearest ladies' room, shook her head. "Sorry. Do you speak English?"

The response was a squeal. "Finally! Another American!" The girl floated in on a cloud of strong perfume, dragging an enormous, expensive designer suitcase behind her, which she immediately dropped on the floor between them and shoved into a corner with a foot before plopping down onto the seat opposite. She grinned at Rissa. "I was only asking if you were planning on hogging this carriage all to yourself, or could I come in."

Since the young lady was already in and well ensconced, Rissa took her inquiry as a rhetorical question. Maybe some company wouldn't be all that bad, she reasoned, especially company who spoke the same language. She smiled. "Make yourself comfortable."

The newcomer didn't need to be invited. She rummaged through her handbag and withdrew an MP3 player and a pair of headphones, which she immediately donned. Sprawling across the seat as only a teenager could, she closed her eyes and was soon nodding in time to the beat of music so loud that, in spite of the headphones, Rissa could identify it from across the carriage as hip-hop.

Rissa took advantage of the interloper's closed eyes to examine her with a writer's innate curiosity. From the close-cropped hair, which was straightened and bleached to a startling platinum blond, to the stretchy purple camisole that most women would have worn as underwear, to the thigh-length denim skirt and brand-name sneakers, the girl looked every inch the trendy American teenager. An array of rings, bracelets, and other adornments—including an amethyst nose ring set in gold—gleamed against her dark skin. She could see the edge of a tattoo peeking saucily out from under the scooped neckline of the camisole.

Her amused smile was upgraded to a grin. At twenty-five, she was sure that there could not even be a decade between her and the girl, but times changed so fast. She always did her best to keep track of what was engaging the interests of young women, especially since she made a living writing for them— or had, anyway, up until now.

One habit that she had picked up in the few years she'd spent writing freelance articles for women's magazines was the ability to pull eye-catching stories out of thin air, like a magician yanking a rabbit out of a hat. It was something she did everywhere, applied to almost every encounter and situation, almost without thinking. She squinted at her new traveling companion.

Hmm.

Hip-hop and hearing loss: is there a connection?
How to choose the nose ring that's right for you.
Makeup: When does "just enough" become "too much"?

"Whatcha looking at?"

The voice made her jump. She hadn't realized that while she had been indulging herself in examining the girl, she had been looking right back at her under those thick lashes. She felt her face flood with heated embarrassment. "Uh, oh, sorry. I didn't mean to stare. I was thinking, uh, like you, how nice it was to meet another American."

The girl accepted her little fib without question. "Yeah. I know what you mean! Nice to hear the native tongue being spoken. Especially coming from somebody who looks like yourself, you know? I mean, there are lots of Africans in the big towns, like Marseille, and a whole lot of folks from Algeria and Morocco, but it's real good to meet an *American* sister. Know what I'm saying?"

Rissa knew exactly what she was saying. Traveling always opened you up to a wide range of cultures and peoples, but there was something warming about meeting one of your own, especially when you were just a bit homesick. She decided that, since it seemed that she and the girl were going to be traveling companions, at least for the next few hours, it would be appropriate to introduce herself properly. She held out her hand. "I'm Nerissa Young."

The girl did likewise. Rissa could feel her many large rings bite into her palm under her surprisingly strong grip. "Frankie Maynard."

An unusual name for an unusual creature, Rissa decided. "Frankie?"

Frankie rolled her eyes. "You don't even want to know what it stands for! Trust me!"

She was really beginning to like this girl. "Frankie it is, then."

Evidently, the connection was mutual. Frankie set her headphones down and came over to sit next to Rissa. Her strikingly clear, honey-colored eyes—although almost obscured by thick clumps of purple mascara—were bright and friendly. "So, what kind of name is Nerissa?"

"It's Indian, after my grandmother."

Her eyes grew even wider. "Indian? No kidding? You mean, like in westerns?"

Rissa shook her head and laughed. "I mean, Indian, as in Mumbai, India. That's where my grandmother was from."

"Oh." She appeared to be processing this information very hard, searching Rissa's face for signs of her mixed heritage, hemming and hawing to herself as she did so. "I can see it! I can see it in your eyes. And you've got this fabulous long black hair. That's not a weave, is it? It's all yours, right?"

"All mine. Home grown." Rissa accepted her scrutiny with good humor, even when Frankie said, "Anybody ever tell you you'd be real pretty if you'd just put a little makeup on?"

Even though her companion's exuberance should have warned her to be prepared for anything, Rissa was a little taken aback by this last comment. "Uh, no. Not that I remember."

Frankie half-reached toward her oversized handbag. "Well, I'm telling you. You want me to make you up?"

Now, that would be taking things too far! Rissa held her hands up in front of her face in a self-protective gesture. "That's okay. I'm fine. Thanks!"

Frankie wasn't giving up so easily. "Sure? I make up all my friends at school."

"Positive."

Frankie tried not to look too disappointed. "Okay, Nerissa. But if you change your mind…."

"I promise I'll let you know," she answered solemnly, although her unspoken addendum to that promise had something to do with weather reports in hell. To soften her refusal, she added, "But call me Rissa. Everyone does."

"Okay. Rissa. I like that even better." Frankie was beaming again. Then a thought bowled her over, and the next thing Rissa knew was that her wrist was being held prisoner in Frankie's excited, sharp-nailed grip. "Rissa! You're Rissa Young! The writer chick!"

Busted, Rissa thought. Obviously, Frankie was one of her readers, something she had hardly expected to come across this far from home. Normally, she preferred to remain under the radar, but since the cat was already well out of the bag, she confessed. "Yes, I am." She tried not to wince when her admission caused Frankie's grip to tighten.

"That's awesome! I adore you! I read all your stuff! Look!" Mercifully, Frankie released her grip on Rissa's arm, leaped up and grabbed her bag, dumping half its contents onto the seat opposite: perfume, CDs, empty water bottle, half-eaten candy bars, a cellular phone, and an assortment of other items, until she retrieved a handful of popular Black women's magazines from the bottom. "You wrote this!" She opened one of them and waved the evidence in front of Rissa's nose, reading the heading aloud as she did so. "*Eleven Good Reasons You Don't Need a Boyfriend.* You wrote that, didn't you?"

"Yup. That was me."

"I loved it! It was *hilarious!*"

Hilarious? Now *that* wasn't an adjective she usually heard applied to her writing. "It wasn't really meant to be funny," she tried to explain, but that was like whispering into a windstorm.

Frankie went on, "I mean, who doesn't need a boyfriend? Men are so awesome. Who'd be crazy enough not to want one?"

Some of us get by, Rissa thought ruefully. *Especially those of us who are so damaged that they aren't even worth the attention of a man in the first place.*

She didn't have time to dwell on such painful thoughts, because Frankie had this advice to give, "You could have stopped at ten reasons, though."

"I *had* eleven," Rissa explained. "So I just went ahead and wrote them all down."

Frankie accepted this without argument. "Oh. Okay." Then, with lightning speed, she changed gears. "I'm hungry. You hungry?"

Starving, Rissa wanted to say. In her penniless state, she'd had to cut down her meals to two a day, and those consisted of fresh baguettes, split with a penknife and wrapped around pieces of French cheese that she bought by the chunk in small corner grocery stores. Apart from the

occasional all-you-can-eat servings of café soup and crou-
tons, anything more than that would have been extravagant.
But she was too embarrassed to admit that, even to someone
as nice as Frankie. So she shook her head. "I'm fine. I had
a big meal before you got on board, a few stations back."

Frankie didn't seem to be buying that. "You sure? Because
the restaurant car's just a few carriages down." She pointed
to her right. "Thataway."

"I'm fine," Rissa repeated firmly. "You go ahead."

She persisted. "I'll buy, if you like. I've got my brother's
credit card. He's *loaded*."

Ah, Rissa thought. Thus the source of all those expensive
accoutrements. A loaded brother was surely a nice thing to
have, especially one who let you use his credit card. But she
couldn't allow anyone to buy her a meal, not like this. Things
might be rough, but they were soon to get better, and at least
she still had her pride. "No, thanks," she said, a little abruptly.
"You go ahead."

Frankie showed no evidence of feeling snubbed. She simply scooped up her wallet, chirped, "Okay, see ya," and left
the carriage.

Alone again, Rissa returned to looking out the window.
From the small, folded railway map in her pocket, she could
tell that they were just a few more stops from Perpignan, a
small town that almost grazed the Spanish border. Therein lay
her last chance at salvaging her trip, earning enough money
to get back on her feet, and, hopefully, enough to buy her a
ticket back home to the States. It was the town on which she
had pinned her last hope, because she wasn't fooling herself;
as much as she was waiting patiently on her credit cards and
other financial documents to be replaced, there wasn't that
much left in any of her accounts Stateside, either.

Major surgery laid waste to anyone's nest egg. Her hand

went unguided to the lower curve of her tummy, where, just under the waistband of her jeans, a small, horizontal scar lay. A couple of inches of pale, just-healed skin was the only evidence left of the vicious disease and the devastating surgical solution that had robbed her of any hope of ever bearing a child. But as crushed as she had been by her diagnosis, it had only brought her news that she had feared and anticipated since her early teens, when she had watched the cancer take first her mother, then her aunt, and then, more recently, her only sister. Genetics were a dice shoot, and it seemed that the women in her family had had a few lousy games.

The tears had flowed for a long time after her surgery, and she had wept not just for herself but for the children who would never be anything more than angels resident in her heart, denied the chance to become flesh. The soul-destroying loss left her unable to write, or even think. Soon, the familiar streets of her own neighborhood, its sights and sounds, and the echoing emptiness of her own apartment became too much to bear. Three months after her release from hospital, she broke the lease on her apartment, shot off notifications to the editors of her usual magazines informing them that she was on hiatus, and removed the little that was left of her savings from the bank, pumping all she had into a trip to Europe that she had hoped would bring her the sense of balance that she had lost—or, at least, that the change of scenery would bring distraction from her grief.

It had been working, too, until—

The door barreled open again, and Frankie re-entered with her arms piled so high with packages and containers that she had great difficulty balancing them all. Rissa leaped to help her before the majority of them hit the floor. There were bottles of French spring water, juice and sodas, packages of sandwiches, packets of potato chips and caramel corn, chocolate, and fruit. Rissa couldn't refrain from laughing. "What's all this?"

"Food," Frankie puffed before plopping back down onto her seat.

"I can see that, but you aren't going to eat all that, are you? It would take days."

"It's for you," she responded. "Most of it, anyway. Eat what you like now and take the rest with you."

She'd bought all this for her? Rissa blustered in surprise and embarrassment, "But I told you—"

"I know what you *told* me," Frankie retorted. "But I know what I *see*. And you look hungry." She chose a wrapped sandwich of dried country ham and emmental cheese and handed it over with a bottle of soda. "Here. Eat up."

Rissa had to bite back her embarrassment. It did look good, and she was half-starved. She allowed common sense to prevail, and took the items. "Thank you," she said sincerely.

Frankie tossed her a bag of chips. "Open up the sandwich and empty that right in there. It's delicious." She proceeded to demonstrate with her own sandwich.

Rissa drew the line right there. "I think I'll just have mine straight."

"Suit yourself," she answered through a mouthful of chips and sandwich. When she was able to speak clearly again, she asked, "So, Rissa, where in the States are you from?"

"Philadelphia."

Frankie pumped one hand above her head. "Philly in the house! You know any rappers?"

Rissa shook her head ruefully. "No, sorry. Can't say that I do."

Frankie looked disappointed, but not for long. "We're from San Diego. Me and my brother, Evan. Although he sort of lives here, most of the time, since his wife left him. He's got his business in San Diego, a boat-building business. Pleasure boats. For rich people."

"Uh-huh?" Rissa encouraged between bites.

"Yeah. And I spend most of my time there, in boarding school. He makes me come over to spend every school vacation with him, though, just so he can keep an eye on me." She wrinkled her nose. "He's a real fussbudget. Honestly, like an old lady. 'Where were you? Who're you going to see? What time are you going to be back?'" She rolled her eyes and mimicked. "He seems to think I'm a handful."

"Really?" Rissa tried not to break out in laughter.

"Really. He's boring. Old, old, old, and *boring.* That's why his wife left him. Went and stuck her in this village by the sea just because he wanted to open up another *atelier,* a boat workshop, here, too. When he could have bought a house in Paris, where the action is. Or at least Nice, if had to be near the water *that* badly! You should see the place he's got, way out in the sticks. No night life, if you don't count hanging out in stupid little cafés and watching people wander past. At least his ex-wife knew how to party!"

"So you'd rather be in San Diego?"

"Got that right. Can't wait until I'm eighteen. I can tell you, he won't be dragging me back down here anymore."

"What about your parents?"

The sparkle in Frankie's eyes dimmed so quickly that Rissa immediately wished she hadn't asked the question. Frankie opened her sandwich and examined its contents carefully before answering. "They're gone. It's just Evan and me. We're all we got."

"I'm sorry." Rissa wondered whether *gone* meant that they had died, or that they had left their children to fend for themselves, one way or the other.

Frankie dismissed her condolences with a shake of her head. "It was a long time ago. It's all right. Evan takes care of me okay. And we're not completely alone. There's our grandparents. Grandpapa's French-Caribbean, from Martinique. Married to a Frenchwoman. They live just outside Nice. That's where I'm coming from. Went to stay with her for a few days. Grandmaman always insists."

"Did you enjoy it?"

Frankie shrugged. "It was okay." She steered the conversation away from that topic with, "So, what happened to your money?"

Rissa was taken aback by the suddenness of the question. "Excuse me?"

"Why don't you have any money?" She pointed at Rissa's sole knapsack, sitting forlornly on the floor next to her. "That's all you got, isn't it? And I know you have a good job, so something had to have happened, right? Don't be shy. You can tell me."

After a week of being entirely alone, with nobody to talk to, Rissa's natural reluctance to talk about herself gave way to the need to share her frustration. "I was robbed. I was just leaving Paris when I met these three college girls, and they seemed nice. I guess I needed the company, because by then I had been on my own for weeks. We rode down to Marseille together, and decided it would be more economical to share a suite in a rooming house than pay for individual bedrooms. And it was working out fine, for a while. They partied harder than I do, and didn't seem all that interested in the museums and the sightseeing, but they were friendly and I liked them. And then I don't know what went wrong...."

"They rolled you?" Frankie guessed.

Rissa nodded. "One night we were sharing a bottle of wine and laughing, just four girlfriends, having a good time, and the next morning I woke up and everything was gone. Camera, cash, credit cards, and most of my clothes. Everything."

Under her breath, Frankie hissed a word that a girl of her age had no right using, and then she commiserated, "I'm so sorry for you."

"And they left me with the bill for the room. It wiped me out. I spent the last of my money on that."

"You coulda skipped on the bill," Frankie suggested helpfully. "Wasn't there a back door?"

Rissa smiled at the ludicrous thought. "I couldn't do that. It wouldn't have been right."

Frankie didn't bother to argue. Instead, she asked, "So, you train-hopped down to Montpellier, and now you're going to Perpignan? Why? Why don't you just go home?"

"Can't. They took my return ticket, and when I checked, the airline told me it had been cashed in. I don't have enough to buy a new one. All I really have is my rail pass, and at least that gets me around. I'm going down to Perpignan to a job interview. One of my magazine contacts set me up with an English bookstore there."

"The one downtown? Near the river? Oh, I know it! I shop there all the time!" She pointed at the magazines she had produced earlier. "That's where I got those!"

"Well, the interview's tomorrow, and it looks good. If I earn enough money there over the rest of the summer, I should be able to make it back home." She finished her story in a gust, and then fell silent, winded from the effort of so much self-exposure.

"And where are you sleeping tonight?"

God knows, Rissa thought, but she put on a brave face. "I've been staying at hostels for the last week, and they gave me the names of a few there. So don't worry, it won't be a problem."

Frankie snorted. "Hostels, huh! Those things are awful little flea-bags. Don't tell me you think they're okay!"

"They're not that bad," Rissa defended. "They're simple, but they're clean and fairly safe. I'll manage."

Frankie set her half-eaten sandwich down on her lap and looked determined. "You aren't sleeping in any hostel tonight."

Rissa panicked. "Why not?" She couldn't imagine what

she meant by that. Did Frankie know something she didn't about the hostels at Perpignan? Would they be closed? Full?

"I said you're not sleeping in any ratty old hostel. Because you're coming home with me. Evan won't mind, I promise."

A Man, and His Castle:
How To Get Past the Dragon at the Moat

Rissa was nonplussed. Spend the night at Frankie's house? With an older brother who was cold, strict and humorless? She didn't think so. She cleared her throat. "Frankie," she began.

Frankie smelled a refusal coming and hastened to cut it off before it could become sound. "Don't even! I don't wanna hear it. You're coming home with me, 'cause I said so."

After such a long time fending for herself alone in the country, the generosity in the offer moved her. "You're very kind, Frankie, and I like you a lot. But I don't think your brother would appreciate you bringing home a stranger like that. It's not safe. You don't know me at all!"

"It's my home, too," she retorted. "And you're my friend. I can bring home whoever I want." She thrust out her lower lip like a small child, petulant at being refused something she wanted.

Rissa found that she couldn't chew her sandwich any more. She put hers down as well. "I couldn't, Frankie."

Frankie wasn't taking no for an answer. She whipped out her cellular phone and dialed a number. In a matter of moments, she began prattling in French so convoluted that Rissa had no hope even of following its gist, although the frequent glances in her direction left no doubt that she was at least one of the subjects of the conversation. When she was done. Frankie shut the phone with a click and look satisfied. "He says it's okay. He's sending someone to pick us up. So don't worry about it, okay?"

As Rissa stood on the platform with Frankie, watching their train chug cheerily down the track toward villages like Banyuls and Collioure, she was overwhelmed by a mixture of hope and trepidation. To be truthful, she was surprised that Evan Maynard had given in to Frankie's request. From what she could gather, he was a man of another generation, who had found himself, through whatever circumstances, being a father figure to his baby sister, who was probably the child of their parents' old age. Men who were that set in their ways didn't take kindly to strangers, especially not stranded strangers seeking a place to stay.

It was too late to change her mind and beg off now, anyway, as the long summer day was already beginning to fade. It would soon be dark, and she didn't quite relish the idea of looking for lodging at this hour. At least the Maynards' invitation would offer her a good night's rest in a clean bed, so that she would awaken fresh and ready for her last-ditch interview. If that failed, well...

Ten minutes passed, and then fifteen. The time was amply filled with Frankie's excited prattle, as she commented on people passing by, occasionally sharing a few snippets of gossip about some of the townspeople she recognized. Rissa found that she wasn't expected to add anything more to the conversation than the occasional "Uh-huh," and "Really?" and Frankie was perfectly happy.

Eventually, though, she had to ask, "Who did you say was coming for us?"

"His name's Corbin. He's a local, a Catalan. Wait till you see him. He'll knock your socks off. He's gorgeous!"

"Catalan, huh? He would be cute." She had to admit that she herself had found her eye drawn by the handsome Catalan people, natives of the Catalunya region that straddled the border between the North of Spain and the South of France. They were swarthy and dark-eyed, with sharp cheekbones and strong Hispanic features. Well worth the occasional turned head. "And he's a friend of your brother's?"

"Sort of. His business manager. He's in charge of the *atelier* most of the time, especially when Evan's in the U.S. He said he'd be right over."

"*He* said?"

"*Evan* said," Frankie corrected herself hastily. "But he's coming from a little way off, out of town."

Rissa tried to squelch the nasty feeling that poked her in the stomach at that very moment. Before she could say anything, Frankie snapped her fingers as though she'd just remembered something, and reached down into her cavernous bag, pulling out a large, floppy purple tam adorned with a silk rose and crammed it down onto her short hair. In response to Rissa's puzzled look, she said apologetically, "It's like this: Evan doesn't know I, um, changed my look. I thought I'd soften the blow a little."

So her brother wasn't expecting the half-inch-long, platinum blonde look. She should have known. She wondered idly what other blows needed softening, but was distracted by a shriek from Frankie, and the girl threw her bags to the ground and dashed across the platform, arms open wide, to throw them around the shoulders of a handsome young man who had appeared through a doorway. The only thing Rissa could do was gather up all their things as best as she could and drag them in their direction.

"Bisous!" Frankie squealed, and kissed the young man on each cheek in the manner of the southern French. He smiled patiently, seemingly used to her intensity. He was fairly small in stature, as were many of the local men Rissa had seen passing by, just about as tall as she. His smooth chestnut hair grazed his shoulders, and was tucked behind his ears. His sharp nose was almost hawkish, but attractive in association with his broad, full-lipped mouth. He looked just under thirty. He returned the kisses on both of Frankie's cheeks, and murmured a greeting.

It was only when Frankie finally let him go, that he appeared to notice Rissa. He introduced himself with old-world solemnity and flourish. "Corbin Sáenz i Merino." He held out his hand.

Rissa shook it. "Nerissa Young. Nice to meet you."

Corbin's English was heavily accented with the rolling *r*'s and strong gutturals of the region. "Very pleased to meet you. Did you have a nice trip?"

"Very nice, thank you," she responded politely.

"I am very happy to hear this," he told her, although his brown eyes had already dismissed her. He gathered up all the bags, even amidst Rissa's protests, and led them out of the station. "This way, *Mesdemoiselles*."

A whirl of activity followed, as they piled into a large, solid SUV and were ferried along rapidly darkening streets. The town gave way almost immediately to countryside: craggy hill faces, adorned with precise rows of grape vines, and occasional expanses of scrubland. Soon, Rissa could smell the salt in the air, telling her that they were very close to the sea. Then they turned off the main roadway onto a much narrower road posted as private property on both sides.

"We're here!" Frankie yelled over her shoulder from the front seat, interrupting her steady stream of chatter aimed at Corbin.

Rissa perked up, looking around her more keenly. The property they had entered was low-lying, and well maintained. A great deal of effort had been put into keeping the landscape as natural as possible, allowing it to fit into the rest of the countryside without becoming as wild and as overgrown. The driveway went on for almost half a mile before the house even came into view, and when it did, Rissa drew her breath.

It was not as large as she would have expected it to be, given the size of the land on which it stood, but it was stunning nonetheless. Under the golden bath of floodlights, the perfect marriage of country charm and modernity was spread out before her. Stucco walls were supported by rough-hewn wooden beams, and the red clay shingles above them contrasted with their warm, buttery yellow. Blooming flowers and tall cacti rose from among the large, smooth white boulders that surrounded the house, and windows were open throughout, inviting inside the sweet scent of the night air. Lanterns hung from wrought-iron posts, swaying in breeze that caused them to flicker like candles. The house immediately sent a new headline for a homemaker's magazine article popping into her writer's brain: *Money Doesn't Need to Scream—Sometimes It Whispers.*

"This is it," Frankie said again, leaping down from the car and nervously patting her tam to make sure it was in place. The look on her face made Rissa feel sorry for her. She looked like a child who had been up to quite a bit of mischief, and who had returned to face the music.

"Ladies, you may enter. I will take your bags inside."

"I can carry mine," Rissa said at once, suddenly shy about having someone else burdened with her things.

Corbin didn't even glance in her direction. "Nonsense. *Pas du tout.* I will take your bags inside."

She decided not to argue further. "Thank you."

"My pleasure." The young man exchanged looks with Frankie, and then he said, "Evan will be nearby. Good luck."

Was the man such a dragon, Rissa wondered, that even his employees knew that Frankie was afraid of him? Indignation rose inside her. Well, if he thought he was going to bully a helpless little girl tonight, he had another thought coming! She felt Frankie's small hand slip into hers, and her protective instincts grew two-fold. "Don't worry," she whispered. "I'm here."

"This way," Frankie whispered back.

Rissa let herself be led around the house to the side, where the faint sounds of a radio played lively Catalan music. As they approached, a splendid European vehicle came into view: its gleaming paintwork deep blue as the Mediterranean, chrome gleaming, body sleek, close to the ground, almost aquatic in form. She half expected it to enclose itself in a transparent bubble, transform into some sort of modern submarine, and propel itself toward the nearby sea. She wasn't much of a car aficionado, but even she could tell that this one was special.

Then the sounds of the radio were drowned out by a double roar that scared Rissa half to death. Her startled mind couldn't understand what could possibly make such a horrific noise, and before she could think any further, two huge blurs charged at them.

Dogs, Rissa realized in panic. Big ones. She looked around but there was nowhere to run. Animal power collided with human flesh, sending them both sprawling onto the ground. She could hear Frankie's high-pitched voice above the excited grunts, but whether she was screaming or laughing, she couldn't tell.

A wet, sloppy tongue insinuated itself into her ears, and then dragged itself across her face, stopping to explore her eyes, nose, and then, to her horror, her mouth. She gagged, and flailed in her own defense, but the two hundred pounds of excited dog flesh seated upon her chest refused to budge.

"Plato!" The authority in the voice stopped the animal dead in its attempts to smother her, and then she felt it being hauled off by a man who had come to stand above her. "Sit!" the man barked, and Plato instantly dropped his haunches onto the paved walkway. "Down! Stay!" Plato followed the commands, letting his head fall onto his paws, and was happy to lie there and smile at Rissa. She found that she was able to breathe once again, but she wasn't out of the woods yet. The big dog was still a mere two feet away, and she had no way of telling whether that smile said "nice to meet you" or "I'll get you next time."

And then, there was the question of the man standing at her side, looking down.

Rissa squinted up at him, abashed by her vulnerable position, unable to move—and awed by what she saw. Even flat on her back, she could tell that he was taller than average. He was wearing jeans that fit into the tops of leather workboots, and a plain white vest which, like his jeans, was smeared with car oil. The vest did nothing to hide the bulging of the muscles in his arms and shoulders, his smooth skin the color of warm, nutty cinnamon toast, and the fine smattering of hair across his almost bare chest. He had the long, graceful limbs of a natural born swimmer: in fact, his entire body seemed as linear and as aquadynamic as the vehicle on which he had been working.

The man carefully wiped his hands on a towel pulled out

of his jeans pocket before bending down and offering her his hand. She took his proffered hand, still overwhelmed.

"*Ça va, mademoiselle?*" he asked gravely. His voice was exactly what she would have expected to hear rising up out of a chest that deep.

Rissa looked down at herself. Her grubby jeans and T-shirt had been made all the more disreputable looking by the stomping of those huge paws, and her face was slick with dog spit, but she suspected she would survive. "Uh, *oui. Merci.*"

"Talk American! She doesn't know any French!" By this time, Frankie had gotten over her joyful reunion with the other behemoth, and came to her side, panting from the exertion of rolling around on the ground.

"Dante! Down! Stay!" the man said to the second dog, without even raising his voice. The animal joined its companion meekly, and watched them, also smiling that enigmatic dog-smile. Now that the chances of being eaten alive seemed dim, Rissa could appreciate them for what they were: two beautiful, perfectly bred boxers. Dante, the one that had just arrived, had a sleek brindled coat with a white breast and paws, and Plato, the monster that had checked her out as an alternative to his dinner was a perfect, creamy white all over. Pink tongues hung out of drooling mouths, and stumpy tails wagged.

For a while, nobody said anything: everyone just looked at everyone else. The lanterns strewn around shed enough light for her to examine the mechanic who had helped her up, and for that, Rissa sent up a silent prayer to the lantern-gods, because he was well worth looking at. Evan Maynard's employees seemed to be better looking than average!

Like the rest of him, his features were smooth, linear and perfectly formed. His hair was cut close to the scalp, with his hairline razor-marked to precision. His mouth, though unsmiling, was beautiful; his nose, cheekbones, jaw, everything just seemed to…fit. And those eyes! Rimmed by thick dark lashes, they were startling against the backdrop of his skin, as they were an unusual shade of golden brown. Almost like honey. Almost like…Frankie's.

Exactly like Frankie's.

Rissa gaped.

She leaned slightly toward Frankie and whispered in horror, "I thought you said your brother was *old!*"

"He is!" Frankie whispered back. "He's *twice* my age, and I'm *seventeen!*"

Rissa would have laughed, if she hadn't been so flabbergasted at the enormity of her own misunderstanding. *Remind me never to trust the judgment of a teenager,* she told herself. They stood before him like two naughty schoolgirls before a wrathful high school principal.

The next person to speak was Evan, who, fortunately, had either not heard or had chosen to ignore her exchange with his sister. In fact, he seemed to have decided to ignore Rissa, now that it was evident that she was not going to be mauled to death on his property. He addressed himself entirely to Frankie, not even looking in Rissa's direction. "Well. So the prodigal daughter returns."

Frankie was both guarded and petulant. "Don't start with me, Evan."

"I have to start with you, Francesca, because you've been A.W.O.L. for two days. You've worried me half out of my mind! Not to mention Grandmaman! Since you left Nice she's been calling me up twenty times a day to make sure you got back safely! Where the heck were you?"

"Cannes, okay? It was no big deal!"

"Cannes?" he echoed incredulously. "What were you doing in Cannes?"

"I was coming home, Evan, honest! But I got off the train

in Cannes just to have a little lunch. And there was this beach party…."

"A beach party that lasted two days?" Evan wasn't buying it.

Frankie licked her lips. "Well, the next thing I knew, it was late, so I checked into a hotel to spend the night. And the next morning, I went shopping, and sort of lost track of time… ."

"Shopping, huh? I suppose that explains where my credit card disappeared to."

"I only borrowed it!" Frankie protested. "And I hardly used it. Just to pay for the hotel and one bag of clothes! One little suitcase! That's all!"

By this time, Rissa was wishing she could melt into the ground and disappear, rather than stand around and bear witness to a family dispute. Part of her wished she could step in and defend Frankie from her brother's rage, even though she knew that he was quite right. The other part of her wished that the dogs *had* snapped her up. At least she wouldn't have been put in this awkward, uncomfortable, fly-on-the-wall position.

Evan Maynard looked as though he was trying his best to stay calm, because when he spoke next, his words were rational and level. "Sis, listen. It's not about the money. It's not about the shopping or the hotel bill or anything like that. It's about your safety. You understand my position. We're well known in the community. People know we have money, and, besides, we stand out. We don't exactly blend in with the French or the Catalans. You never know who's watching, or what their intentions are. You never know—" he threw a hard glance at Rissa "—who to trust and who not to."

Rissa bristled. What was that nasty look for? Did this man think she had some ulterior motive for coming here?

Frankie stamped her foot. "I do know who to trust. I'm not a kid. I'm—"

"Seventeen. I know. And I suppose when I was your age, I thought I knew everything, too. But you don't. I was worried about you. You could at least have called. You could at least have answered your phone when *I* called *you*."

Frankie looked down at her feet. "I, um, didn't get any of your calls."

"I wonder why."

"Dead cell site?" Frankie proposed hopefully.

Evan snorted, but didn't bother to tackle that obvious untruth. "And you could have told me you were coming in tonight. You know I'd have come meet you at the station. I'd have *wanted* to come."

Frankie's face was a comic mixture of defiance and defeat. "I tried. I called you over and over, since we passed through Montpellier. But you didn't answer."

With a sweeping motion, Evan unclipped his phone from his belt, gave it a cursory glance, and then clipped it back on, saying dryly, "Funny. No missed calls. Dead cell site, you think?"

"Probably," Frankie said, commendably calm in the face of her brother's sarcasm. "Good thing I got Corbin, eh?"

"Good thing," he echoed.

Rissa had been following the conversation with a sinking heart. Her suspicious were correct. If Evan hadn't known that Frankie was coming, then Frankie obviously hadn't spoken to him about her. And that meant she was here without permission. An uninvited guest—but not for long. She was leaving right now. She wondered how best to interrupt the conversation, while a cease-fire seemed to have been declared between brother and sister, to take her leave. She wondered even more frantically what sort of transport she would get to take her back into town, and, once there, what she would do next.

Evan chose that moment to address her. "And what's your

name, Miss?" The question held a hint of accusation. "And where are your parents?"

Rissa's hand went up unbidden to her hair, which was caught up in a disheveled ponytail, her once-smooth bangs a nest of flyaways. Surely, in spite of her lack of make-up and more sophisticated attire, she didn't look that young! She started to tell him he was mistaken. "Mr. Maynard, I'm twenty-five—"

But Frankie took that burden upon her own shoulders. "She's not a girl, Evan. She's a grownup! Her name's Rissa Young, and she's my friend!"

He didn't apologize for his gaffe. Instead, he continued to critically assess her face. "Rissa?"

"*Ner*issa," Rissa corrected. She considered offering to shake hands, but the look in his eye told her it would be a bad idea. One hand remained at her side, while the other clutched her handbag securely to her chest.

"I met her on the train," Frankie offered helpfully.

"I see." Accusation grew into mistrust.

You don't see, Rissa wanted to say. *I didn't invite myself along. I didn't just turn up. I thought you had given permission....*

Oblivious to Evan's irony and Rissa's discomfiture, Frankie barreled on. "Yes. She's from Philly. And she's staying the night. I invited her, Evan, so she's staying. She's got to. She has no money and someone stole all her clothes and stuff. And her camera. And her plane ticket. So she can stay, right?" There was a mortifying pause in which Rissa briefly considered the most efficient means of making herself disappear, and then Frankie asked again, *"Right, Evan?"*

Whatever calm had come over him in the past few moments went out the window. Evan's ire rose again. "Francesca, what did I tell you about this?"

"This is different!" Frankie protested.

"How is it different? What makes this different from any other time? I keep telling you: you can't keep picking up strays!"

Picking up strays?

"But she's *destitute!*" Frankie's pretty face was scrunched up, as if she was about to cry. "And she's my friend!"

In irritation, Evan tossed aside the hand towel he had been holding and put his hands on his hips, frowning down at the driveway, as if trying to deflect a glare that would otherwise turn his sister to stone. He was fighting a losing battle with his temper. "Frankie, people don't make friends in a matter of hours. What *can* happen in a matter of hours is that you can pick yourself up some hangers-on who latch on to you because they think you're a soft touch. What I keep trying to drill into your head is that there are people out there who can smell money on you better than sharks can smell blood in water! You'll always be a target, Frankie. The least you can do is make yourself a hard one!"

That did it. Enough was enough. It was time for Rissa to speak for herself, rather than stand here and be treated like something just one step above a pickpocket. She stepped between Frankie and her brother, put her hands on her hips in an unconscious imitation of his gesture, and said, "First of all, Mr. Maynard, I am not now, nor have ever been, either a 'hanger-on' or a 'stray'. It was my belief that I was specifically invited to spend the night here, by *you*." Behind her, Frankie gave a guilty squeak.

Evan's face was like hard, dark stone, but he was listening, so she went on. "And furthermore, I find you rude and insulting. I do not appreciate being talked about like that, least of all to my face. You'll be happy to know that I have absolutely no intention of imposing myself on your home tonight, as the last thing I would ever do is make myself an unwelcome guest. All I ask is for you to be kind enough to

allow me to call a taxi, and then I will be out of your hair."
How she intended to pay for that taxi, she had no idea, but
spending her last euro to get herself back into town was worth
it, even if it meant she would have to spend the night on the
steps at the train station. Anything to get away from this ob-
noxious, distrustful pig!

Evan appeared flustered by her tirade. "Miss Young," he
began.

But Rissa was on a roll. "And another thing! I don't like
the way you speak to your sister! Maybe she should have been
home a few days earlier, and maybe she should have called.
But that doesn't mean you need to bawl her out before she
even steps through the door! She's just a kid. Kids do those
things sometimes. Maybe you could force yourself to be more
understanding!"

At the mention of her, Frankie dashed around to watch the
battle rage between the two, eyes and mouth equally wide open.

Evan didn't take kindly to her comment. "What goes on
between me and my sister is none of your business!" His
handsome face was mottled with anger. "And I do not take
kindly to receiving parenting tips from strangers!"

"You aren't her parent, you're her brother! And it is my
business because…." She glanced across at Frankie who was
watching the discussion with a mixture of excitement and
anxiety. "…Because, like Frankie said, we're friends."

"For all intents and purposes, I am the only parent she has.
And I'm 'bawling her out,' as you put it, because I have been out
of my mind with worry because I haven't heard a peep out of
her since she left our grandparents' house two days ago! She
needs to learn to stop putting herself in harm's way, and if a
lecture every time she wanders off does the trick, well, so be it."

Rissa was out of breath, puffing from annoyance. This
beast was clueless! "So, you're glad to see her?"

He turned away, paced a few steps up, and then a few steps back, trying to rein himself in. "Yes," he said tightly. "She's my sister. I haven't seen her in more than a week. Of course I'm glad to see her."

"Well, you haven't shown it. In my family…" She had to stop and struggle to get her voice past the sudden sharp obstruction in her throat that rose at the thought of the family she no longer had, but she pressed on. "In my family, when we meet each other again after we've been apart, we *hug*." It was part information, part challenge.

Evan continued his pacing, scratching and patting the back of his head as if trying to dislodge a particularly pesky thought. Eventually, he stopped right in front of Frankie. One look at his face told Rissa that he had mastered his anger, and in its place was a sheepish look. "Frankie, I'm sorry."

Frankie only stared at him, speechless.

Evan went on. "I know I was mad at you, but I was only worried. I missed you, and I'm glad you're back. Okay?"

"Okay," she managed in a small voice. Then she found herself being pulled into her brother's arms and held against his chest for several moments.

Rissa had to smile when the indomitable youth stuck her head out from under her brother's arm to give her a triumphant grin and a thumbs-up. When Evan released her, Frankie was still grinning.

There was a warmth in Evan's voice that Rissa hadn't heard before. "Okay, sweetie. Why don't you run on inside, have a shower and get yourself some dinner? Madame Soler baked a chicken. And there's *chausson aux pommes* for dessert."

"With cream?"

"With cream," he answered indulgently.

Frankie flashed a look at Rissa. "Rissa, are you coming?" Her next glance, a more defiant one, was for Evan.

Rissa saw it, and demurred. She wouldn't be caught dead following Frankie into that house, not after her brother had made it clear exactly how he felt about it. "No, Frankie, I can't. I'm grateful for your invitation, but I really have to be going. I'll call you tomorrow after my interview, and we'll talk, okay? I'll see you again, I promise."

Frankie looked as though her cheery mood was about to evaporate once again. "But you have to! You can't leave!"

Before the conversation could degenerate any further, Evan interrupted. His voice was even, but there was enough command in it that not even Frankie could defy it. "Frankie, go on in. Take a shower and get something to eat. Everything will be okay."

She was doubtful. "Promise?"

"I promise. Now, skedaddle. I need to have a word with Miss Young."

Frankie took one last longing look at Rissa, and then skedaddled.

Second Impressions—How To Recover From a First-Meeting Fiasco

When he was sure that Frankie was safely inside, Evan turned to face Nerissa Young once more. He wondered what to say. He'd made a fool of himself; he knew that. And now she was glaring at him suspiciously from under drawn brows. She did look rather young, he thought, forgiving himself for at least one stupid thing he had said to her. Assuming she was Frankie's age! She was quite tall, several inches taller than his sister. Her adolescent hairdo and grungy attire may have contributed to his mistake, but her face was soft, womanly, and definitely belonged to an adult—as did her body. The T-shirt and jeans tried their best to hide her soft curves, but did a poor job. Although she looked slightly underfed, her arms were well rounded, as were her breasts, hips, thighs, and cute, curved bottom. That body certainly did not belong to a girl! If the situation wasn't so tense, he would have chuckled at his own idiocy.

The expression on her face was no laughing matter, however. She folded her arms in an effort to look tough, and said slowly, "Now, about that phone call...."

He was a lot of things, he thought, but one thing he was not was the type of man who threw stranded women off his property in the middle of the night. "Nerissa," he began, and then stopped. Things had gotten off to a bad enough start; he wasn't sure she'd take kindly to being addressed so informally, so he sought her permission. "May I call you Nerissa?"

"You can call me anything you want," she answered tightly, "as long as you let me make that call."

"I can't let you do that. We're quite a way out of town, and it would be quite some time before any taxi would be able to make its way out here—if one would be willing to come at all. Besides," he considered her financial predicament, and added tactfully, "they can be quite expensive."

"A bus, then!" she countered desperately.

He shook his head regretfully. "I'm sorry. The nearest bus route is miles away, and they've probably already stopped running for the night: most of the minor routes close early." Her face was the picture of misery, so he hastened to say, "Please, do me the honor of being my guest tonight. I apologize for my rudeness. Even worry over my sister is no excuse for what I said. Please forgive me, and come inside. I promise you that you'll be safe and comfortable, and I'll take you back into town in the morning, if that's what you want."

Her shoulders slumped, and he was half sure that she would choose spending the night outside in the scrubland over entering the house with him, but then reason forced her to say, "Thank you. I'm sorry for imposing—"

"It's not an imposition, I assure you." He beckoned. "Come. Follow me." She threw her handbag over her shoulder and fell meekly into step with him. He slapped his thigh, summoning the dogs. "Dante! Plato! Come here!" They immediately leaped up from their prone positions and trotted after him, tongues hanging. Evan noticed Rissa warily eyeing them, so he hastened to put her at ease. "They're really quite harmless, once they know you're a friend. They just get over-enthusiastic sometimes."

"I noticed." There was a flash of humor in her voice, and that made him feel better. Maybe she wasn't entirely trauma-tized by the events of the evening.

He let her precede him into the house, carefully watching her face for her reaction. In his experience, some people used your home as an indicator of how much you were worth; others as an indicator of who you really were inside. Into which category would she fall? He was surprised by how fer-vently he hoped it would be the latter.

He'd had the house built six or seven years ago, but had ensured that it was a detailed imitation of a traditional country house of fifty years ago, with the exception of the state-of-the-art amenities such as central air, a sophisticated security system, and wireless network connections in most rooms. He loved his home; it literally lifted his spirits every time he stepped inside. The interior was enveloped in a comfortable masculinity: large, hand-made local furniture, natural fabrics throughout, stucco walls and a high roof supported by wooden beams. The floors were covered with tiles from a local artisan, as pottery was one of the strengths of the region. Throughout most of the house, the palette was earthy, in shades of brown, gold, burnt orange, and yellow. They combined to work their magic on him, soothing when he needed to be soothed, and invigorating when he needed a pick-me-up.

He waited as Rissa let her gaze run around them, pausing at the pieces of art on the walls and the sculptures scattered about on shelves and side tables. "Local art?"

"Most of it." He pointed to one of his favorite pieces, a large painting that dominated the living room wall. "I picked that up in Collioure, not far from here. It's a tiny village by the sea. A lot of famous modern artists got their start there, trading drawings for food and selling paintings to tourists on the beach. It's home to one of the most often-painted towers in Europe, or, at least, in France."

"I've heard of it." She stopped to run her finger over a small piece of metal sculpture, engaged by its medieval appearance. It was the figure of a hideous, troll-like creature with an obscenely dangling tongue and hellish eyes. It had folded, bat-like wings and way too many claws. He was pleased that she had been drawn so quickly to it. It was one of his treasures.

"That one," he explained, "is from Carcassonne, one of the oldest surviving walled cities in France. It's a copy of a gargoyle from one of the old buildings there. It was made by my housekeeper's nephew. Her name's Madame Soler—she's originally from Carcassonne."

"It's beautiful, in a grotesque sort of way," she chuckled.

"That's what I think." She had an eye for art. He liked that.

But all the while she was drinking in his artwork, she was still avoiding looking him in the eye, so he put an end to the tour, and hastened to get her to her room so that she could make herself more comfortable.

"This way," he said, and led her up a passageway to the guest room. Before he could open the door for her, he saw Corbin emerging from Frankie's quarters.

The younger man flushed. "I put the ladies' bags in their rooms," he said to him in Catalan, and then repeated himself in English for Rissa's benefit.

"Thank you." Evan responded in Catalan, a language he had picked up from the locals rather than through any formal classes. He enjoyed the robust marriage of French and Spanish, and the expressive gestures that accompanied it. After centuries of being bickered over by and shunted back and forth between the French and Spanish governments, the

Catalan people had developed a personality of rebellious pride that intrigued him. "I'll talk to you in the morning, Corbin. You can wrap it up for the night and get going." His voice was curt, but he was more than a little ticked off that Corbin had allowed Frankie to sucker him into going to meet them at the station without saying anything. He could only surmise that Corbin had sought to aid and abet her in her attempt to delay facing his anger for a few moments more, but it was not up to Corbin to make that decision. He'd have to let him know that in the morning.

His workshop manager nodded and hurried away, leaving him alone with Rissa once more. He slipped back into host mode. "This is your room. You should find everything there: shampoo, conditioner, soaps, towels, and dressing gowns. If you need anything, just let me know. I assume you have laundry that needs doing?" He asked this last part delicately, not wanting to offend her, although judging by her scruffy condition, and if what Frankie had said was true, he was sure that she would probably not have had access to such creature comforts for a while.

He could see the hasty, untrue "No" forming on her lips, but then she thought the better of it and confessed, "Yes, yes, I do."

"Not a problem," he said briskly. "Just leave it outside the door and I'll make sure it's taken care of." Madame Soler, his housekeeper, had already left for the day, so he'd probably wind up doing the washing himself, but he was afraid to let on, for fear that pride might make her hold on to her dirty laundry and miss the opportunity to get some clean things. He'd done enough backpacking in his day to know how much little amenities such as clean clothes could mean when you were on the road.

He only wished she didn't keep looking at him as if he were about to pounce. He really must have made a bad impression on her out there! He wondered what he could do to change that. She could barely lift her head to speak. "Thank you, Mr. Maynard. I'm truly grateful—"

He interrupted. "Evan, please."

This time, she did lift her head, and looked at him directly. He noticed then how dark and beautiful her eyes were, with a slight Asian cast to their almond shape. But they were rimmed with fatigue and an unfathomable sadness. "Thank you, Evan."

He wished he could do more to take that look of exhausted despair away, but a clean bed and a hot meal was all he had to offer. "Once you're all cleaned up and feeling better, join us in the dining groom. I'm sure Frankie's there already, making inroads into the chicken." His smile was warm and comforting. "We'd better hurry."

She looked as though he'd invited her to a hanging. "Oh, no, really. Thank you but I'm not…" she paused, and he could read the effort on her face to verbalize the polite lie "…hungry." She finished miserably. "I ate on the train."

If you had anything more than crackers and soda on that train, Evan thought, *I'll eat my shoes.* It was obvious that she was mortified at the thought of sharing a meal with him, after all the things he'd said about her. She'd rather sit in her room and eat soap than go outside and admit to being hungry. He gave in gracefully, loath to make her feel any more uncomfortable than she already did. He'd find a way to get her to eat if it killed him. "Okay, then. I'll leave you alone. But if you need anything, you'll let me know, right?"

"Right."

He stepped back out into the passageway, joining the dogs who were patiently awaiting his return. "Don't forget that laundry," he reminded her.

"I won't," she said in a small voice.

* * *

By the time Rissa hauled herself out of the bathtub, her fingers and toes were doing a pretty good imitation of a bunch of raisins. She was sure that she had been in the bathroom for at least an hour and a half. It felt so good to be clean again! And Evan's guest bathroom was luxury itself. The porcelain sunken bath was hand-painted all around the rim in old-fashioned tea-roses, but equipped with very modern jet sprays that had the rose-scented bubble bath churned into a thick foam in minutes. Hand-dipped beeswax candles filled the air with the sweet, delicate smell of honey, and the counter was crowded with an array of shampoos, organic facials, scrubs, razors, shaving gels, and even a pedicure kit. When she finally emerged from the bathroom, she was washed, conditioned, pedicured, and manicured. Her brows were suitably tamed, her legs fuzz-free, and her face deep-cleansed, toned, and moisturized. After weeks of trailing around Europe feeling increasingly like roadkill, she looked and felt human again.

God bless Evan Maynard!

Even the terry bathrobe was gorgeous, with a pile so thick her fingers disappeared into it up to the first joint. The bedroom was in complete harmony with the bathroom, a perfect collusion of charm and modernity. The bed was easily wide enough for her to sleep on it sideways, if she so desired. There was a writing desk, a bookshelf with a thoughtful choice of books in English, French, Catalan, and Spanish, a television, a computer, and a CD player. Rissa went over to the far wall, which was shrouded by floor-length linen curtains, and pulled them back.

The glass doors looked out onto a small patio where Evan's guests could sit and enjoy the sunshine either in any of the white-painted wrought iron chairs or in the large double hammock that rocked invitingly in the breeze. Beyond it, lit up by overhead lanterns and submerged floodlights, was the prettiest swimming pool she had ever seen. Even from where she stood, she could see that it was tiled in a dazzling range of blues, from the palest of sea-foams to the deepest lapis lazuli. The mosaic pattern undulated like ocean waves, even though the surface of the water was still. At the end facing the sea, the water lapped over the edge in a mini-fountain, creating the illusion that the pool actually emptied into the Mediterranean.

Evan, it seemed, liked to surround himself with nice things. Maybe the ogre that had roared at her when she had intruded on his space had a softer, more sensual side.

The tap on the door almost made her swallow her own tongue. The house had been so quiet, she'd thought that everyone had turned in for the night. In hindsight, the silence was probably more due to the solidness of the walls than to anything else. She went to the door. "Yes?"

"Nerissa."

Evan! She'd hoped she didn't have to face him again until morning! She opened the door with trepidation. "Yes?"

Immediately, there was a snuffle at thigh-level, and Dante and Plato tried to nose their way into the room. A single command from Evan halted them, sending them to the floor in a submissive position, but their eyes were still fixed longingly on Rissa. She consoled them with a pat on each nose, and then returned her focus to Evan.

He, too, had taken the time to clean up. Gone were the dirty jeans, vest, and workboots, and the layer of automobile oil that had led her to assume that he was his own mechanic. He was wearing another pair of jeans, this one impeccably clean, but which hugged his body as affectionately as the one before, and a plain navy T-shirt. His feet were bare. He was holding a tray laden with food and drink, and a small, folded white item. She looked at him quizzically.

"You must be hungry, Nerissa. Frankie says you came all the way from Montpellier. That's quite a journey. And train food doesn't exactly fill you up. Please, eat something."

The smell of roast chicken killed any thought of protesting. She took the tray without hesitation, looking it over eagerly. There was a large breast of chicken, sprinkled with rosemary, a square of what looked like turnip pie, a baked potato with a heaping dollop of herbed butter, baby carrots and peas, and a small pastry that smelled of apples. Next to it was a glass of white wine and a bottle of spring water. Her stomach leaped for joy. Her "Thank you," was heartfelt.

"My pleasure." He pointed at the folded white cloth. "I brought you a clean T-shirt to sleep in. It's a bit big, because it's mine, but it's fairly new. I thought you'd need it for the night, until your own things come out of the wash."

How did he know she slept in a T-shirt? Then she remembered the laundry and her skin grew hot. She'd assumed that the housekeeper would have done it…but come to think of it, she hadn't seen hide nor hair of the mythical Madame Soler since she had arrived. *Don't tell me he did my laundry,* she groaned inwardly. That would be too embarrassing! "Thank you," she managed again.

He seemed to know what had crossed her mind, and shrugged it off, signaling her with his eyes not to make a fuss. "Eat, Nerissa."

She set the tray down on the desk, dying to dig in. As she did so, he turned to go. "Have a good night."

"Wait!" She called after him before she could stop herself. He halted. "Yes?"

"Would you…like to come in?" Now, what had she gone and done that for? Common courtesy? It was, after all, his house. He could go wherever he pleased. Or maybe she simply needed the company. Apart from Frankie, she had barely had a conversation that lasted more than five minutes since those college girls had abandoned her a week ago.

"Thank you." He re-entered without argument and sat on the edge of her bed, crossing one bare foot over the opposite knee. The bed sank under his weight. "Eat," he urged.

She didn't have to be told again. He sat in silence while she did her meal justice, not venturing to make conversation until she began her dessert. The apple tart was so good she almost moaned.

"So, Frankie tells me you're a writer?" was his opening gambit.

"Yes. Freelance. For magazines, especially women's magazines."

"Anything I've heard of?"

"Maybe. Most of them are quite popular." She named a few of the better known ones.

He nodded in recognition. "Yes. I know those. My ex-wife had subscriptions to a few of them." He mentioned her almost matter-of-factly, without a flicker of emotion on his face.

His ex-wife. Rissa wondered briefly what kind of woman she had been. It was a beautiful home; how much of the design, and everything that filled it, had been her idea? And what had happened between such a young couple? What could possibly have made her leave a house that looked like that, and a man who looked like this? Frankie had said that she had left him because he was boring, but then again, Frankie said a lot of things. She suspected that *boring* was not a word that anyone could conceivably apply to Evan.

He didn't wait for her to find a suitably non-committal response to his remark. He asked, "So, what kind of articles do you write?"

She felt almost embarrassed by her answer. "Girly things, self-help articles." She rolled her eyes and quoted: "*Nine Days To a More Interesting You.* That kind of thing."

"It's not what you really want to write?"

"Not anymore. I've put it on indefinite hold while I—" She glanced involuntarily at her laptop perched demurely on a chair. "I've started a novel." Now, why'd she gone and told him that? She hadn't told *anyone* about that! She felt her face get hot.

He leaned forward, interested. The small movement made the muscles of his torso flex under the confining shirt. Rissa had to drag her eyes away. It might have been fatigue, or it might have been the fact that he was sitting on the edge of that enormous bed in this sensual, enticingly comfortable bedroom, but that small gesture made her squirm.

"What kind of novel?" he asked. He read the hesitation on her face, and smiled. "Too late to back out now. You've already let the cat out of the bag, so you might as well go ahead and tell me."

For some reason, she *wanted* to tell him. Maybe it was a desire to validate herself in his eyes, so that he would take her seriously, and not as the "stray" that he had labeled her. So she said assertively, "I'm writing a children's novel."

His brows shot up, and his face took on a warmer aspect. "Why a children's novel? You like kids?"

"Love them," she said sincerely.

"Do you have any?"

"No." She was glad that her negation didn't sound abrupt.

"But you want to have some, someday?"

The scar at the base of her tummy tightened at the question, like a small, vicious mouth biting into her skin, reminding her of its presence. It didn't matter how deep her desire to raise a whole brood; thanks to her illness, not even desperate wanting would ever make it so. She shook her head and managed to reply, "I did, once. Now…I don't think that would be possible."

"Career?" He sighed heavily. "It's such a pity that so many women think they have to choose between the two."

He was so wrong! Her eyes were burning, and she hoped it wouldn't show. "No, not that."

He probed no further, but instead said complacently, "Maybe one day, when the time is right for you, you might change your mind. Children are wonderful."

She didn't think she had the strength to challenge his presumption about her being able to change her mind, so she turned the question over on its head and lobbed it back at him. "Do you want to? Have kids, I mean."

His smile was indulgent. "As many as possible. This is a beautiful place to bring up kids. Lots of space for them to run around. When I built this place, I imagined it filled with the sound of children. I designed the garden to hold swings and slides, and provide ample hidey-holes and pretend forts. And then there's our family legacy; I come from five generations of boat-builders. If I have no one to pass it all on to, nobody to learn my craft, then it's all been wasted."

"I don't think it will be wasted," she said sincerely.

"I hope not. I hope that God will be good to me, and bless me with a great big brood of my own." He looked wistful, almost sad.

In her mind, question tumbled upon question. Why hadn't he and his wife had any? Why did he look so pained? He was young, wealthy, and very attractive. Surely he would have any number of fertile young women lined up on both sides of the Atlantic eager to fulfill the role of mommy to the children he so much desired. What had happened? What *hadn't* happened?

He returned to the original subject as if he didn't want to

dwell on that particular one. "So you've come to Europe seeking inspiration for your book." He stated it as a given.

She exhaled heavily, throwing her hands up in the air. "No, not really. I needed to get away from the States for a while. I needed time to think, to regroup, to use the popular term."

His voice was soft, and not unkind. "Running away?"

Her lips twisted wryly. "I guess you could say that." Running away from pain, ghosts, and a bleak future.

"Bad...relationship?"

There was no man in the picture; there hadn't been for quite some time, and there wouldn't be in the near future. He himself had said it. What men wanted was their legacy. What man would settle for an aching, empty shell of a woman? But she couldn't tell him that. "No, not a man. Just a few bad things coming one after the other. I lost my sister last year—"

His condolences were immediate. "I'm so sorry."

She nodded. "Thank you. And then I was...ill for some time. So when I got well enough to travel, I did what anybody who's had a life-changing experience would do. I sold everything, packed up, and came to Europe." She laughed almost self-deprecatingly. "I started out in Amsterdam, then Brussels, then Paris, then Marseille. I was headed for Nice, but I was robbed."

"You know, I wanted to ask you what had happened to all your money, but I didn't want you to feel awkward. Like you were under interrogation." He frowned. "Did they hurt you?"

By this time, she was done eating, and carefully put away the remnants of her meal. She got up, spurred by nervous energy, and began pacing. She felt him following her with his gaze. "Only my pride, and, I guess, my faith in human nature. I met three young American girls, college girls, and we decided to stick together. I liked them, and I thought they liked me. We shared a suite to cut costs. Things were going fine, I thought—and then one morning I woke up, and everything I had was gone."

"Sometimes, youngsters just don't see the harm they cause by their high-jinks. They see the little picture—the booze or clothes or whatever it is they did with your money. But they don't see the damage they do to the person they've hurt." He looked genuinely sympathetic. "What are you going to do?"

Survive, she thought determinedly. *However I can.* "I came to Perpignan for a job interview tomorrow afternoon. At a bookstore in town. An English language store."

"I think I know it. You think you'll be able to make a good living there?"

"It's not much, but it'll feed me and help me raise the money to fly back home in a few months."

Evan rose to his feet and approached her. He stopped just before her, making her halt in her restless pacing. His honeyed eyes held hers steadily. "You'll be okay." He sounded more confident than she felt.

"I guess so." She tried to sound positive. "It's not a *promise* of a job. It's just an interview, but…."

His eyes speared her through like a moth on a drawing pin, and she would have tried to wriggle away, had she not been so mesmerized. "No," he said. "You *will* be okay. I mean that. I don't know how, but…let me think."

Before she could express her puzzlement, he stepped away, and the spike on which he had held her fast suddenly let her go free. The relief left her limp.

He was moving fast, toward the door, as though propelled by an idea. "I'll let you be now. I've peppered you with questions, and I know you must be tired. I'll see you in the morning, okay?" He took the empty tray, setting the T-shirt he had lent her down carefully on the bed.

He was right; she was exhausted. She ruffled her now-dry hair and stifled a yawn brought about by the power of suggestion. "I will. Thank you again. Good night."

He halted in the open doorway. Beyond, the two dogs, who had been waiting patiently on their master to emerge—or, Rissa thought, on a second chance to bolt into the room—looked at him with eager anticipation, waiting for his attention to swivel their way. He whispered a soft greeting, sending them into paroxysms of delight, and then, when he spoke his final words to Rissa, his voice was just as soft.

"Sweet dreams," he wished her.

"Thanks," she managed. "You too." Then she hastily shut the door.

Evan returned the tray to the kitchen, not bothering to wash up, and, instead of heading to his room, slipped out a side door. Dante and Plato, knowing what was coming, eagerly followed, yelping softly with excitement, and jostling each other for the chance to be closest to him. It was quite late, and the summer sky was sprinkled with bright stars. This, to him, meant that the wind was coming down from the nearby Pyrenees, as a wind coming off the sea usually brought with it a fog that often obscured his view of the sky.

Poolside, he stripped, leaving on just his shorts as a courtesy to his sister and her guest; for most of the year, when he was alone, he always swam naked, whatever the hour. He preferred the feel of the water on his bare skin. Swimming, he believed, was something you should do unrestricted. He swam every night as a rule, last thing before bed. It relaxed him as well as kept him in shape. He had little use for gyms; the water was all he ever needed. Most nights, he made twenty laps. When he was especially disturbed, or, like tonight, when he needed to think, he made thirty.

He cannonballed into the deep end like an eight-year-old, sending up a tremendous splash and wetting the pool furniture and the deck, and the dogs leaped gleefully in after him.

They played for a while together, galumphing around in the deep end, batting about a ball and some floating pool toys, and then he got serious, developing the steady rhythm that he preferred, moving cleanly and silently through the water with movements reminiscent of his childhood obsession with dolphins. The dogs kept pace with equal skill, cleaving the water like seals. His body settled, finding its ease, performing almost without his command. He counted his laps. *Five…six.* All the while, his mind buzzed.

This Nerissa was a puzzle. He would freely acknowledge that he had been nasty to her when she had arrived, but that was a reaction based on his previous experience with Frankie's choice of friends rather than anything else. At least he had done what he could to make amends for his original slight.

But there was more there, some terrible hurt that he sensed but couldn't understand. She'd lost her sister, and she said she had been ill. That much was evident: there was a thinness about her, not so much in a physical sense, as though she'd lost a great deal of weight, but in the sense that she seemed to have spread herself too thin, stretched to the edges of her endurance. There was something in her eyes that yearned for rest, and for solace.

Eight…nine.

He wished he could help. The fact that she was little more than a stranger didn't make that impulse any less urgent. By nature, he had always been caring. As a child, he had spent his hours combing the beaches in his native San Diego, picking up wounded sea-birds, mending wings, hand-feeding lost fledglings, nurturing them until they were strong enough to take care of themselves. When he was older, he'd volunteered in any number of marine wildlife ventures, from freeing stranded whales to rescuing sea-turtles tangled in fishing nets. This was no different, he tried to tell himself—except that in this case the object of his concern was not a gray, two-ton mammal in mortal danger but a beautiful, sad-eyed young woman.

Twelve....

And then there was Jeanine. He couldn't believe he'd mentioned her to a stranger. While his ex-wife's name rarely passed his lips, her presence was always felt. She was a part of him as surely as if her name had been tattooed across his chest. Even though he had methodically and meticulously removed every trace of her presence from his home since she had left three years ago, he thought of her often, especially when Frankie was here.

He saw a lot of Jeanine in Frankie. Some of it was good: her ability to approach anyone with courage, regardless of their position, age, or status; her sense of fun; her charm; and the ease with which she made friends. Jeanine had always been the perfect hostess, able to liven up any gathering, draw even the most reticent guest out of himself without effort.

But then, there was more. He never thought of himself as a loner, not exactly; he enjoyed company as much as anyone else. But Jeanine took her love of parties to another level. She craved constant stimulation, and would do anything to draw attention to herself, through the way she dressed, the way she laughed, and the way she maneuvered any conversation around to focus on herself. Shopping was an addiction, and her tastes were for the best. When there was no further room for any more of her luxurious purchases, she had blithely thrown out or given away what she had, used or not, and then started all over again.

She enjoyed the company of men. As willing as he had been to trust her to respect the bonds of matrimony, her taste for glitter drew her to constantly haunt the finest entertainment centers of New York, L.A., London, Venice, Florence, Paris, and Nice, and, since most of the time he had been obliged to stay back and attend to his business, there was no way that Evan could have been assured of her conduct. Unwilling to know the truth, he had never asked her, preferring to close his eyes and trust even when intelligence and common sense told him that his trust was misplaced, rather than open himself to the anguish of knowing.

Seventeen...eighteen.

But it was the impact of Jeanine's behavior on Frankie that disturbed him the most, not what it had done to their marriage. When Frankie had come to live with them, after their parents' deaths, she had only been eleven. A vulnerable age for a young girl. To her, Jeanine was all glamour, all beauty, all grace. Enjoying the young girl's adoration, Jeanine did not hesitate to share with her tales of her adventures, planting seeds into that fertile young mind that, to Evan's horror, were now beginning to germinate.

Stealing his credit card to go on shopping sprees, flirting shamelessly with boys, sneaking out to parties, running off to Cannes without calling...he supposed that to some extent that was normal teenage behavior. But the snowball had begun to roll downhill, and, in spite of what Rissa thought, he was the only parent Frankie had, and it was his job to ensure that he put a halt to it, before things got out of hand. It gave him nightmares to imagine Frankie growing up without a steady, stable female influence, and what would happen if, years from now, she woke up, looked at herself, and realized that she had become someone she didn't like?

He had to do something. Now.

As he swam, an idea formed. First, appearing as a niggling sensation at the base of his neck, and then growing, forcing its way upward and forward into his consciousness. He stopped dead in the water, paddling to keep himself afloat, and the dogs halted as well, turning back to return to his side. It seemed so simple. Two birds, one stone. There was a way he could help Rissa, and apply a stopgap measure to his own predicament at the same time.

On impulse, he lifted his eyes toward the guest room, which faced the pool. There was just a single, dim light burning within, and the curtains were securely drawn, but even so, he was sure he saw movement. A shadow. He narrowed his eyes, trying to focus, trying to make out her silhouette. He wondered idly if she had donned his T-shirt, and how it had fit. He imagined the stark white material against her beaten-bronze skin, and the way the fabric would skim over her generous curves.

Behind the curtain, the shadow started in surprise, and then darted hastily from the doorway.

Evan smiled, chest rising and falling as his breathing returned to normal.

Rissa had been watching him, just as surely as he had been watching her.

The Many Moods of Men: When To Get Close, and When To Stay Clear

As it turned out, the mythical Madame Soler really did exist after all. Plump, round-faced and dark-eyed, she appeared within moments of Rissa's rising, making her wonder if the tiny housekeeper had been hovering outside the door, waiting for signs that she had awoken. She brought with her a basket filled with her carefully folded laundry, and, as they were cool to the touch, Rissa deduced that they could not possibly have spent the morning in the dryer, confirming her suspicion that Evan had done them the night before. The less she thought about *that,* the better.

Madame Soler didn't speak a word of English, and, as Rissa's French was not much better, they managed to communicate with a series of gestures and monosyllables—as well as a neatly written note from Evan inviting her to enjoy breakfast on the main patio, and informing her that he would be coming to take her into town just after eleven.

Rissa looked at her watch. It would be a quick, late breakfast indeed. She must have been tired, because it was already ten o'clock. Rissa thanked the older woman, had herself a hasty bath, dressed in her freshly laundered clothes and hurried to the patio.

There was no sign of Frankie, but Dante and Plato were very much in evidence. After showering her with affection and saliva for several minutes, they were happy to flop down at her feet and enjoy the sunshine while she had her breakfast.

In the daylight, she was more able to appreciate the glorious grounds that the patio overlooked. There was an air of carefully planned chaos about the garden: along white stone paths, colors rioted. Succulents poked up from among pink, purple, orange, and white bougainvillea, and vines clambered over smaller shrubs and bushes. A mimosa tree shed its bright yellow flowers onto her head as she ate, and birds chirped at each other from its branches.

She was truly going to regret leaving such a beautiful, peaceful spot, but she had known that it would only be for one night. That had been asking much of Evan in the first place. Any minute now, he would return, and then she would say her goodbyes to Frankie and be transported without ceremony to the real world, which is where she belonged. At least this evening, if all went well, her position would be more assured. There was a good chance that she would be able to obtain a week's advance from her employers, so she would be sleeping somewhere clean and comfortable come nightfall.

The sound of Evan's car engine, as the splendid machine pulled up, was like a panther purring as it rolled over to have its belly rubbed. Rissa went rigid, praying that his pleasant mood of the night before hadn't worn off. He parked in the driveway, and when he emerged from the driver's seat, he was smiling. He was sleek, lean, and clad in his perennial jeans. This time, a cotton shirt had taken the place of his vest, and its long sleeves were rolled up as a nod to the summer heat. His honeyed eyes were hidden behind thin, smoky sunglasses, but she could still tell that they were focused on her. Rissa's insides flip-flopped.

"Morning," he greeted her.

"You mean, *bonjour,*" she corrected, smiling back inanely, glad that he seemed cheerful enough.

"You're right. A beautiful language for a beautiful French morning." He gave the dogs a perfunctory pat on the head and then took a seat across from her, folding his arms and leaning on the tabletop.

"That's about all the French you'll get out of me," she responded regretfully. "Apart from *fromage,* that's as good as it gets."

"We'll have to settle for English, then—at least for the time being. Maybe while you're here, you'll add a little more to your repertoire."

While she was here. Considering her predicament, it wouldn't be a whole much longer. She tried not to let her spirits dip. "Thank you for having me," she said politely. "And for breakfast."

"Anytime. Was breakfast okay?"

She patted her tummy appreciatively. "More than okay! I'm stuffed! I thought the French got by on a cup of coffee and toast?"

"The French do. I do. But I figured that if I'm entertaining one of my fellow countrymen, I should put out an American spread."

"Well, it certainly was a spread. I don't know if I'll be able to stand." Then she had a thought. "Where's Frankie? I haven't seen her this morning."

Evan laughed outright. "This is my sister you're talking about. She hardly ever surfaces before noon, and then she has something to eat, and then three or four hours of lessons. I usually don't see her before evening."

"Lessons? What kind of lessons?"

"French, for one. Even after being in and out of France several times a year since we were kids, and with two French-speaking grandparents, Frankie still speaks the most awful street dialect you can imagine. If you knew what she was saying, it would curl your hair. She doesn't care about the inherent beauty of the language. She reads the classics like a child swallowing nasty medicine."

That sounded like Frankie. "What else?"

"Spanish. She likes that, mainly because she loves when I drive her down into Spain. Barcelona is her favorite city. Mine too. But she refuses to speak a word of Catalan. She thinks it's harsh."

"I like the sound of it," Rissa said immediately. "Even though I don't understand a word."

"I like it, too. It's dynamic and rebellious. And very old." He returned to the subject of Frankie's tutelage. "Frankie has her SATs later this year, too. That's pretty much how she spends her afternoons. She doesn't necessarily like it, but she's wise enough to know that it's good for her."

"That's good." The vision of the temperamental, rebellious teenager floated before her eyes, purple tam with its cheeky rose perched on top her head. That reminded her. "Uh, before you see her again, there's something you should know."

"Uh-oh." He took his sunglasses off and resignedly laid them on the table. "Lay it on me."

"She's, uh, cut her hair."

He squinted reflexively. "How short?"

Rissa bit her lip, reluctant to rat on her friend, but hoping that if he was better prepared, maybe the shock of seeing her minus the tam wouldn't precipitate a fight. "Very," she said succinctly.

He gasped. "She shaved her head?"

"Not exactly." She held her finger and thumb half an inch apart, indicating the current length of Frankie's crowning glory. She waited for the explosion.

When it did come, it was a gust of laughter, rather than a roar of anger. "Tell me you're joking."

"Nope. Sorry."

"Aw, now that's sad. She had the thickest, longest, most gorgeous hair. Our mother's hair. Why'd she want to cut it all off?" He rubbed his forehead, bewildered. "What will this girl do next?"

"Well, there's more."

He collapsed onto the table in mock resignation. "God, tell me now and be done with it."

"She's blond."

"Dirty blond, right?" he asked hopefully. "Brownish?"

"Platinum."

"Oh, good grief," he muttered, but at least he looked resigned rather than upset. Then his mouth quirked. "That, I've got to see."

She was glad that he wasn't mad, but she hastened to ensure that Frankie wouldn't suffer any fallout from her having spilled the beans. "You'll take it easy on her, right, Evan?"

"Of course. It's her hair, after all. I guess I'll get used to it, just like I got used to the tattoos and the piercings. In the long run, it's pretty harmless."

She sighed gustily, relieved. "Good. She was worried that you'd be ticked off."

"I try only to get ticked off over the important stuff." He cocked his head and gave her a critical, searching look. "You really like my sister, don't you?"

"Of course. Why? Don't you think she's likeable?"

He waved his hands in his own defense. "No, no, you

know that's not what I meant. It's just that you only met her yesterday."

"Sometimes," she reminded him, "people just click."

His reply was long in coming, and while she waited, Rissa felt his gaze, like light fingertips, flutter across her face, brushing her eyes before moving down to her mouth. Defensively, she drew in her lower lip. Finally, he said, "Yes, I guess they do just click. But does that mean that it will turn into something real?"

Why was he still staring at her? She gulped. "If you work at it."

Whatever he was searching for, he seemed satisfied that he had found it. He let her off the hook. "So, are you ready to go into town?"

She knew that that had been his purpose for coming, but she still felt a sense of disappointment. She tried to put a brave face on it as she stood up and hauled her knapsack and laptop out of the chair next to her. "All ready. I will get to see Frankie again soon, right?"

"Sure you will. Very soon." He looked quite confident in his assertion. "I was thinking I could take you to lunch in the town center. Would you like that?"

"Lunch? I just had breakfast!"

"Well, I still have to stop off at the boatyard first to attend to a few things. I could give you a quick tour. After that, maybe we can walk around town for a bit, and then eat."

"My interview is at two," she reminded him.

He nodded. "I haven't forgotten."

It seemed that that was all she was going to get out of him for the moment, as he began to lead her to the car. She followed, head buzzing. A visit to a boatyard, a tour of downtown Perpignan, and lunch, all in the company of this incredibly disturbing man. She tried to quell her excitement. It wasn't

as though he was taking her out; he was merely being courteous. He'd help her get her bearings, make sure she was fed,
and then leave her to her own defenses with his conscience
clear. That was the way life was.

But for what it was worth, she decided, she was going
to enjoy it.

The boatyard was located at the extreme end of Evan's
property. It was surprisingly small. It consisted of a short
pier, at which a beautiful leisure boat called the *Sardana* was
moored, an office, a covered working area where, as far as
Rissa could determine, only two boats were under construction. They were in an advanced stage: the hulls were already
built, and four or five locals were busy clambering in and out
with their tools.

"That one's mine," Evan said, pointing to the *Sardana.* "The
Sardana is the traditional dance of the Catalunya. It's a fascinating dance, very lively. At one time, not so long ago, when
the Spanish were trying to quell the Catalan culture and force
it to become assimilated, it was banned, but nobody ever paid
the ban any mind. The people kept on dancing. I like that: re-
bellion is good, if it comes from a position of righteousness. And
I like the way it makes me think of a boat dancing on the waves."

"I don't know anything about boats, but it's gorgeous," she
said.

He'd replaced his sunglasses, but the pride in his eyes was
still evident. "It's a work of art. Handmade from stem to stern.
It was one of the last projects I worked on with my father."

She was dying to find out what had happened to their parents. Frankie had been reluctant to say, but Rissa was sure that
it would go a long way toward helping her understand the
nature of the relationship between the siblings. She wondered
if it would be bad form to ask.

She didn't have to. Evan saw the question in her eyes. "My parents were avid sailors. They were still very young, both in their fifties, when they disappeared."

"Disappeared?" she echoed. An uneasy ripple ran through her. How did two people just disappear?

He nodded soberly. "They'd gone on a long trip, starting off at Nice, and headed around the Horn of Africa. My father called it the adventure of his life. He and Mom had been planning it for a very long time. They were used to shorter journeys— through the Caribbean, along the West Coast of the U.S., around the Greek Isles, places like that. But the Horn is an especially difficult region. There are experienced sailors who would balk at the prospect, because it's so unpredictable."

"So why did they want to go?"

"They saw it as their Everest, their great challenge in life. They'd already done so much. Raised two children, taken my grandfather's small business and made it into a thriving family enterprise, and built some of the most sought-after pleasure boats in the business. They wanted to do something just for themselves. So six years ago, they set sail on the *Castillet,* the sister boat to this one. It was a much larger, better equipped vessel. We made it ourselves, too.

"And everything went beautifully. My parents were having a wonderful time. It was never intended to be a direct trip, from one port to the next. They wanted to see as many countries as they could. Tunisia, Egypt, Turkey, Cyprus...." He enumerated on his fingers. "They kept a journal, took lots of photographs and videos, and sent them back home to me at every port they visited. They checked in with me by radio every evening, just to let me know that everything was okay, and to tell me how their day went."

Evan had been leading her toward the workshop with determined paces, gravel crunching under his feet, but now he stopped abruptly. Rissa waited for the rest of his story. "Then one evening, about nine weeks into their trip, they didn't call. As a seaman, I can tell you that a missed check-in is a very serious matter. And I knew that my parents wouldn't have missed a call for no reason. Something had to have happened. I tried calling them all through the night. I sent out a distress call to all boats in their area. They'd left Alexandria, and were headed for the Suez Canal. I tried to raise the authorities in that general vicinity, pleaded for help from Egypt, the Israelis, anyone who might have news of them. Nothing. The American embassies in the region coordinated a search with the other governments, but after two weeks everyone gave up."

Rissa faced him. She longed to lay her hand on his arm, but was afraid it would be out of place, afraid she would offend him. So she clasped her hands behind her back, nails gripping into her own flesh. "And…did you ever hear anything?"

"No, nothing." From the look on his face, six years had done little to ease the hurt.

"I don't know anything about sailing. What could possibly…?"

He lifted his shoulders heavily. "I don't think we'll ever know. There were a few squalls that night, within a few hundred miles of where they were last located, but nothing serious enough to have sunk a ship. My father would never have allowed himself to run out of fuel. It could have been a mechanical failure or some sort, or a collision. But no wreckage was ever identified, although that's not proof positive that it never happened. It could have been pirates, mercenaries. That goes on more often than you would imagine, even today. Especially in regions such as that. We'll just never know."

"So then there was just you and Frankie."

"Yes, just us. I was twenty-eight, a newlywed, and she was eleven. I was left with a business to run on both sides of the ocean, and a sister to care for. Our grandparents wanted to take her, but she didn't want to go. For her, France is somewhere you visit, not somewhere you live. So she spends most of the year in boarding school back home, at least until she graduates next year. Then she's a free agent, and whatever she chooses to do with her life, she'll have my support."

"She hasn't gotten over your parents' passing," Rissa observed.

"No, she hasn't. She refuses to believe they're dead. I don't know how she has rationalized it, but she only refers to them as 'gone.' She truly believes that they will walk in the front door one day, and we'll all be reunited."

"You don't."

"No. As much as it kills me, I'm realistic. I've conducted my own searches, tried to locate their boat, or parts of it, on the black market, gone down every possible avenue, including modern slavery, but I've never found a shred of evidence that suggests they didn't perish at sea. I've accepted that."

One hand rebelled against the other that was holding it back, and she reached out and touched him. His flesh was firm and warm. He neither flinched nor pulled away. "Evan, I'm sorry."

He put his hand over hers and squeezed it lightly. "Thank you." Then he broke their tenuous contact, resuming walking once again. "Come, let me show you around."

As they walked through the small workshop, the rich scents of wood, brass, and polish filled her nostrils. The few machines visible were rudimentary, and there was a surprising absence of automation: no conveyor belts, no rows of parts waiting to be slipped into their rightful place. The men working around her barely acknowledged her presence, pausing only to glance up and down at her in the manner of their countrymen, give her an appreciative wink or quirk of the brow, and then return to work. She felt as though she were wandering through an artist's workshop, rather than a factory. Eager to absorb as much as she could, she listened intently to Evan's explanations, feeling honored when he allowed her to stroke a strip of leather or feel the weight of a brass ornament in her hands.

They finally stopped at the entrance to the offices. "You'll have to excuse me for a few minutes, Rissa," Evan said. "I just have to check on a few things with Corbin, and then we can go." He encompassed their surroundings with a sweep of his arm. "Feel free to have a look around, or you can sit in the lobby, if you prefer. But if you want to stay outside, watch your head and stay clear of anything moving."

She wasn't sure if he was joking about that part, but after a few seconds' deliberation, she decided that it was better not to risk it, so she slipped into the lobby behind him while he disappeared around a corner. It was small but well kept; the walls were decorated with copies of old maritime maps, and a few prints of well-known paintings of the region, including one that she was sure was by Dali, and another by Picasso. A large fish tank took up most of the space in one corner, and Rissa bent over, propping her hands on her knees to support herself, and watched the brightly colored freshwater fish as they darted in and out among the clumps of weeds, rocks, and plastic fish toys scattered about. The tank was like a miniature undersea world of a bygone era: sunken galleons, broken amphorae, gold coins, and tiny weapons. Rissa smiled. That tank had been put together by someone with a sense of whimsy, and she was willing to bet dollars to donuts she knew who it was.

It seemed as though everything she saw around her, here and at the house, bore Evan's fingerprint. Every painting on the wall, every book on the shelf, every plant, every piece of furniture spoke of good taste, a careful, ordered mind, and a quiet harmony with nature. The more she discovered about Evan, it seemed, the more she wanted to know.

Before she could muse over that fact much longer, she heard raised voices coming along the passageway where Evan had disappeared. The words were certainly not in English, but their heat and volume left no doubt as to the anger behind them. Rissa halted, feeling like an intruder, wishing desperately that she had taken the option of putting life and limb on the line by staying in the workshop, anything to avoid the uncomfortable position of being a witness to an argument in which she was not involved.

Evan emerged first. He stalked out, strides long and back straight, a bunch of documents clenched in his tightly curled fist. Corbin followed, face ruddy with anger, spitting Catalan out of his mouth like nails. He was driving home a point, punctuating it with one fist pounded into the other.

Whatever Evan said in response had an air of finality to it, because Corbin said nothing more, except for a bitten-off affirmative. He threw his hands up into the air in a very Latin gesture of frustration, snatched the papers that Evan held out to him, frowned down at them, and then looked up, bright eyes locking with Rissa's embarrassed ones. "Mademoiselle Young," he acknowledged her, dredging up his old-world courtesy with some difficulty. "Nice to see you again."

In the absence of the thunderbolt that Rissa had been praying to strike her dead rather than leave her here in this private moment between the two men, she coughed, and managed a greeting. "Hello, Corbin. Nice to see you, too."

Formalities over, Corbin nodded, once at her and once at Evan, spun around on his heel like a soldier at a passing-out parade, and marched back up the passageway, conveying his disgust at his final orders by slamming the door to his office. The noise reverberated through the small lobby.

Rissa eyed Evan warily, wondering if his residual anger was going to spill her way. It wouldn't be a pleasant trip into town if he was going to be scowling all the way down! And what about his proposed tour of Perpignan? Would he be in any mood to do that? Disappointment made her shoulders slump.

Evan shook his head to clear it, and blew slowly out through pursed lips. Then, like a chameleon changing color to adjust to a new branch, he seemed to morph back into the same relaxed, affable host who had escorted her in. He took her elbow and guided her back out into the sunshine before he said anything again. His touch was firm and courteous, almost impersonal, but she found heat rising to her face and neck all the same. It was the first time he'd touched her since the evening before, since he had come forward to rescue her from the ignominious position in which his dogs had left her on his garden path. She hoped that he would be dense enough to put her flush down to discomfiture at having witnessed their argument.

Maybe he had, because he said, "Don't worry about that," as he made sure she was properly seated in the car. "I hope it didn't embarrass you too much. It wasn't as serious as it looked; men in business argue like that all the time. It's just that we have a different way of doing things from women. You tend to put more emphasis on *how* things are said rather than *what's* being said. We men, we thrash it out loud and clear, and get it out of our systems. By tomorrow, it will all be forgotten." He climbed in next to her, and the car sank under his weight. The car was so low-slung that, had she not driven across with him in the first place, she would have been afraid that it would have scraped the gravel underneath as they drove off.

"What was it about?" she ventured to ask, and then added hastily, "If you can tell me, that is."

"Oh, it's no secret. As a matter of fact, Corbin will beef about it to anyone. He's been approaching me with an offer of partnership for a long time, at least as far as the workshop here is concerned. This one is legally entirely mine. The ship-yard in San Diego is a private company, originally owned by my grandfather, and then my father, but now controlled by a handful of shareholders, presided over by myself."

The car swung gracefully onto the coastal road, its sea-blue mimicking the dazzling Mediterranean along which it trav-eled, and white leather interior evoking the sea-capped waves that slammed against the cliffs. The coastal road was wide enough not to cause Rissa any unnecessary nervousness as to the several sudden curves. From time to time, she glimpsed a passing train moving purposefully by. It was a glorious day.

Evan continued, "Anyway, Corbin has worked for me ever since he left college. He's my right-hand man, and a good businessman. Too good, actually. For him, business is more about getting to the bottom line quickly and less about the trip there. The big difference between his philosophy and mine is this: the way I see it, a career and a reputation are things you build over a lifetime. Wealth is something you accumulate through patience and careful investment." He threw her a sideways glance. "In my case, I had help: it took generations for our business to get to the point where it is, because my father and grandfather had the same philosophy."

"But Corbin wants to get rich quick."

"The quicker the better. Not that there's anything wrong with that, per se. And I'd be the last person to prevent him from trying. That wouldn't even be motivation enough for me to refuse to share leadership in the business with him. As I said before, he's a good businessman, and a very hard worker. It's the way he wants to do it that worries me."

"Which is?"

His scowl returned momentarily. "Which is to cut corners on the way we build my boats, and that, I won't stand for. The boatyard in San Diego is a purely commercial operation—we make high-quality, affordable boats through a number of processes, many of them automated. We emphasize efficiency, safety, good looks and durability. Over there, you can buy a boat from our showroom or place an order, and have your vessel in a week or two.

"But this workshop, my *atelier*, is an entirely different species of creature. It's more of an artist's studio than a production line. We never work on more than two boats at any one time, no matter how urgent the demand, how important the client, or how much money they offer for a rush job. That's my first rule. I insist that my workers have the time and space to attend to every detail.

"Second, automation is kept to a minimum—with the exception of what's needed for the engines and instrumentation, of course. That part's always ultra-modern, the best that the client can afford. The boats themselves are built by craftsmen, the upholstery stitched by hand, woodwork and leatherwork hand tooled. The people who buy these boats are clients who are looking for something special. They look for utility *and* art, all rolled into one vessel."

The top of the car was down, and the warm air blew through Rissa's hair, ruffling her bangs, lulling and seductive—but nowhere near as lulling as the pride in Evan's voice as he talked about his business. "They're beautiful boats," she confirmed.

"Yes, they are. And to be fair, Corbin's suggestion wouldn't diminish their beauty much on the outside. He just thinks that there are a lot of shortcuts that we could take on parts of the work that aren't immediately visible. Like the undersides of the upholstery. The interiors of closets, hidden corners. Using glue where we now use nails, staples where we now use stitches, that sort of thing. Overall, it would shave a few days or weeks off of each boat's construction timetable, save on salaries for my employees, and nudge the profits up a bit over time. And to tell the truth, many of his changes wouldn't be apparent to most clients, except to those with the most discerning eye. We could get away with it, if we tried."

"But you'd know, deep down." She understood exactly how he felt. It was like being confronted with the temptation to rush down a piece she was writing because a deadline was creeping up on her. She might be able to send off an acceptable piece, see it published and get paid for it, but she would know deep in her heart that she could have done better. When you really had pride in your work, something like that left a bitter taste in your mouth.

"I'd know, deep down," he echoed. "So that's where it stands between us. I won't back down, and neither will he."

"And he doesn't like that," she observed.

"No, he doesn't."

Evan let the matter drop, and for the rest of the journey concentrated on pointing out landmarks both small and large, giving her bits of information about the plants that draped the sloping hillsides in color, about the small domestic winemakers in the area, and about anything else that popped into his head that she might find of interest. Rissa listened, as interested in what he had to say as she was in the sound of his voice. They swung away from the coast and turned inland, and the greenery gave way to the town.

"Perpignan proper," Evan announced. He looked across at her and smiled. "Ready?"

Tips and Tricks for Warming Her Up When You Need Her To Say Yes

Evan pulled up in one of the roomy downtown parking lots, unreasonably excited by the prospect of showing Rissa around his adoptive home town. As they exited the vehicle, he watched her look around, craning her neck and turning from side to side as she tried to take everything in. He loved Perpignan with his whole heart: the wide-open spaces, the narrow, cobbled roads, the collision between Latin and French cultures, and, most importantly, the expressive and fiery people.

As he led Rissa onto the sidewalk at the town's main thoroughfare, the first question that tumbled into his mind was: which of all the wonderful nooks and crannies he held dear should he show her first? The second was: why was it so important? He'd only met this woman yesterday, and it hadn't been the most pleasant of meetings at that, but even once he factored in the fact that they had gotten over that hurdle reasonably unscathed, he was inordinately anxious for her to like the town as much as he did. Okay, so maybe his bright idea to take her around was partly intended to seduce her into a state where she would be comfortable enough with the town, and with him, to accept the proposition he'd dreamed up last night. For his sake, or, rather, for Frankie's, it was vital that she say yes. If playing tour guide for the day and turning on the charm was what it took, so be it. He wasn't above using a little butter to grease the mechanisms of the human will when needed.

But there was more. It wasn't just about softening her up to get her to see things his way. He wanted her to like Perpignan, in the way that a man introducing a special friend to a group of strangers wanted them to like her, too.

"What's that?" Rissa snatched from his mind the indecision as to where to begin their tour by pointing excitedly up at an enormous red-brick edifice that dominated the entire town center. It was an ancient castle, complete with ramparts, slitted windows, and elaborate metalwork throughout. It stood surrounded by well-tended lawn and perky flowers, much of it reflected in the river that sauntered past, bisecting the town center.

"That's the Castillet. It once marked the entrance to the town, back in the days when all this was surrounded by medieval walls. It's as old as the Bastille in Paris, more than 600 years old, actually." He pointed at the barred windows. "It even used to be a prison for a while. Imagine being locked away in *that*." That thought had crossed his mind several times as he went about his business in town. The castle, though beautiful, had a brooding sense of majesty that imposed itself not only upon the landscape, but upon the minds of all who gazed upon it.

Rissa felt the same way. She looked up and shivered. "I don't know why, but I get the eerie feeling that someone's got a bow and arrow trained right at my heart." She put her hand up to her breast as though to protect the organ, drawing Evan's gaze downward. She was wearing a pretty cotton peasant blouse, embroidered around the neckline and wrists, over a deep blue skirt that just about made it to the knee, baring slender, shapely legs that ended in sandaled feet. Hardly what one would normally wear to a job interview, but he assumed that it was the best of the few remaining articles of clothing left her by the scamps that had cleaned her out. The blouse was held together at the throat by a drawstring and tassels, which dangled between her breasts. The defensive hand idly stroked the curve of her left breast. The material was thin enough to suggest that maybe she didn't like bras much. He inhaled sharply.

She caught the sound and her deep brown, tip-tilted eyes flew to his, slightly suspicious, but slightly—something else. She snatched her hand away from her breast as though he had laid his hand upon hers, and ruffled her lustrous black bangs to hide her confusion. The effect was charming.

He cleared his throat and tried to focus on her comment. "Relax. It's probably just the ghost of an old Catalan soldier. Don't worry about it."

She gaped. "It's haunted?"

He smiled to let her know that he was half pulling her leg. "Aren't most castles?"

"I guess," she conceded hesitantly, but still kept a cautious eye on the upper windows of the Castillet. Then, she noticed something else. The flag of the Catalunya whipped proudly in the wind, its four bars of blood red in striking contrast to the background of gold. "Why aren't they flying the French flag?" she wanted to know. "Don't they think of themselves as French?"

"Of course they do. They are as loyal to their nationality as we are to ours, except that they are in an unusual historical position. Legally, and politically, they're as French as anyone from Paris or Provence or Calais. But these are people whose bloodlines harken back to a race that fought determinedly against cultural invasion from both France and Spain. And even though things have changed, their region has been split up like the spoils of war, they still hold their history dear. They haven't forgotten who they really are deep down."

He pointed at the flag. "They call that flag the 'Blood and Gold'. It's the ultimate symbol of ethnic pride. You'll see it in stickers on car bumpers, on badges stitched onto their chests, on scarves wrapped around their throats. You'll find the French flag flying high on all the official buildings, but this is the one they pin over their hearts."

"It must be strange," she mused, "to experience something that almost amounts to cultural schizophrenia."

"I understand them perfectly. I've been there myself; maybe that's why I love them so much." He decided that it was time to start walking, so he turned toward the sidewalk, leading her up along the right bank of the languid Basse river, which bisected the town, separating the luxurious cafés, bookstores and *bijouteries* from the smaller, slightly shabbier, and, in his opinion, far more interesting quarter. The sidewalk was elevated along the riverbanks, which lay about twenty feet down. Both banks were carefully tended, grass neatly mowed and flowerbeds laid out with geometric precision. A bridge or two offered the means to cross from one bank to the other, or simply provided a convenient space to stop in the middle and gaze down at the scudding clouds reflected in the water below.

As he walked, he began to explain himself. "I know what it's like to have two cultures colliding inside me. My paternal grandfather is what they call in Martinique a *chabin,* half white, half black. His wife, my grandmaman, is a white French woman. He migrated to the States as a young man, to transplant a small boat-building business that had been in his

family for more than a century. My father was born in the
U.S., as was I, but I spent much of my life tracing a perpetual triangle in the Atlantic: America, Martinique, France.

"I love all three, for different reasons. I sail to Martinique
on the rare occasions when I have the time to take a vacation.
I fly back to San Diego every six weeks for a board meeting
and to consult with my operations manager over there on how
things are going. I have a house there, and when I'm there, I
call it home, just as I do with my house over here. I speak four
languages, and love them all for different reasons. I think of
myself as a Black man, but that doesn't mean that I've turned
my back on my French heritage, because to do that would be
to deny my grandmother and her ancestors, and I love her
dearly." He paused to take a breath, hoping that she understood what he was saying.

"So you feel torn," she said sympathetically.

She didn't get it! He tried to clarify. "Not at all. I feel like
a whole person, made up of a lot of parts. I don't consider any
part of who I am to be any more or any less than any other
part. I think we should all be proud of every drop of blood
that mingled together to make us what we are. To do anything
less would be a form of self hate."

Rissa looked at him critically, as if she hadn't expected to
hear anything that reasonable come from him. Maybe she still
harbored an image of him as irrational and prone to sudden
bursts of anger. He'd planted that seed in her mind with his
treatment of her last night, and his fight with Corbin in her
presence this morning had watered the seedling. He'd have
to fix that.

He sought to illustrate his point by bringing it closer to
home. He let his gaze sweep slowly over her. Her features certainly held evidence of another bloodline, and the almond
shape of her eyes, the waves in her glossy, jet hair, the fineness

of her bone structure and the perpetual pout to her lips told
him that India was its most likely source. "I'm sure you know
what I'm talking about," he suggested. "I'm sure you think
of yourself as a confluence of races, rather than belonging to
a single one."

She laughed, and seeing those full lips pulled back like that
did something weird to his gut. "'Confluence of races,'" she
quoted him. "I like that. You should have been a writer."

"There's always time," he murmured.

"Well, actually, I see your point, but I have to say that I've
never thought of any part of myself as belonging to India, or
of India belonging to me."

"Why not?" He was truly puzzled. "It's there in your face,
and your hair, and your eyes. It's in the tone of your skin, like
copper chimes in the sun." *And in the sudden flare of your hips
and the perfect roundness of your breasts.* He kept the last two
observations to himself; it was too nice a day to be slapped
in the face by an outraged female.

"'Like copper chimes in the sun,'" she mimicked. "You're
on a roll now."

"Thank you. Coming from a professional, that's something." He bowed his head briefly with mock gallantry.

"Unlike you, I've never been to India, and I never knew my
grandmother. She died when I was very young. I don't remember her. So our situations aren't the same."

"Oh, okay." He was almost disappointed that that potential connecting point between them had collapsed.

"But I understand how you feel," she added hastily.

"Good," he told her. *Very good.* Empathy led to trust.

As they walked, the broad roadways dramatically narrowed, and the paving underfoot transformed to square cob-
blestones or rough bitumen. Grungy apartment buildings
leaned in toward each other, and, overhead, wet clothes

dangled from clotheslines strung across the road from window to window. Women in housecoats propped themselves up on their elbows on the railings of balconies that seemed to be no more than two feet square, gossiping with their neighbors. Inside the buildings, children squealed with laughter.

A couple approached from the opposite direction, a portly, middle-aged woman dressed in a navy burka, her face and body almost completely covered in fabric. Finely worked silver filigree adorned the rim of her veil. The husband wore unusually warm clothes for the weather, including a jacket, tie, and a battered overcoat. As they passed each other in the narrow street, Evan registered Rissa's surprised stare as she noticed that the woman's lips and eyes, just visible through the netting of her veil, were heavily tattooed with blue symbols and patterns. The husband was equally unreserved about staring. He glanced quickly down at Rissa's bare legs and then gave her an affronted glare. Rissa returned the stare with a defiant one of her own.

"North Africans, most likely," Evan explained. "Perpignan doesn't have a whole lot of brown-skinned inhabitants, of course, but you'll find a larger concentration of them here than in most other quarters. Mostly from the French West Indies, North Africa, and the Middle East. Some migrant workers, some second and third generation French citizens who haven't been able to overcome their situation."

She looked around with renewed interest, and then pointed at a small shingle hanging in a doorway. "Look, a Senegalese restaurant!"

"I know the guy that owns it. Food's pretty good. Cheap, too."

"I'll remember that," she said humorously.

Eventually, they came upon a small square that seemed to be more of a meeting of several narrow roadways than anything else. Compared to the quieter back streets through which they had passed, it thronged with activity. Rickety market stalls were haphazardly scattered throughout, many arrayed with mounds of brightly colored fruit and vegetables. Some stalls sold fresh fish out of plastic pails filled with shaved ice, others, an uncanny variety of olives from wooden barrels. Housewives rummaged through heaps of clothes looking for a bargain, and the air rang out with the combined sounds of French, Catalan, Spanish, Creole, Arabic, and any number of African tribal languages. Evan watched Rissa carefully for a reaction to the mayhem.

He was not disappointed. She slapped her hands to her cheeks and exclaimed, "Oh, my God!"

He was smiling with pride and the desire to share this pleasure with her. "One of my secret haunts. I come here all the time, especially when I'm in the mood to cook. You game?"

"Oh, you bet!" She went directly to the olives and other preserves, peeping into the barrels in amazement. Apart from the black, pimento-stuffed, and plain olives that usually line grocery shelves back home, there were olives stuffed with almonds, anchovies, garlic, or pickles, either dry-cured or floating in oil or water, flavored with cumin, coriander, rosemary, or cardamom. The vendor, whose head-scarf was so elaborately wound that he looked top-heavy enough to topple over, grinned expectantly. Evan asked Rissa whether she liked olives.

"Love them! I feel like I've died and gone to heaven!"

"Good. I make a mean olive tapenade with salade niçoise and crusty bread. We'll get some and have it for dinner."

"But I won't—" she began to remind him.

"Shh," was all he said. Ignoring her puzzled look, he made his selection, transacted business quickly with the vendor, and moved on to a seafood stall he normally visited. As they approached, a commotion broke out. A whip-like brown eel had escaped the confines of its white plastic prison, slithering onto the dry sidewalk and flopping frantically about for several moments before gratefully tumbling into the water-filled drain and making a dash for freedom toward a nearby canal. Unperturbed, the hefty, red-faced woman in the stall squatted, her tree-trunk calves making it difficult, and scooped up the miscreant, throwing it back into the bucket without flinching.

"Ugh," Rissa shuddered. "If I ever had even the slightest inclination to try eel, that's pretty much killed it for me."

"They're an acquired taste," he informed her with a straight face.

"I won't be acquiring it."

He persisted in his mischief, pointing to what looked like a bowl of pinkish-white, star-shaped flowers. "What about baby octopi? Sauté them lightly, sprinkle them with a little—"

"Nope."

He laughed, and let her win. "Okay, just some fresh tuna and anchovies for the salad, then. Coward." He paid for two small packages, added them to the shopping bag filled with olives, and guided her through the rest of the small market to his preferred stalls, buying all the fixings for tonight's dinner. When they'd made the circuit, he stopped and faced her. "Enjoyed it?" He resisted the urge to cross his fingers.

Her eyes were shining. "Yes! It was so…different."

"That, it is." They'd managed to kill what was left of the morning, and the lunch hour was long past. "What about lunch now?" he suggested. "I know just the place. No eels, unless you specifically request them."

"Are you kidding? I've barely digested that whopping breakfast I had back at the house!"

"Not in the mood for a little French cuisine?"

"Don't know where I'd put it!" She jokingly patted her hip, which was far from plump, if that was what she was implying by the gesture.

"You're not going to tell me you're fat! From where I stand, you need a little fattening up, actually. Haven't you been taking care of yourself?" Then he remembered jarringly that she had told him that she'd been ill for some time. Maybe that accounted for the sense he had, when he looked at her, that she'd lost a layer of herself. Not wanting to kill the jovial mood, he tried gentle persuasion. "How about a sandwich, then? It's nice outdoors, we can eat and watch people go by. And you don't have to finish it if you don't want to."

She considered his suggestion for several moments, and then gave in graciously. "I think I can squeeze one in."

"Good. Follow me."

The look on her face when he made an about-face and headed back into the market was too precious to be missed. They stopped at the stall of a wiry, bare-armed Tunisian vendor who was busy poking at links of merguez sausages sizzling in a cast iron skillet over a low gas fire. Sections of fresh baguettes toasted nearby. The smell of the hot, spicy meat made Evan's mouth water. He lifted his brow at her, challenging. "Think you can handle that?"

She was too stubborn to balk one more time, even in the face of evident doubt, and the taunt of "coward" that he had tossed at her still rankled, so she cocked a brow right back at him. "Bring it!"

He lifted two fingers at the vendor. In response, the man nodded and worked quickly, seizing two segments of bread, and piercing a hole through each, end to end, with the handle of a large wooden spoon. Sticking each sausage onto the end of a fork, he dipped them first into a bowl of ketchup, then into a bowl of mayonnaise, and then inserted one into the tunnel he had made in each piece of bread.

"Kill me now," Rissa murmured weakly. "Get it over with."

"It's not over yet," he promised. Sadistically, he nodded in response to the vendor's unspoken query, as the man lifted a half-squeezed tube of *harissa,* a paste made of red chilies and spices guaranteed to corrode metal. They came in mild or extra-hot varieties. He indicated the latter when Rissa glanced away for a second. The vendor got the joke, grinning broadly at Evan, and added a generous squirt to each sandwich.

Rissa took hers gingerly. "French hot dogs, huh?"

"You could call 'em that."

They found a park bench and he plopped his purchases down, encouraging Rissa to sit. "I'll be back in a jiffy," he promised her.

He was, bearing a bottle of red Banyuls wine and two plastic cups. "Nothing completes the whole experience of dining al fresco as a nice, rich wine. Sorry about the cups, though," he added, although he wasn't sorry at all. Plastic cups made it fun.

"Wine goes with hotdogs?" she enquired, not buying his remorse.

"Wine goes with everything," he countered. A penknife that he always carried on his belt dealt easily with the cork, and he poured out two glasses. *"Salut."* He handed hers over and lifted his.

"To your health," she responded, and drank heartily. She took her first bite of hotdog—and grimaced. "What in the name of…what did you make him put in this?"

"Harissa. Arabic hot sauce. Like it?"

"Love it," she gagged, and stubbornly took another bite of her sandwich before washing it down with generous gulps of wine.

Evan was unable to keep a grin off his face. She was gutsy and adventurous. He liked that, and she got extra points for looking cute even while she struggled against the pressure of the steam building up between her ears. They finished the rest of their meal in comfortable silence, enjoying the vantage point that allowed them to observe shoppers as they wandered about the market place, made their purchases and left. The level of the wine in the bottle dipped.

Evan was content, enjoying both his lunch and her company. Then she finished her meal, rummaged through her bag for a breath mint, handed him one and looked at her watch with a decisive air. "Thanks for lunch," she began, "and the tour. But—"

He froze. It was almost time for her to head off to her job interview at that bookstore down in the town center. He couldn't let that happen; he needed her. If he didn't stop her now, he'd lose her, and his bright idea would blow out like a candle in the breeze. Whatever he had to do to make her stay, he'd have to do it fast.

"I think Frankie's got a boyfriend," he blurted, startling both himself and her.

She stared at him, dumbstruck, blinking rapidly in an attempt to process the remark, put it into context. "Huh?"

He wanted to slap an exasperated hand to his forehead. *Smooth, Evan, real smooth.* That wasn't exactly how he had planned to begin making his case. But he'd already set his course, so he followed it. "I suspect Frankie's got a boyfriend. It's really beginning to bother me."

"Why?" She still hadn't recovered from the shock of the comment leaping at her straight out of left field.

"Why do I think there's a boy, or why is it bothering me?"

"Why, both?"

"She's suddenly become secretive. Spending hours in her room at night chatting online, when she used to hang out with me before bed, making popcorn and watching movies. Now she heads off on these all-day shopping trips with little to show for it. Runs away to late night parties. Dashes outside with her cell phone to take or make calls."

"Typical teenage behavior," Rissa diagnosed.

"Maybe. A bit of it, I suppose. But my instinct says there's more."

"And why—"

"It bothers me because she's too trusting, attaches herself to people too fast, thinks she's more grown up than she really is...."

"Brings home *strays* to spend the night," Rissa couldn't resist adding pertly.

He hung his head slightly at the sound of his own words being hurled back in his face. "Yes, sometimes. That, too."

Rissa swiveled in her seat, pointing her knees in his direction. "She's *seventeen*, Evan," she reasoned, as though that made it all any better. "They *do* that. Boyfriends are a part of any normal girl's life."

"I know, I know! And I'm not challenging her right to have one. It's just that she's fragile; she has a lot of emotional baggage, what with losing our parents the way we did, and spending half her life in boarding school away from my protection. A *girls'* school at that, so she hasn't had much chance to learn about boys even under supervised conditions. I don't want anyone to take advantage of her. You understand?"

Rissa thought about it for a while, and then grudgingly gave him the benefit of the doubt. "So, who's this boy?"

"I have no idea! Most likely some youngster from one of the nearby villages, or maybe even Perpignan itself. It's only just begun, but it's escalating way too fast. I can sense it. She may think she's in love, but I don't think she has any concept of the pitfalls love brings. I don't think she's even capable of grown-up love. And I hate the idea that somewhere out there there's a young man willing to take advantage of her ignorance and naiveté to his own...." He waved his hands, searching for a term that wouldn't even offend his tongue as he said it "...ends," he managed lamely. "You know what I mean?"

"I know what you mean. But, Evan, at that age, they do experiment—"

"My sister is not a lab-rat," he snapped, knowing that the analogy was ridiculous even as he said it.

She saw his point, but persisted in defending Frankie. "But you're not being fair. Think back," she proposed reasonably, "to when you were seventeen. Didn't you...experiment, too?"

"Yes," he conceded miserably. "But a lot of water has passed under the bridge since then, and I know things now that I had no inkling of at the time. There are so many dangers—disease, heartbreak, and a lot worse. She has her whole life ahead of her. I'm not going to sit back and take a chance on her muddling through it on her own. She's my *sister!*"

"And I'm sure the young ladies you, um, were acquainted with back then had brothers, too. They were someone else's sister, and someone else agonized over them in much the same way. But didn't they do okay, in the end? And aren't you being unfair to this boy, whoever he may be? Maybe he really likes her, too. Maybe it's not what—"

"I'm sorry if it sounds sexist, or if this seems like a double standard to you. And don't start preaching at me about the Madonna-whore complex either, because, to tell the truth, every man suffers from it in some small way. Sure, in the past I may have set a few other men worrying about their sisters, but I can't go back and fix that. And Frankie is the only one I've got, and I'll do whatever it takes to make sure she's safe and happy."

To his relief, she didn't argue the point further. "What are you going to do, then?"

There it was: his opening. He had to make his proposal now, and make it in such a way that she couldn't turn him down. He reached down into his pocket and withdrew an envelope, and handed it over to her.

She took it, frowning in puzzlement, not even looking inside. "What's this?"

"Open it." She hesitated, and he urged her further. "Open it, please. Trust me."

She broke the seal of the envelope and withdrew its contents, fanning out the small sheaf of large-denomination bills in astonishment. "What am I supposed to do with this?"

"Don't go to that interview, Rissa." He removed his phone from the clip on his belt and held it out to her. "Call and cancel. I'm offering you a better job."

She looked down at the money in her hand, and as the wind ruffled the edges of the bills, she was able to estimate their value without actually having to count. It was a tidy sum.

"I'd like you to work for me," he reiterated.

The look she gave him was hard, suspicious, and bordering on outrage. "As *what*?"

Moral Dilemmas: When the Wrong Thing Seems Like the Right Thing To Do

Rissa put the money carefully back into the envelope, and laid it down between them on the bench. What was Evan up to? Whatever it was, it smelled funny. There was more money there than she'd lost last week, almost as much as she'd had when she'd started out on her trip. What could he possibly have that he wanted, that was worth that much? She reddened slightly when an obscene thought popped into her head.

Evan saw the flush, guessed its origin, and hastily denied her unspoken accusation. "No, no, nothing like that! It's totally above board, Rissa, I promise!"

"There are an awful lot of euros there, Evan." She wasn't sure she even wanted to know what plot he'd dreamed up, with her in a starring role.

"I could make it U.S. currency, if you like," he offered. "I just thought that this was more convenient."

He was being deliberately dense. He had to be! "That's no[t] what I meant!" she snapped.

"No, I know. I'm sorry. I'm just nervous. This is impor[-]tant."

"What is?"

"My sister. I told you that."

"And what do you want me to do for your sister? She already has a tutor."

"She does. That's not the service I had in mind."

She leaned forward, her face near to his, and asked slowly and carefully, so that there was no misunderstanding the note of menace in her voice, "And what, exactly, is the 'service' you had in mind?"

"I need you to watch over her. Be a companion, or a chap[-]erone, whatever you want to call it. Guide her along the right path. Most importantly, make sure she doesn't get into any sort of trouble."

"With that boy."

"Correct."

She was aghast. What he was proposing was sickening. He was going to pay her huge sums of money to follow a seven[-]teen year old girl around and make sure she didn't make ou[t] with some neighborhood kid? "And submit written reports to you each night, I suppose?"

"No. But I do expect you to tell me if she's involved in any[-]thing more hazardous that the normal teenage shenanigans."

"You want me to rat your sister out?" she shrieked.

"I want you," he replied equally slowly, equally carefully, "to be a companion to my sister, and offer her guidance in [a] matter that I think only a woman can. Keep her company, keep her out of trouble, and help me get her back to San Diego i[n] one piece at the end of the summer. In exchange," he pointe[d] at the envelope that sat between them, "you'll receive a simila[r] sum of money, in cash, every Friday. There's enough there to help you get back on your feet for the time being. Get some new clothes. Whatever it is you lost. And when it's time for Frankie to fly back to the States, my offer includes a ticket home, right back to Philly."

"You pig!" she exclaimed. She couldn't believe he was suggesting something like this! She'd had such a good time with him today, she'd actually begun to like him. She'd begun to think that the authoritarian, controlling, self-appointed father figure he'd seemed to be last night was actually a combination of her own distorted perception and Frankie's penchant for exaggeration. But she was wrong. He *was* as bad as he'd seemed last night. "You want me to be your sister's little Rent-A-Friend! I don't believe this! You think you have to pay me to be good to her?"

"You *are* good to her. And good *for* her. I know you care about her, and she likes you. That's the only reason I've asked you. I certainly wouldn't ask this of anybody else."

"What do you think Frankie will say? She already thinks you're a controlling stick-in-the-mud. How do you think she'll feel when you tell her you've bought me off for the summer?"

His face hardened, leaving her no doubt as to the seriousness of his assertion. "I won't. And neither will you. That condition is non-negotiable."

"So," her voice dripped with sarcasm, "all I have to do is stay close enough to your sister to spy on her and thwart any little romantic rendezvous she might have in mind, report back to you on any suspicious activity—"

"Any *dangerous* activity," he corrected.

Rissa continued, her outrage unabated. "—Lie to her, and in return, you pay me this huge sum of money every week. Is that all?"

"That's not exactly how I'd prefer to see it, but, I guess, that's all."

"You must have a pretty low opinion of me."

"On the contrary. Like I said, I'm only asking you this because I have a very high opinion of you."

"Oh, thank you. I'm so glad to hear it. And, your high opinion notwithstanding, you believe I come at a price."

"Everyone does, one way or the other," he answered reasonably. "You just need to find out what it is."

That did it. Rissa shot to her feet, shouldered her handbag, and looked around in agitation, trying to remember the way they had come. She found it, and stalked off.

Evan scooped up the envelope and was after her in a flash. He came abreast of her easily. "Rissa, don't."

"You make me sick."

"You've misunderstood! I love my sister. This isn't about you or me or right or wrong. This is for her sake."

"And she'll thank you for it later, huh?"

"When she's old enough, and wise enough, maybe. But what I'm really hoping is that she never even gets to find out what I did. And that depends on you."

She pointed down a narrow, cobbled street. "This is the way back to town, right?"

"It is, but—"

"Good. I have an interview in twenty minutes." She cut her eyes at him. "For a *real* job."

She felt his hand come down on her arm, halting her in her tracks, and spinning her to face him. His fingers dug into the soft flesh of her bicep. She could have fought him off, or screamed just loudly enough to embarrass him into letting her go, but the urgency in his voice and the fire in those honey eyes held her riveted.

"Listen to me, Rissa. This is the best option you have open to you right now. As far as I know, bookstores pay minimum wage. And if you're lucky enough to get an advance out of them, more power to you. But no matter how you budget, it's still going to be very tough going for the next few months. I'm offering you comfortable accommodation, three squares, and a ride back home at the end of your stay. You can sleep late, swim, and sit on the patio, under the trees, and work on your novel until my sister's classes are over. Then you have the rest of the evening to enjoy her company." Then he added, as a weighty afterthought, "And mine."

"Enjoy *your* company? Me? Like hell! You're deceitful, manipulative, and…and…" *And funny, and impulsive, breathtaking to look at.* She stopped railing.

He brushed off her slight. "Where were you planning to sleep tonight, Rissa?"

"Same place I was planning to sleep last night. In a hostel."

"And what are you having for dinner?"

Visions of her dismal gastronomic future floated across her eyes. All she had to her name were the few miserable snacks that Frankie had bought her on the train yesterday. In contrast, she could almost smell the rosemary-encrusted breast of chicken she had enjoyed last night. Some contrast! She hung her head, teetering on the brink of defeat. "That's blackmail."

"If you like." He didn't look the least bit ashamed; in fact, he seemed confident that he had already won. He held out his hand, palm up. In it was the envelope. "But the choice is yours." Then, he added ironically, "No pressure."

What could she do? She was broke, hungry, and had no place to go. On the one hand, she could perpetuate the struggle, go to her interview, hope she got the job, find a place to spend the next few nights, and fill her belly with bread and cheese until she received her pittance on Friday. On the other, she could return with Evan, back to clean sheets, lavish meals and a long soak in that awesome rose-scented bathroom. Enough money to buy her all that she'd lost, and then some.

A means to get home. All in exchange for keeping the company of a young girl she already intended to see again, keeping her from harm…and lying about it.

When you thought about it, was there really any choice in the matter?

Her hand rose as if it didn't actually belong to her, taking the envelope from him, and slipping it into the pocket of her skirt. She didn't know what to say, so she settled for "Thank you."

"Thank *you*." He looked relieved, as though a huge weight had been lifted. "You made the right decision, Rissa. You won't regret it."

"I hope so," she answered miserably. Deceit was not her strong suit. She extended her hand again. "It's an unholy bargain, if you ask me. But I suppose we should shake on it."

He took it, but instead of grasping it briefly in an informal gesture of agreement, he turned it over, palm down, and brought it to his lips. It could have been for him a purely European habit that he had acquired through time spent here, a casual thing, but for Rissa, it was unbelievably sensual. She was not prepared for the warmth of his mouth against her skin, the long moment that he lingered, or the spine-jarring tremor that he sent racing through her.

Let go, let go, she begged silently. *Oh, God.*

He lifted his head, but did not release her. His thumb idly grazed the spot where his lips had touched, and his index finger was directly under the pulse point at the inside of her wrist. She knew he could feel her blood pound through it.

"I'm grateful that you understand my position." His voice was raspy, like sandpaper on velvet. "I hope I can be of service to you some day in return."

She blustered, trying to cover up her discomfiture. "I'll… I'll tell your sister…tell Frankie that you invited me to stay on as an act of…kindness." Then she added, "Then you'll be a hero in her eyes."

He released her at last, shaking his head slightly. "I don't need to be a hero. I just don't want to be the villain."

Rissa felt suddenly tired, as if, once the tension caused by her uncertainty about her position had been removed, the nervous energy that had sustained her over the past few days oozed out. "Evan, if you don't mind…."

He understood immediately. "You need to get back."

"Yes, please."

"Of course."

They turned in unison, he hitching up his shopping bags to make them more comfortable to carry, and she absently patting her skirt pocket to reassure herself that the money was still in it, even though she had placed it there only moments before.

They were almost back at the parking lot before he said, "For what it's worth, Rissa, I would never have turned you out on the street today, even if you'd decided to turn me down. I'm not that callous. You are always welcome at my home, for as long as you need it."

She rolled her eyes. *Now he tells me.*

Frankie was ecstatic. "You're staying? Cool!"

The evening was warm and clear, so Evan had decided that they would have dinner out on the patio. Only the proximity of the sea and the whirring fans overhead kept the summer heat to a tolerable level, and two or three citronella torches in the garden held the bugs at bay. As promised, Evan had prepared dinner, using much of the fresh produce that he'd bought in the market earlier. Now that he'd gotten his way, he'd been pleasant, almost charming, joking with his sister and explaining, in great detail, the origins of the wine they were having with dinner. Rissa enjoyed his conversation for the most part, but still couldn't stave off the uneasy feeling that she'd been hoodwinked.

Even the dogs seemed happy to see her again. Throughout most of the meal, they had made a great effort to carefully divide their time and affection between all three humans before finally settling down at their master's feet.

Rissa was flattered by Frankie's delight, but still ill at ease with the conditions of her accommodation, especially when Frankie asked, "And you got the job at the bookstore, right?"

Rissa shot a glance across at Evan from over the top of her glass. The look he returned was steady and unperturbed, but held in it a measure of warning. She was taken aback by the ease with which the lie rolled off her tongue. "Your brother was kind enough to lend me some money to tide me over until I get my bank cards back. So I thought I'd pass on the job so I'd have enough time to enjoy Perpignan."

Frankie pumped her hand in the air in triumph. "I told you he was cool!" she exulted, although she'd said no such thing. She leaped up from her chair and ran around the table to fling her arms around her brother's neck, kissing him on the cheek with a loud smacking sound. She beamed across at Rissa. "We can do all sorts of stuff. I've got a million things to show you. We can hang out on the beach all day!"

"Which in your case," Evan clarified, "doesn't begin until late afternoon. Rissa being here isn't a license to cut your lessons."

"Aw, man!" she protested.

"Don't 'Aw, man' me, sweetheart. You know you have your—"

"SATs to take in a few months. Yeah. I know." She made a face, but her glee was undiminished. She addressed Rissa again. "We can go shopping for new clothes for you. I know some great places in town. And we can get massages at this spa on the bay."

"Just as long as you don't take her to your hairdresser,

Blondie." Evan playfully ruffled Frankie's short, bleached locks. "I couldn't stand to see another crowning glory go."

Frankie laughed, smacked Evan open-handed at the back of his head, and dashed back to her seat before he could return the compliment. "Thanks for not being mad."

"Why should I be mad? It's your head."

"But you weren't even surprised. You didn't even do that blinky thing with your eyes when I came out to dinner with my hat off. I was half-sure you were going to bawl me out."

Evan lifted his brows. "'Blinky thing'?"

"You know...." Frankie did a hilarious imitation of Evan registering a combination of astonishment and outrage. "That thing you do."

"Ah." Evan grinned. "Thanks for bringing it to my attention. If I really look half as bad as you make out, I'll try to keep a handle on that in the future."

"Do that," Frankie said solemnly. She stabbed her fork into what remained of the hunk of blueberry cheesecake that they were having for dessert, leaving it standing upright like a tower, and then tilted her head to examine her sculpture critically. "It's almost as if...." She stopped in her tracks and looked at Rissa. "You warned him, didn't you!"

Rissa hesitated, wondering whether it would be better to 'fess up or plead innocent. Eventually, she admitted, "Well, I thought it would be better to prepare him for it. So that when you got around to taking off that tam of yours, he'd be less, uh, taken aback."

"You did that for me?" Frankie beamed. "You are too, too cool!" Everyone seemed to be "cool" to her tonight. "I'm so glad you're here." She shot Evan a look that attempted to be only jokingly hostile, but failed. "At least now I have *somebody* on my side."

Rissa hoped her guilt didn't show.

* * *

Over the next several days, Rissa settled into a comfortable routine. True to Evan's prediction, Frankie never emerged from her room before midday, claiming that while at boarding school the dragons therein tortured her repeatedly by forcing her to get up at six every morning, seven on Sundays, so that while she had the chance, she was putting as much into her sleep bank as possible.

Evan made a point of having breakfast with Rissa, even waiting around until she got up, so she pretty quickly learned to set her alarm to ensure that she was up and dressed at a decent hour, for fear of keeping him from important things down at the boatyard. She also found herself dressing a little better for breakfast than she usually did, glad that she and Frankie had made several forays into town to buy clothes. She told herself that she was a guest in the man's house, and it wouldn't do for her to slouch outside to breakfast with her hair in disarray and nothing on her feet. That wasn't how her mother had raised her. She would not have admitted—not even if you slammed her fingers in a drawer—that she was also motivated by the desire to pass muster, as Evan had taken to short lapses into silence when he would do nothing but scrutinize her slowly and thoughtfully. It didn't seem to matter that these examinations made her squirm like a bug on the end of a pin; in fact, he seemed to find her discomfiture amusing, as though he was challenging her to either comment, tell him to cut it out, or return the stare in spades.

In spite of that, she looked forward to breakfast, not only for the fabulous fare that was always laid out, but because it was virtually the only time that she would be alone with him, except for the few moments in which Madame Soler ghosted in, delivered their meal, and ghosted back out with their empty plates. Apart from that, her time was spent with Frankie, roaming the town, watching movies and cable television, or surfing the Internet together, and as much as she enjoyed Frankie's company, the girl was constantly revved up, seemingly incapable of a single contemplative moment.

On the other hand, Evan brought her American newspapers, and they would sit across the table from each other and read over their coffee, occasionally commenting on current events. He always enquired after his sister, and was happy to note that there seemed to be absolutely nothing going on, as far as Rissa could ascertain, that he should be concerned about. Rissa only managed to overcome her gnawing unease over having to deliver these reports by reiterating over and over to herself that there was no harm in a brother asking about his young sister's well-being. The cloak-and-dagger nature of her assignment was, she decided, all in her head.

At night, after everyone had had their dinner, and after the three of them had idled away a few hours together watching movies or playing video games—or rather, after Evan had been soundly beaten by Frankie in the game of her choice—each female retired to her bedroom, and Evan went outside to take his nightly swim. Frankie hated the idea of swimming, especially at night; as far as she was concerned, pools were for lounging next to, and soaking up the rays, not for actually getting wet in. As for Rissa, she made fair use of it during the day when she wanted to take a break from working on her novel, which was coming along very well indeed. She found that the repetitive, rhythmic motion of swimming helped simultaneously to clear her mind and to sharpen it, allowing her, when her dip was over, to return to her work more focused than before. She understood why Evan swam every night with religious fervor.

What she didn't quite understand was how she had gotten into the habit of hiding in her room, her face pressed to the sliding glass doors facing the pool, to watch him do it. She was quite sure that he had caught her on that first night, when she'd discovered him there quite by accident. She'd been caught up in the beauty of him, his crisp, deliberate strokes and the way he moved through the water like a slender, dark fish, even as his dogs churned up the water behind him, and found herself not just glancing out but staying to watch. And then he'd paused mid-stroke, as if he'd noticed her in spite of the darkness of her room. She'd dashed away from the doors, hot with embarrassment, hoping that her being discovered was more a figment of her imagination than his reality. But she was back the next night, and the next, and every one thereafter.

To her credit, she wasn't stupid enough to do her Peeping Tom routine with her room lights on, thus giving herself away by her silhouette. Whenever she heard those first few splashes outside, and his playful commands to the dogs, she made a big show of shutting down for the night, turning off her bathroom lights, the overhead lights in her room, and then, finally, her bedside lamp, until there was enough darkness to allow her to comfortably take up her position. Each night, she counted his laps with him, quickly developing the ability to tell just what kind of day he'd had by the number of repetitions.

If she was deluded enough to believe that he was unaware of her clandestine observation, more fool she, because one night, he called her on it.

Sweet, Sexy Things To Do
on a Steamy Summer Night

She'd turned away, just for a second, to attend to some inconsequential thing, and returned to the door, only to hear him say, just inches from her face, "Come swim with me, Rissa. The water's great."

It was a good thing that she had a strong heart, because the shock of finding him standing on the other side, when moments before he had been jostling for pool space with Dante and Plato, would otherwise have meant the end of her. She choked off a shriek.

His whisper was repentant. "Sorry, I didn't mean to startle you. I thought you'd seen me coming."

She blustered. "How would I have...." *Aw,* she groaned to herself. *Busted.*

He confirmed her diagnosis of the situation by saying, "Come on. You're driving me nuts, lurking in the dark there every night. If you want to get into the pool, get into the pool. Didn't I say you had the run of the house?"

"I was not lurking," she protested indignantly. "I was just…." *Admiring the view* would have been the most truthful answer, but it was not one that she was prepared to give.

He didn't want to hear it. "Doesn't matter what you were doing. Whatever it is, stop. Get your swimsuit on, and hit the water. The temperature tonight is positively amniotic. You'll love it. You'll sleep like a baby afterward."

What? Put on her swimsuit and actually get into the water? While he was *there?* He had to be kidding. She backpedaled furiously. "I'd hate to disturb you…."

"More than you're doing lurking there like some sort of ghost?"

"I told you, I was not—"

She could see the dark shapes of his knuckles outlined against the glass as he rapped on it. "At least pull aside the curtains so I can talk to you. I feel like you're in purdah, and I'm not allowed to see your face behind your veil."

Bravado got the better of caution, and she drew the curtains back. "Better?" she asked tartly.

He ignored her sarcasm. "Much." He rapped against the glass again. "Better still if you open the doors. And for God's sake, turn on a light before one of us gets hurt."

She clicked open the latch on the doors, allowing him to slide them back with a single, fluid movement, and then reached up and flicked on a switch, flooding both her room and the guest patio with soft, white light.

He was dripping with water, his customary dark shorts plastered to his body. A smattering of dark hair lay flat against his bare chest, their swirly pattern reminding her of swan's down. But then, she shouldn't have been looking. She dragged her gaze up to eye level.

"Well?" His hands were on his hips, his legs spread apart, challenge in every inch of him.

"Well, what?" she countered, although she knew very well "well what". It seemed a handy way to play for time.

"Well, are you going to get your itsy-bitsy, teeny-weeny, yellow polka-dot bikini on? Or do you prefer to swim in the buff?"

She was scandalized. "Never!"

"You don't know what you're missing," he said ruefully. "Talk all you want about the right to vote and the right to free speech, but true freedom is splashing around butt-naked in your own backyard pool when you know nobody's looking."

Curiosity killed her cat. "You mean you...." She encompassed his body with a wave of her arm, and then vaguely pointed in the direction of the pool.

He didn't seem the least bit put out by the question. "When I'm alone, sure. These shorts," he snapped the waistband briskly against his belly, "are for your benefit. And Frankie's. Wouldn't want to scare either of you."

Rissa choked on her laughter. "Scary, huh?"

He shrugged, grinning broadly. "Well, at least perturbing." Then he returned to the original subject. "So, how's about that bikini?"

"I don't wear one." At least, not anymore. Prior to her surgery, she had no qualms about squeezing into a few ounces of material whenever she was near water, although she did draw the line at a thong. But now, she was shy about baring the scar at the base of her abdomen, so she settled for slightly less revealing bathing attire.

He lifted a brow. "Really? I had no idea you were so modest."

"Not modest," she answered. "Practical."

He gave an exaggerated groan of exasperation and impatience. "Rissa, whatever it is, get it on. Even if you like to

swim in jeans and a sweater, army fatigues, space suit, whatever. Get dressed pronto, and let's get out there before the
water starts to get cold. Don't be a spoilsport. I…want your
company." He dropped the drama, becoming dead serious.
"And you don't mind mine."

She hesitated. She wasn't a complete idiot, and neither
was he. The night was warm and intimate, and the pool,
even more so. They would be alone out there, and the
rhythm of swimming was more than a little reminiscent of
other, more intimate rhythms. She knew that he had been
watching her, just as she had been watching him, evaluat-
ing him, sometimes enjoying the unspoken awareness that
passed between them across the breakfast table, or which
zinged back and forth when they bumped into each other in
the house.

The way she saw it, she had two options. She could choose
to decline his invitation, shoo him back out of her room, and
go wisely to bed like a good little girl, and put an end to, or
at least postpone, the impending reality of intimate contact
that had been on both their minds almost since she got there.
Or she could show him—and herself—just what she was
made of, meet his challenge and accompany him outside—
and let nature take its pleasant course.

Her decision didn't take long. She spun around and headed
for the bathroom. "I'll change in there."

He seemed pleased but surprised. "Didn't think you had it
in ya, Young."

She gave him what she hoped was a long, deliberate, put-
him-in-his-place look. "That, and then some."

He was unfazed. "Glad to hear it." He stepped fully into
the room, looking around himself as if it weren't a room in
his own house, eyes moving from her open laptop on the desk,
to the few scattered magazines on the bed, and to the clothes

thrown over the back of a chair, as if her castoff belongings offered him insight into who she really was. "I'll wait here."

"Don't sit on my bed and get it wet," she instructed.

"No, ma'am." His cheeky grin belied the meekness of his tone.

Rissa hurried into the bathroom, fingers pulling at the buttons of her clothes even as she pulled the door shut. She took her swimsuit down from the shower curtain rack where she had hung it to dry that morning, and donned it hastily. Frankie was the one who had insisted that she buy the hibiscus-pink and tangerine tankini, even though Rissa had argued that it was bright enough to signal a passing ship. The boy shorts left just half an inch of the lower curve of her bottom bare, although the waistband rose to her navel, meeting the hem of the tank top nicely. The top had spaghetti straps and flexible underwiring for that Wonderbra effect—not that she needed it. She almost chickened out and wrapped herself in one of the big, fluffy guest towels, but refused to surrender to the impulse, throwing it over her shoulder instead.

When she emerged, she caught Evan peering at the screen of her laptop, both hands clasped behind his back as though each was trying to restrain the other from touching the keyboard. He jumped guiltily.

"If you were hoping to catch a look at my novel, forget it. It's got a password on."

"And I suppose it'd do me no good to casually ask you the name of your first pet?"

"Nope. I'm smarter than that."

"Darn." Then he caught sight of what she was wearing and forgot all about weaseling her password out of her. There was nothing but appreciation in his eyes. "Hmm. Fetching. Even if it isn't a bikini."

"Oh, be quiet." She swatted at the backs of his legs with

the towel, and he complied, keeping a lid on it until they reached the side of the pool, where the dogs were waiting patiently. They leaped up at their approach.

The pool certainly looked inviting. The submerged lights made the elaborate tilework on the bottom glow, and the whisper of the water as it flowed over the beautifully crafted waterfall edge was Zen-like. The rocky edge of the cliffs leading to the beach was screened off by a circle of trees, but the brooding sea was visible beyond and between them. It was a dark night, even though the new moon had fully risen, and the night birds and insects kicked up a ruckus. It was a perfect night for swimming. Evan gestured toward the pool with elaborate courtesy. "After you."

"Thanks." Rissa let her towel fall to the ground and regarded the water solemnly for a moment. This was it. There wasn't much leeway to turn back now, so in she went. In went Evan, and in went Dante and Plato: splash, splash, splash, splash. She broke the surface of the water and took a deep breath, laughing out loud. "It's delicious! As warm as bathwater."

He popped up next to her. "Told you." His face was just two feet from hers, and he was smiling at her, glad that she was enjoying it. Then he flipped backward, arms up over his head, and resumed his laps, leaving Rissa to her own devices.

Not wanting to disturb his routine, and being more of a paddler than a swimmer, she was happy to stay in the shallows, clowning around with the dogs, who generously brought her their toys and patiently trained her to throw them across the pool so that they could fetch them and bring them back. They seemed quite pleased with the pace at which she learned, because soon she found herself engulfed by a deluge of beach balls, floating bones, and pool noodles.

"You'll tire out way before they will," Evan warned her.

He finished his laps and glided over to stand next to her, water dripping down his face and chest.

"I'm sure." She tossed a bone overarm across to the deep end, and they charged gleefully after it.

"You throw like a girl," Evan commented.

"I am a girl," she reminded him.

Tiny droplets of water glittered on the ends of his lashes like miniature gemstones as he swept his gaze along her body, from the slick dark hair that clung to her neck and cheeks, to the pink-and-orange swimsuit, which glowed like a beacon in the pool lights. "I noticed." He jerked his chin toward the edge of the pool. "Come, sit on the edge with me. Let the dogs throw their own toys for a while."

She followed him obediently to the side, her heart thumping, awareness of him growing with every passing second. In the stillness that surrounded them, broken only by the cheeps and chirps of the night creatures and the lapping of the water, it seemed to her that they were not just alone in the garden, but alone in the universe. It was a delicious feeling. He offered to help her out, but she demurred, clambering out unaided. Unperturbed, he hauled himself out and sat next to her, reaching for her towel and handing it over before sitting beside her, dangling his legs in the water just as she was doing. She wrapped the towel around her shoulders and hugged it, even though it was still very warm out.

The silence was comfortable. When he chose to break it, he said, "So, are you going to tell me what it's about?"

She feigned puzzlement. "What?"

"Your *chef d'oeuvre*. Your masterpiece."

"No. Telling spoils the writing. Didn't you know that?"

He shook his head gravely. "Not being a writer, I didn't."

Her response was equally grave. "Well, it does. The magic of the writing is in the telling, and if you talk about it before you tell it to the page, you diffuse some of the energy. Then when you get around to writing it down, you've lost something."

"Well, I'd hate to make you do that. I'll cut you some slack and be quiet."

"Thanks for understanding."

He nodded, and surveyed the canine goings-on in the water for a bit, before he said, "At least tell me the genre."

He wasn't going to give up, so she indulged him that much. "Fantasy."

"Oh, are you going to give Harry Potter a run for his money?"

She laughed. "I doubt that! But I've always had a thing for magic."

"Any dragons in it? Flying serpents?"

"No, but there's a giant worm."

"How giant?"

"Giant," she said emphatically.

"A worm you say?" He looked as though he wasn't sure whether she was pulling his leg or not, but took her at face value. "Does it eat anybody?"

"Not yet, but that's an idea."

"That, I've got to read."

"You'll get the first bound galley off the press," she offered.

"Looking forward to it. Ever wrote any magazine articles on the subject?"

She feigned ignorance. "Giant worms?"

"Magic."

She thought for a while. "Not unless you count stuff like, Ten Ways To Get Him Under Your Spell, or Curse The Competition: Witchery For The Workplace."

He grimaced. "Egad."

"I know!" She simulated sticking a finger down her throat, and backed it up with a realistic gagging sound. "It's a living, though."

"Are you going back to it? Writing for magazines?"

That wasn't something she'd thought about much, but as far as she could see, she didn't have much of a choice. "I'll have to, when summer's over." *When I have to leave this beautiful, beautiful place. And you.*

He seemed to understand. "Summer's only halfway through," he reminded her softly.

"I know."

He changed subjects abruptly. "How's Frankie doing?"

"You mean, have I noticed any suspicious activity?"

He conceded without a trace of embarrassment. "Yes."

She shook her head. "No, and she hasn't given me so much as a hint. We have a lot of fun together, and as far as I can tell, she's a normal, happy teenager, even though she thinks you're a little severe."

"I do what needs to be done," he said mildly. Then, "She's crazy over you. She thinks you're 'da bomb,' and gives you 'mad props,' whatever that means, for almost everything you do and say."

"They speak a different language these days, don't they."

"They sure do. Frankie makes me feel ancient."

"Frankie *thinks* you're ancient. The evening I met her, on the train…" She paused, remembering the unpleasantness of that first night, but those were bygones, so she went on, "She led me to believe you hobbled around on a walking stick, had a hunchback, and a single remaining tooth."

"Oh, good Lord. Well, there's a lot of space between us, in terms of age. I think Frankie took my parents by surprise late in their marriage. And I guess that, as her authority figure, I must come off as much older than I am. Theoretically, in the strictest terms, I *am* old enough to be her father."

She laid her hand on his arm. "But you're not."

"I have to be."

She accepted his determination as being born out of a sense of familial responsibility, so she didn't bother to argue with him. "Well, rest assured that I am doing the best I can. I do spend as much time as is reasonable with her, but there's just so much that I can do without becoming her jailer, and so far, so good. But as far as her telephone contacts and Internet activity are concerned, what she does at night when she closes her door is beyond my control."

He sighed gustily. "I know. I guess, if that's all there is to it, then I'm okay with that."

She suggested, a little too sharply, "Well, if you really think you have to, there are a zillion varieties of software you can install on her computer, and her phone, to let you follow every word she writes or says, know who she's talking to, when, and where."

He looked hurt by the unspoken accusation in her voice. "You know I'd never do that. All I'm doing is trying to balance my concern for her well-being with respect for her privacy. I'm sorry you don't see it that way."

He looked so aggrieved that she was ashamed of her sarcasm. "Sorry."

For a moment, she wasn't sure if he was going to answer. Then he said, "Let's put that one to rest, okay?"

"Okay."

The silence resumed, but this time, an element of tension had crept into it. For want of something better to do, she feigned an intense interest in the dogs' activities, until even they got bored, clambered out of the pool, and wandered off to sleep. He cut through the quiet with a question a full five minutes later. "You still mad at me?"

She turned her head. His face was inscrutable. "I'm not mad at you, Evan."

"Come over here, then."

Thump, thump, thump. Her heart did somersaults. There was barely three feet of space between them, so "coming over" would entail winnowing down that space to nil. It would mean touching him, deliberately and expressly, without the excuse of accidental or casual contact. She almost laughed outright, in delight, anticipation—and derision. He wanted *her* to go to *him?* Make the first move, take the first risk? Hardly.

She tilted her head with more than a hint of challenge. "Why don't *you* come over *here?*"

He hedged, playing with her for a while, drawing out the anticipation. "Tired. My arms and legs are rubber from all that swimming." He lifted his feet out of the water and patted his legs for emphasis, schooling his features into what he hoped was a mournful expression.

This time, she did laugh. "Right. Oh, poor baby." She dusted her hands off briskly, and pretended to be about to get up. "In that case, I guess we'd better call it a night. You go get some rest."

His response was galvanic. "Like hell," he muttered, and crossed those three feet so fast she barely had time to register the fact that he had moved. His hands were on her upper arms, holding her fast. "You aren't going anywhere."

She was playing with fire, but she loved the heat of the flame. "Says who?"

"Says me," he growled back.

"Bully," she managed to grunt, just before he kissed her.

Wow.

Their kiss was sweet and soft, gentle and enquiring, friendly and open. He tasted of pool water, even though they had been out of the pool long enough to have become reasonably dry. She'd known for so many days that it was coming, and wondered what it would be like when it finally did, and it was nothing like she had imagined. It didn't have that rock-your-world quality she had come to expect from first kisses; instead, it was simple and caring and comfortable. It just felt right.

Their only points of contact were their lips, and his hands upon her taut biceps, and, once he was assured that she would not attempt to wriggle free, they caressed rather than re-strained, moving along her smooth skin, forefingers hooking experimentally under the spaghetti straps of her swimsuit and pulling them down an inch, so that her shoulders were bare. He released her arms completely, running his thumbs along her shoulder blades, making her shiver.

He broke the kiss and murmured, almost to himself, "I was wondering when we'd get around to that."

"Me, too," she countered playfully. "Took you long enough."

He answered honestly. "I wasn't sure how welcome it would be, considering."

"Considering what?"

"Considering the low opinion you seem to have of me."

She hated to think that he could sense the misgivings she sometimes had about him, even when she knew his intentions were good. She tried to reassure him. "I don't have a low opinion of you, Evan. It's just that—"

"Don't have a low opinion of me? You act like I'm the Big Bad Wolf!"

"What'd you expect, with all that huffing and puffing?" she blurted.

He looked comically taken aback, and could have tried either to defend himself or return fire, but instead reached out and traced the shape of her lower lip with his thumb and said, "Rissa, let's not argue. Not tonight. Look up." He used the same hand to tilt her chin up until she was looking into the heavens, curious to find out what he wanted her to see. It was a dark, clear night; sea and sky were one and the same, except for the billion glittering points of light that stood out against the blue-black velvet overhead. She frowned, puzzled. "Look up at what?"

"Perfection. It's a perfect, peaceful, endless summer night. It's beautiful." His upturned gaze swiveled downward to her face again. "You're beautiful. The last thing I want to do with you right now is fight."

He was making a whole lot of sense, and any potential squabble was immediately forgotten. She watched as he picked up his towel, folded it carefully into a rectangular pad, laid it down on the tiles, and patted it invitingly. She wouldn't have been able to stop herself from smiling if she tried, and responded to his wordless invitation by lying back, placing her head on his makeshift pillow. Against her back, the deep blue glazed tiles bordering the pool still held the warmth of the sun, even so many hours after its setting.

"Comfortable?" he asked.

"Very." She was still smiling.

He stretched out next to her, so close that she could feel his legs brush against hers. He propped himself up on one elbow, leaning over until his face obscured the sky that had so recently been the subject of discussion. "Good." His mouth came down on hers again, and this time, the kiss was different. It was less experimental, more frank, openly sensual. The tip of his tongue slid between her lips, not probing, but more as an offering, lying still for her to do with it as she wished. She grasped it with her teeth and sucked on it, causing a groan to escape him.

In spite of the length of time he had spent in the pool, his skin was warm under her fingers. She wrapped her arms around his broad back, pulling him down into her embrace, so that his torso was pressed against her breasts. Under her fingers, the ridges of muscle knotted and unknotted, feeling to her touch like marble wrapped in lambskin. From his back and shoulders, her hands drifted downward to his waist, which gave the illusion of narrowness in contrast to his chest, but which, in fact, was solid, substantial. Down farther still to his lower back and hips. He was nothing but muscle, taut and trembling.

Inside, she felt a growing hunger, more similar to the yearning she usually felt for food, rather than for a man. She wondered what his skin would taste like, what the texture of his skin would feel like under her tongue. She wanted to consume him like ice cream on a hot day. Then, her desire lurched in a completely different direction; she wanted to make a dent in his defenses, break down his control, leave her mark on him. Make sure she had his complete attention. An imp of mischief caused her to slip three fingers just under the waistband of his damp shorts, and rake her fingernails across his skin just at the point where the swelling of his hard, utterly perfect backside began.

He spasmed in shock and broke their kiss, gasping. "What the—!" He struggled for air.

"Sorry," she told him, although nothing could be farther from the truth. "The devil made me do it."

"Did he, now?" He recovered from the shock of her assault and shifted position, straddled her hips, and lowering his body until she bore a substantial amount of his weight. If he had intended it as a punishment for her assault on his senses, he was way off base, because the hard, jutting ridge against her pubis elicited nothing but delectable shivers. "What else does he want you to do, the rascal?"

"He's got nothing to do with what I want," she told him. She wriggled so that he was pressing just right against her point of pleasure, and sighed. To ensure that he did not take it into his head to move away from this, the sweetest of spots, she let her hand fall against one cheek of his bottom. "This was all my idea."

"Good idea," he murmured, and resumed their kiss as if it had never been interrupted. It was harder, more intense, more demanding, his teeth bruising the soft inner skin of her lip, grinding against her teeth, enamel colliding with enamel, his tongue now a blade, slashing through any thought of resistance that she might have harbored.

Then, brutally, before she thought she'd had enough, he took his mouth away, but consoled her by burying his face against her neck and inhaling deeply. "I've been wanting to know how you smell, close up."

"And how do I...." she began to ask, and failed, because the rough texture of his late-o'-clock shadow against the soft skin of her throat was making her crazy. She made another attempt. "How do I smell?"

"Like...yourself, I guess. Warm. Sweet." He sniffed her skin like a gardener appreciating his prize orchids. "Hungry."

Her whole body was a pool of warm liquid. "What am I hungry for?"

He lifted his head from the hollow of her neck. The eyes that held hers steadfastly were no longer their characteristic amber. They had stolen the darkness clear out of the sky. "You tell me."

She was beyond denial, pretense, and false pride. She reached down and grasped his left hand, bringing it to her mouth, drawing one large finger slowly inside. Before releasing his hand, she gave a single nip at the webbing between his fingers. His breathing tripped over itself. She crooked one leg around his hips, giving herself even greater contact with him, and more leverage. She pressed upward, and released—and then did it again. Slowly, repeatedly, rhythmically. He didn't press back against her, for fear that his rhythm might throw her off hers, and disrupt the delicate balance of her quest. He merely held her close against him until she found what she was seeking. Her body shook, and her short, sharp cry was muffled against his chest.

"Easy, now," he murmured.

A fine sprinkling of sweat broke out on her skin, and as her tension ebbed, she relaxed against the tiles again. He still hovered over her, stroking the damp hair away from her face. "You okay?" he asked.

"Okay," she confirmed, although she was much, much more than okay. Her arms felt heavy and limp, but still she managed to wind them around his neck. She didn't want him to pull away just yet.

He had no intention of doing any such thing. He dusted her cheeks with kisses, and then moved downward to her shoulders and the tops of her breasts. He cupped them with his hands, enjoying their firmness and their weight, and then, almost reluctantly, released them to slide his hands further down. With his palm flat against her belly, he stroked her in circular movements, stopping briefly to explore her navel with a curious fingertip before moving further still to the curve below.

Toward the high waistband of her swimsuit bottoms, and the rough-edged scar that lay beneath it.

"No!" Rissa reacted without thinking, knowing only that she was loath to see the expression on his face morph from an almost sleepy sensuality to surprise, curiosity, and even, possibly, revulsion. This wasn't the time for questions. This wasn't the place for explanations. She was jolted into a sitting position, and skittered backward, away from him, both hands pressed to her abdomen. "Don't!"

Beans—When To Store Them, and When To Spill Them

Evan drew back as if he had been shot, mortified by her outburst. What had he done? One moment her body had been purring beneath his like the engine of a Bugatti, and the next, she was staring at him, wild-eyed, with her hands across her body as if she were trying to protect herself. He felt like a sexual opportunist. Shame burned within him.

He reached out and took up the towel that had served as her pillow, unfolded it, and held it out to her. She took it wordlessly, and wrapped it around herself.

"I'm sorry. I didn't mean to offend you. I thought you wanted me to…." He was both flustered and angry, but more at himself than at her. "I thought you wanted me to touch you like that. I'm sorry if I was wrong." He wished that some miracle would obliterate the next few awkward moments, so that he would find himself whisked away to the privacy of his own room, where he could recover from his humiliation alone.

She had recovered from her initial outburst, and strove to placate him. "No! You weren't wrong. I mean, it wasn't your fault. It's not what you think. It's not that I didn't want you to touch me."

Could have fooled me, he thought, *skating away from me like I'd pounced on you from some dark alley.* But he gave her the benefit of the doubt, and asked patiently. "What is it, then?"

Her eyes downcast, she hedged, "I just reacted, that's all."

He wanted to move closer to her once again, the better to look into her eyes while he asked, but he was afraid that, in the frame of mind she was in, any move toward her might send her away, screaming bloody murder. "I know you just reacted, but to what? Did I move too fast? Did I touch some sort of nerve? Did I step over some sort of line in the sand that I didn't see? Help me out here, Rissa."

She wet her lips. "No, there's no line. And no nerve. You did nothing wrong. It's just that, well…" She searched in vain for her next words, and then threw her hands up in the air. "It's my problem, and I'll deal with it on my own. Okay?" She stood up almost reluctantly. "It's really late, Evan. And it's getting cooler out. Maybe we should go inside."

This time he did get close to her, standing in such a way that he barred her direct retreat to her room. He didn't need to lay a hand on her to prevent her from moving. "Not so fast. We've got something going on between us—or about to go on. You knew it from the start, and I did, too. You wanted me back there. Am I right?" He asked this without a trace of conceit.

She answered without a trace of coyness. "Yes."

He nodded in confirmation. "And I wanted you. I still do. So if there's something that's getting in the way of that, then it's my problem, too."

She sighed wearily. "No, it's not. It's nothing you need to

concern yourself with. Honestly," she tried to sound more cheerful, "I'm fine. I'm just tired. So can we just drop it?"

The last thing in the world he wanted to do was drop it, but he never forced anything upon a woman; not his company, not his attentions, and not his curiosity. He was graceful in his concession of defeat. "Okay, Rissa. You win." He touched her lightly on the elbow to get her to turn to face her room, and began to guide her toward it. "I'll walk you to your room, then. Maybe a good night's sleep will do us both a world of good. Things will all look clearer in the morning."

"They will," she agreed, but there was doubt in her eyes.

When they got to the half-open glass doors that led from the patio to her room, she stopped and turned to face him, almost awkwardly shy. Waiting. What should he do? he wondered. Kiss her goodnight? Offer his hand? What was the accepted etiquette for such a muddled situation? But his body knew the answer to that question, and he found himself wrapping his arms around her in a warm hug that wiped away the tension of the past few minutes. She returned the gesture, squeezing him against her breasts and uttering a soft sigh, as if she had not been held like that in a long, long time. When they released each other, she looked herself again; the dark, troubled look had left her eyes. That made him feel much better.

"Goodnight," she told him.

"Sleep well," he wished her sincerely, and waited until she had slipped inside and locked the doors securely behind her.

Then, like a shadow, he disappeared into the shrubbery, taking the long way around the house to his own quarters. He hoped that sleep would, indeed, come quickly for her, even though he knew that he would have no such luck. Unresolved sexual tension left him restless, but his mental turmoil made him even more so. He knew that there would be little sleep for him.

A year or two ago he would have sought to release that

pent-up energy and calm his frazzled mind by leaping onto his low-slung sea-green-and-chrome Italian motorbike and tearing up several miles of the winding coastal road, even at this late hour, seeking solace in the merciless assault of the wind in his face. But rational thought won out over the reckless impulse; it was late, and the last thing he was doing was leaving two females alone and asleep in his home while he went out trying to reenact a scene from some bad biker movie. Responsibilities were, after all, responsibilities, and, besides, he was getting too old for that nonsense.

So he took the saner option, and entered his own suite via a patio that was a larger version of the one that led to Rissa's room. The dogs were asleep close enough to the door that he had to step over them to get inside. They felt him nearby, and snuffled in their sleep, but, not sensing any danger, did not awaken.

He stripped down immediately, even though his shorts were by now bone dry. Butt naked, he took a shot glass down from his minibar and poured himself a whiskey. He drank it, neat, in one go, and then poured himself another one which, hopefully, he would be able to make last a tad longer. He sat in one of his huge leather armchairs and tilted it back into the reclining position and carefully balanced the glass on the arm of the chair.

Now, he could think.

Rissa. For no reason that he could fathom, serendipity had thrown her his way. This was good, not just because she provided a golden opportunity for him to keep his sister from harm even when he could not be around, but also because, to be honest, he liked her company. He liked her.

Though that in itself could pose a problem. Like any healthy man his age, he loved women and loved being with them, and had been fortunate enough to have had a few relationships since his divorce. Some had ended amicably, some had ended badly, but, eventually, they had all ended. That was the way things were, he philosophized. Relationships were meant to be enjoyed, and when they were over, you just had to find the courage to move on.

One thing he had never indulged in, though, was the presence of a woman while his sister was here, spending time with him. That violated his sense of propriety, and, as old-fashioned as it might seem, he didn't think it was a good example for Frankie to see a woman overnighting with him while she was around. He was sure that Frankie, being no fool, was perfectly aware that he indulged his right as an adult to enter into sexual relationships with women if he so chose. That right did not, however, extend to waving that fact in her face. Previously, if he had been involved when she was due to visit, he had simply put the relationship on hold until she left again. Some women hadn't taken too kindly to that, but those were the sacrifices he was willing to make for what he saw was right.

So, if things were going the way he sensed they were going with Rissa, how did he treat with starting a relationship with a woman who was living right in the house with them? He'd promised Rissa that things would look clearer in the morning. Now, he wasn't so sure.

With some difficulty, he shoved the dilemma from his mind, and clicked the television on, just in time to catch a rerun of a college basketball game, beamed across the Atlantic to him via satellite. He allowed himself to become engrossed.

Nine minutes into the second half, he heard the faintest of knocks, startling him so much that for a brief second he was unsure whether it was coming from the patio or his bedroom door. Then it came again, less faint than before. Bedroom door, definitely.

"Yes?" He was cautious, even though the person on the other side could only be one of two people.

"Me." Rissa. Her voice was a whisper.

He leaped out of the armchair and almost broke his neck trying to make it to the door, and then remembered just as he began to twist the doorknob that he was hardly dressed for company. "Hang on," he whispered back, rummaging through his stuff for something to cover his nakedness. He settled on a pair of jeans, and dragged them hurriedly on, willing to go commando for the moment. Then he opened the door and let her in.

She was as hastily dressed as he, appearing to have dragged something on before leaving her room on impulse. His diagnosis was underlined by the almost bewildered look on her face as she looked around his room, as though she was not too sure how she had managed to wind up there in the first place, and even further surprised that he had actually let her in.

When she didn't say anything, he probed. "You okay?"

"I couldn't sleep," she said by way of explanation.

"Me neither."

"I saw the light on under your door, so I thought…." She gnawed on her lip for several moments before she finally confessed, "I couldn't sleep because I didn't want you to go to bed thinking that what happened out there was your fault."

He was not the kind of man to re-hash old discussions, especially not embarrassing ones. As far as he was concerned, that topic was put to rest, and he certainly wasn't keen on raising it from the dead. "Don't beat yourself up over it, Rissa. It's not worth it. It's over and forgotten."

"No," she said firmly. "It's not over. There's something I've got to tell you."

A creepy unease ran through him; he knew that what he was going to hear would not be pleasant, but if she was willing to share, he was ready to listen. "Okay, then. Sit down. Let's talk."

She dropped onto the nearest spot, which just happened to

be his still-made-up bed, but the moment she did so, she thought better of it and leaped up as though it were on fire, opting instead to sit in the armchair that he had so recently vacated. He tried not to smile. He sat on the bed, as it was the closest to her. "Okay, shoot."

She had been rubbing her hands together nervously, but then pressed them determinedly against her thighs to halt their jerky movement. "I'll cut to the chase," she said bravely.

"I'm listening," he told her gently. "You're safe." He wanted to touch her on the back of the hand to emphasize this, but resisted the urge. She was skittish enough already.

"When I first came here, that first night, I told you that I'd been ill."

"I remember."

"And that I'd lost my sister last year."

"I remember that, too," he told her gently.

"Well, a few years ago, we lost our mother, too. And an aunt."

He frowned. That was too much loss for someone so young. "What—?"

"Cancer." She spat out the name of her mortal enemy. "It took all three of them."

"I'm so sorry," he said sincerely.

"And then it came after me. Genetics can be a real pain in the tail, I'm telling you." She laughed harshly. "A disease like that can choose a family to torment, and pick them off one by one, like birds on a wire. But it didn't get me. I gave it the fight of its life, and I kicked it."

"Good for you. Are you okay now?"

"I'll live," she answered matter-of-factly, and then frowned. "But I didn't get off without a scratch. My nemesis got its pound of flesh. Literally."

That eerie sensation at the back of his neck intensified. "What do you mean?"

"I had to…" She stopped. She tried again. "They made me…" She cursed and got to her feet, and stood before him. "I'll have to show you." She eased up the hem of her top, and in the dim light of the bedroom lamp, he could barely see, just below the curve of her belly, a small, horizontal scar, recently healed, pouting at him like a rude, mocking mouth.

Then, he understood. "Oh, Rissa."

Her words came in a rush. "That's why I backed away. I didn't want you to touch me there, and feel that ugly, awful thing. I didn't want to see the look on your face when you tried to figure out what—"

"Sweetheart, it's not ugly." He reached out and touched it with his fingertips, knowing that this time she would not pull away. To his touch, it felt small and innocuous.

"What it's done to my life is ugly!" she retorted passionately. "I'll never have children. I love babies. I'd always hoped that some day, once I found the right person, I'd have lots of them. Now I can't. *That's* what's ugly!"

He thought at once of his ex-wife, Jeanine, and the horror she had put him through when she had dangled before him the tantalizing prospect of fatherhood—and then brutally snatched it away, and his stomach turned. He had no way of knowing exactly how it must feel for Rissa, because although the promise of a child had collapsed among the shambles of his disastrous marriage, his fertility remained. For him, there was always time. For Rissa, time had run out. "Honey," he began, but couldn't finish the thought. He wanted to tell her things would be okay, but he knew that was a lie.

She knew it, too. "Don't bother. It's not worth lying about. I know what my position is, and I've come to terms with it. I may not like it, but I can live with it—somehow." She rolled down her top, hiding the scar from his view once again. Her face was resolute. "There. Now you know." She seemed to be waiting for something, and when he realized what that something was, his heart sank. She was waiting for his rejection.

He'd have to show her differently. Still sitting on the bed, he reached up and pulled her down to him. She slumped, unresisting, into his lap. "Did you really think it would make me change my mind about you?"

"It's sort of...upsetting, you have to admit. Unsexy."

"You're sexy," he told her softly. "A two-inch scar can't change that."

She persisted, still needing his reassurance. "But I'm not..." she struggled to find the right word "...whole," she finished.

He hated to hear her say that. "Don't! Don't do that to yourself! It's not true. You're whole of heart, kind in spirit, and sound of mind." He let his hand slide down to curve around her bottom. "And as much woman as I could ever possibly handle. And I want to see where this is going, with us." He lifted his eyes to hers, unashamed of the desire shining within them. "Will you give me that chance?"

He didn't have to wait long for her answer. It came in the form of a soft sigh as she wrapped her arms around his shoulders and buried her face in his neck. They cuddled, not needing to seal their agreement with anything resembling the passionate kisses they had traded earlier. After a while, she yawned in his ear, and that was the signal to bring the night to an end. "Sleepy?" he murmured indulgently.

"Mmm." She rubbed her eyes. "Sorry."

He let her up and then got to his feet. "That's perfectly all right. It's way past any sane person's bedtime, anyway." Trying to dismiss the imp that was needling him to offer her some downtime in his own bed, he escorted her to the door. "You go get some sleep."

She laughed. "Roger that! I don't even know if I'll make it in time for breakfast!"

"Well," he suggested, "feel free to pull a Frankie and sleep until noon. Have brunch instead."

"Sounds like a plan," she agreed vehemently. She reached for the doorknob, but he stopped her as a thought struck.

"One thing," he began. He tried to figure out how to couch his next request in order not to come across as a complete jerk. "About Frankie...."

"Yes?"

"I'd like for us to be discreet, at least for the time being. She's my sister, and she's still a minor, and I'm not in the habit of...carrying on, if you like, in front of her." He hastened to clarify, "It's not that I'm ashamed of you, or that I think we're doing anything wrong. It's just that I'd like to set a good example for her. Understand?" He held his breath.

She seemed to be pondering his suggestion, and he half expected her to lash out at him, call him a hypocrite, much as she had on the day he had made his offer of employment. But to his relief, she nodded, albeit reluctantly, and smiled. "Understood." She opened the door and stepped through it. "Goodnight, then."

He leaned forward, and tried to wipe away the awkwardness with a brush of his lips across her forehead. "Sweet dreams," he wished her.

How Not To Get Stung
When the Con Is On

Rissa did not wake up as late as she had expected, perhaps because her body clock had already grown accustomed to rousing her at the same time every morning. Instead of indulging in the luxury of lounging in bed anyway, contemplating the events of the night before, she dressed quickly and hurried outside, hoping to catch Evan at least on the tail-end of his breakfast. She tingled with anticipation at the thought of seeing him again so soon after her visit to his room just a few hours before. Her hopes were dashed by Madame Soler, who informed her with a range of gestures and patiently careful French that Mr. Maynard had left already, and that he hadn't stopped for breakfast.

Rissa swallowed her disappointment, fiddled idly with her food, and took the dogs for a stroll around the property until Frankie finally roused herself and emerged, yawning as though she hadn't been hibernating for most of the morning. As always, a grin of pleasure split her face when she saw her older friend. "Rissa!" she greeted her cheerily, sounding almost surprised to see her there.

Rissa returned the smile. "Frankie." She tilted her cheek to accept the very European kiss of greeting that Frankie had affected so charmingly. "Sleep well?"

Frankie yawned ostentatiously once again. "Mmm-hmm." She plopped down onto a patio chair. "You?"

Rissa thought almost guiltily of her late night and tried not to flush. "Uh, yeah. Very well, thanks." She tried to redirect the girl's attention before the silly smile threatening to spill over had its way. "So, if you slept as well as you said you did, what's with the yawning?"

Now it was Frankie's turn to flush. She did her best to keep her voice nonchalant. "I was up chatting for a while."

"Oh?" Rissa tried to sound casual. "On the phone?"

"No, dum-dum!" Frankie laughed. "On the Internet! Who chats on the phone anymore?"

Rissa's spider-senses were tingling like crazy. She was willing to bet that the person on the other end of the connection was none other than Frankie's mystery boyfriend. She tried to sound casual. "With a girl? A friend from school?"

Frankie rolled her eyes. "Don't make me laugh!"

"A boy, then."

Frankie picked at the hem of her wildly patterned cropped top. "You could say that."

Mindful of the fact that this was the first real opportunity she had had to actually earn the handsome stipend that Evan was paying her, she probed gently. "Is he from around here?"

"Maybe."

She was tighter with information than a clam, but Rissa wasn't giving up. "Boyfriend?"

Frankie turned exaggeratedly wide eyes on her. "Why?"

Why, indeed. *Because your brother is paying me to spy on*

you, Rissa could have said, but she was almost too ashamed to admit it to herself. So, instead, she said quite honestly, "Because I care about you. And I don't want you to get hurt."

Frankie looked genuinely baffled. "Hurt? How?"

She has no idea, Rissa thought with a pang, just how deep a wound a man—or in Frankie's case, a boy—could inflict upon a girl's heart. Should she explain? As an older woman, wasn't it her duty to explain, to warn? She reached out her hand and gently ruffled the short crop of blond hair before her. "Because sometimes, even when you think everything's fine between you and a boy, things can change overnight, especially when you're very young. And if you're spending as much time talking to him as you say you are, then you must be a little sweet on him."

Frankie smiled a smug, secret smile that Rissa wasn't too sure she liked. She went on bravely. "So I don't want you to… expose yourself…too much…"

Frankie's smile degraded into a smirk.

Rissa was hasty to clarify. "Figuratively speaking, I mean. Emotionally. Leaving yourself open to hurt. When the summer's over, you'll have to go back to school. You'll have to leave this boy, and put a few thousand miles between you. If you allow yourself to get too…attached to him, that might sting."

"Uh, yeah." It was all Frankie could do not to roll her eyes. She stretched her arms languorously over her head, arched her back like a cat on a windowsill, and yawned. "You eat yet?"

"Sort of." Rissa gave in to the obvious change in subject without a struggle, but was determined to approach her once again, and press home her point at the next opportunity, as much for the sake of Evan's peace of mind as for Frankie's best interests. "You?"

Frankie shrugged. "Not hungry."

Rissa nodded, not even bothering to try to cajole her into

getting something to eat. She knew well enough that getting into such an argument with a teenager was futile. "Okay. Well, then, how about you go off to your lessons, and then you and I meet up afterwards? We could go do something in town. Maybe a show? I hear there's a new play on at the Palais, and I wouldn't mind—"

Frankie cut in. "No lessons today." She was grinning as though she'd been playing the penny slots and hit an unexpected jackpot.

Rissa's brows shot up. "No lessons? How come?" If there was one thing Evan always insisted upon was that Frankie should stick to her lesson plan, come hell or high water.

"Yup. Free as a bird." Frankie slipped past her to the patio table, swiped a peach out of the fruit basket, and bit into it. "No lessons, no homework, no boring, boring SAT drills. Nada."

Rissa was still puzzled. "How come?"

"My tutor called. She can't make it. Flu. You should have heard her. She was coughing and hacking like a sick dog. She said it came out of nowhere, and it's awful. So she can't make it, and I haven't got a thing to do all day. Lucky me, huh?"

"Not exactly all that lucky for your tutor," Rissa replied, but she could understand why the youngster would be delighted for the unexpected reprieve from the punishing schedule to which Evan insisted that she adhere. She felt a brief surge of anticipation, though, at the idea of spending the day in her friend's company, instead of banging away at her computer. Her story was stuck in the doldrums these past two days or so, anyway, and it might be a good idea to go out and spend a few hours not pondering over stuffy dialogue and sticky plot points. She smiled. "But lucky for me. So we go into town, yes?"

"Yes, definitely." Frankie slid her arm into Rissa's. "We'll have so much fun!"

"So we'll pass by the Palais and see if we can get tickets to the play?" Rissa asked hopefully.

Frankie made a loud, unladylike retching sound. "Play? We have a whole day to waste in town and you want to see a *play?* No, girl, we have to go shopping! We need new clothes!"

Now it was Rissa's turn to struggle to keep from rolling her eyes. "We go shopping all the time. How many clothes can you wear? What about the stuff you bought last week?"

Frankie dismissed the suggestion with a wave. "What, those pieces of junk? I don't like them as much as I thought I did."

"Last week, you were over the moon with them," Rissa reminded her.

"That," Frankie explained with exaggerated patience, "was last week. Besides, this is important. We have Evan's *cargolade* on Saturday. That only gives us two days. There's going to be lots of people there, lots of *guys,* and we've got to look *slammin'!*" She threw the half-eaten peach up into the air and caught it in one hand, and then tilted her head to one side, eyeing Rissa critically. "You could get yourself something, too. Something nice, instead of…that."

Rissa looked down at herself, distracted briefly by the offhand comment, but struggled to draw her mind back to the question she was about to ask. "We have Evan's what?"

"*Cargolade.* It's, like, a party. A French party, outdoors, like a barbecue, only with snails, and eels, and merguez, and goat meat."

Rissa wondered briefly if there would be anything getting roasted that wouldn't make her gag. "Any burgers?"

"If you like. And lots of guys."

She couldn't help but smile. "So you mentioned. Problem is, I haven't been invited."

"Didn't Evan tell you?"

"It must have slipped his mind," she said dryly.

"Huh. My brother! If it doesn't have leather seats, doesn't float, and doesn't have a polished oak butt, he can't keep his mind on it for more than ten seconds. Doesn't matter. It's on Saturday, and I'm inviting you." She yanked on Rissa's arm, more insistently. "So let's go into town. C'mon!"

Rissa resisted slightly. She wasn't too keen on crashing Evan's party, even if she was a temporary resident, and the event would most likely take place right on the pool patio, just feet from her bedroom door. "Wait, hang on. Hold your horses. What's this party for?"

Frankie shrugged. "It's a summer thing. A ritual. He does it every year around this time. For employees. Like a thank-you for all their hard work throughout the season. One of those employee bonding things. You know?"

"I know."

"And it so happens that it falls on Corbin's birthday this year, so Evan's ordering a cake. Black forest."

Rissa wondered briefly at the incongruity of Evan ordering birthday cake for an employee with whom he was so often at loggerheads. It was a decent gesture, though, and she had to give him credit for that.

Frankie must have seen the look on her face, because she said airily, "It was my idea, actually. The cake. Evan never remembers things like birthdays. I practically have to hint a month in advance for him to remember mine. So I told him he had to get one. He's been a real pig to Corbin lately, so I told him he had to make nice."

"I notice they've been having problems," Rissa said delicately, not wanting to say any more out of loyalty to Evan.

Frankie had no such qualms. "That's 'cause Evan's a mule-headed old fuddy-duddy who doesn't want to admit the world is changing. He wants to go on doing everything like they did in the Dark Ages, by hand, as though machines haven't been invented. Wasting a whole lot of time on one boat when he could be doing three or four. If he listened to any of Corbin's ideas, he'd double his profits in a year. But not Evan! It's his way or the highway. That's how it always is, with everything."

Rissa could see that Frankie was getting agitated, and, besides, she didn't feel comfortable being on the receiving end of a rant against Evan, so she said, "Maybe he thinks he's got enough money already. Maybe he's more interested in craft, rather than profits."

Frankie scoffed. "If he wasn't interested in profits, he wouldn't be in business. And there's no such thing as enough money."

It would be an awful thing to spend their unexpected free day with Frankie in a bad mood, so Rissa hastened to soothe her. "Look, the day's wasting away and here we are, talking about boats and stuff. You're right—I do need some clothes." She held out her hand. "Come, I'm throwing myself upon your mercy. You help me pick out some new clothes, and as long as they don't show illegal amounts of skin, I promise you I'll take your advice, okay?"

Mollified by the prospect of shopping, Frankie smiled. "Okay."

Rissa was pleased that the crisis seemed to be averted. "Good. Let's get our stuff, and then we can hit the road."

But as they went back indoors to gather their things, Frankie couldn't resist one parting shot. "But Evan can fight, fight, fight all he wants. Corbin will eventually wear him down. You'll see."

Rissa doubted it.

As it turned out, the day on the town was just what Rissa needed. She did, indeed, let Frankie talk her into a new summer dress for the party, a mint-green cotton number that swooped down daringly low in the back, while maintaining an almost perversely demure aspect from the front. Their shopping done, they killed a further few hours at a beauty parlor, where they indulged in sea-salt body scrubs, kelp facials, fragrant deep-conditioning hair treatments, and French manicures. They wound up their evening with cheese-cake, seated in the sun's evening glow on wrought-iron chairs, on a *café-terrasse* on the trendy Rive Gauche.

By the time the taxi dropped them back off at the house, Rissa was glowing, invigorated by the day's pampering, and excited by the thought that, with all the attention she had been paying herself, she looked as good as she felt. As they passed the garage, the flash of Mediterranean-blue metal just beyond the doors told her that Evan had preceded them home, a rare event indeed.

Shivers of excitement ran through her. The last time she had seen him, they had been sweetly intimate, and just the thought that he was in the house, and, dare she hope, as eager to see her again as she was him, was thrilling.

She didn't have to wait long. At the sound of the taxi, he emerged from the house, flanked by Dante and Plato, and stood at the top of the stairs at the main entrance, watching them. He was still wearing his usual working gear: close-fitting jeans and a simple shirt, but the shirt was open at the throat, and its cuffs were unbuttoned and rolled up. The over-all effect was relaxed, nonchalant, and very sexy. He held a bottle of Belgian beer in one hand, and as he took a sip, his Adam's apple moved under his dark skin.

She was unable to prevent herself from running a hand self-consciously through her hair. It was silk-soft to the touch, and just ruffling it sent up the slightest scent of aromatic condi-tioners. She wondered if Evan would enjoy touching it, too.

Frankie had dropped behind her, burdened by even more

shopping bags than she. Rissa approached the steps, her face tilted up to his, a smile on her lips. "Evan."

"Ladies." He did not return the smile. In fact, his face was so expressionless that her smile faltered. She had this uneasy sense that something was amiss, but for the life of her, she couldn't imagine what. Her hands tightened involuntarily around the handles of her shopping bags.

She tried again, timorously this time. "Evan?"

Instead of answering her, he turned his attention to his sister. "Francesca, you're in mighty fine form for someone who was wracked with the flu just a few hours ago. Are you all better?" His level tone was more frightening than any emotion.

Frankie scowled and held up her hand in a "just-shut-up" gesture. "Don't start with me again, Evan!"

"I wouldn't need to start with you if you didn't keep on giving me reasons to start. Did you really think you'd get away with it?"

"I already have," she snapped. "I got just what I wanted. A day off. No thanks to you!"

Rissa was bewildered, not fully following the conversation, but getting the unpleasant feeling that she'd stepped right into another family row. "W-what?" she stuttered. "*Who's* got the flu?" She looked from brother to sister and back again.

Evan filled in helpfully. "It seems that my sister called her tutor this morning and informed her that she was unable to have a class today, since she was in bed with a really bad flu. The lady called me this evening to find out how the patient was doing."

Rissa gasped. "*Frankie* had the flu? But I thought…" Understanding dawned. She'd been hoodwinked into aiding and abetting a willful youngster to cut classes. Her euphoria at the events of the day evaporated. Although his face betrayed nothing, Evan was mad, and she knew that she would be tarred with the same brush of irresponsibility as his sister. She hastened to try to fix things. "Evan, it's not as bad as you think. It was just misunderstanding. Frankie just—"

But Frankie decided to speak for herself. "Okay, I lied. I went into town. So what? What's the big deal? It's not as if we were out robbing banks or something. We just went shopping and got our nails done. Is that so bad? Is that a crime? And besides, I don't need you to tell me what to do. I am not a little girl. I'm sick and tired of your stupid classes, and I'm sick and tired of doing homework out of school. I'm going to ace my SATs. I know all the books inside out. My grades are excellent—you said so yourself."

He was gracious enough to concede. "Yes, they are."

"So why do I have to take your stupid, stupid, stupid classes every day?" She punctuated her words by slamming her purchases down onto the stone paving one by one. "I'm on vacation; this is not boot camp. If I want to go shopping, I'll go shopping. If I want to go to the beach, I'll go to the beach. Do you hear? I have a life."

"You do have a life," he agreed. "But you also have a future. And it's my job to make sure it's the best it can be."

Frankie's arms were waving agitatedly. "No, it isn't Evan. It's not your job. It's not your responsibility."

"Yes, it is. I'm your—"

"Brother!" she shrieked. "That's all! You're not my daddy. You aren't anyone's daddy, no matter how much you badgered Jeanine to have a baby for you. You're so stuck on the idea of being a father, and just because she wasn't willing to get fat just because you wanted it, you've decided to use me as your surrogate. Well, you know what? I'm not. I've only got one father, and one mother, and when they find them, and bring them home, they'll tell you, too!"

For the first time, Evan's face lost its implacable calm. He grimaced as though he'd been kicked in the stomach. What-

ever Frankie meant about his not being able to have a baby
with his wife, Rissa felt sorry for him, but she felt even worse
for Frankie. Evan had been right: she still refused to acknowledge their parents' death. She was still hoping that they'd
come home. Rissa was torn between the desire to say something to comfort either one, and slipping away so that this little
family squabble could find its conclusion in private.

She chose cowardice over compassion, and ducked her
head, trying to slip past Evan into the house, but a single
word from him halted her. "Wait."

She looked at him, her every instinct telling her to cut and
run while she still could. "Why?"

"I need to speak with you."

"Why?" Frankie wanted to know. "Why d'you want to
speak with her? What'd she do?"

Rissa couldn't meet Frankie's curious eyes. Frankie hadn't
a clue as to the business arrangement between her and Evan,
and Rissa certainly had no intention of letting on now. She
shook her head, but couldn't speak.

"Nothing. Just a chat. Nothing for you to worry about."
Evan descended the few stone steps between them, and leaned
forward pressing a light kiss upon the crown of his sister's
blond head. "I'm sorry. Let's forget it happened, okay?"

Frankie looked startled that the fight she was fixing for
seemed to have fizzled out. She held her brother's eyes with
her own wide ones. "Huh?"

"Forget it. It's over."

The girl's relief was palpable. She smiled. "Okay."

He smiled back. "Okay. You can go on in, now. I'm sure
you want to try those new clothes on again. Enjoy."

As though their quarrel had never happened, Frankie
beamed, bent forward and collected her bags, and, with a grin
in Rissa's direction, disappeared, leaving them alone.

Alone so that she and Evan could have their "little chat". Rissa folded her arms, preparing herself for his onslaught, but instead, all he said was, "In my study. Please."

She hesitated just briefly, considering telling him just where he could stuff his little chat, but decided that if he wanted to dish out some medicine, with or without a spoonful of sugar, she was woman enough to take it. She followed him mutely inside.

The Delicate Art of Compromise

Evan led Rissa through the house to his study, a room she had never visited before. She followed him silently, a stubborn cast to her face that told him that she was preparing herself for a battle. That hurt him. He had no intention of taking her to task for the scam Frankie had pulled today. While it was true that he had hired her to act as a de facto chaperone, to-day's escapade was minor, and it was certainly not her fault. He doubted that Rissa had any idea as to just how sneaky Frankie could be when it suited her.

He opened the heavy wooden door and stepped aside to allow her to pass. As she did so, he caught a whiff of something sweet and ethereal, but whether it came from her hair or her skin, he had no idea. Whatever it was, it was delectable, and it immediately brought to mind the achingly sweet experience of kissing her last night. It immediately made him want to do it again.

The late evening light was dimming fast, so he moved

swiftly to snap on two shaded lamps, eschewing the harsher overhead fluorescents. In spite of her bristling hostility, she couldn't help but gaze around. In contrast to the sunny Mediterranean hues that dominated the house, this room was infinitely masculine, even somber. It was furnished with huge wooden antiques: a solid oak desk, coffee tables and matching couch and armchairs. One wall was completely covered in shelves, stacked two thick with books occasionally interspersed with model ships, most of which Evan had built as a boy, with the help of his father.

A print of a centuries-old nautical map hung in a prominent place, flanked by a number of smaller documents, framed hand-drawn blueprints of boats, every loving detail sketched in and annotated. A large globe sat on his desk, which, apart from a silver pen and pencil set and the obligatory staplers, tape, and thumbtacks, was spotless.

Evan watched Rissa's face as she looked around, enjoying the feeling of seeing his favorite sanctuary through her eyes. She seemed particularly drawn to the blueprints, and he told her with great pride, "Those were my father's. Some of his best boats." He pointed. "That yacht has been in the America's Cup race four times. That one is owned by a member of the Monaco royal family, and this one was made under special order for a Greek businessman. It's still the jewel of his fleet." She nodded, but didn't say anything, making him feel awkward and embarrassed, as though he'd been trying too hard to impress her.

She turned her eyes upon him, and the wariness in them made his heart sink. She threw her bags down, much as Frankie had before, re-folded her arms, and glared at him.

"Okay," she challenged him. "Go ahead. Get it over with."

He passed his hand over his close-cropped hair wondering what he should say, now that he had requested her presence and received it. He decided that the best way to handle the situation was to begin by allaying her fears. "I'm not looking to get into an argument with you, Rissa."

"Really?"

The tone of her voice should have been a further warning, but he was fool enough to disregard it. "No. Relax. I just wanted to tell you, if you haven't figured it out already, that my sister can be a bit slippery. You just have to be a little more on your guard with her, that's all. Sometimes she says things that should be taken with a grain of salt."

"That so?" Her lips pursed even tighter. She took a deep breath and then let it out in a rush. "Well, you know what? You might not want to fight with me, but I sure as heck am ready to rumble with you!" The fire in her eyes left him with no doubt that she meant exactly what she said.

He gaped. "What?"

"You heard me."

"I heard you, but I don't understand. What could you possibly be mad at me for? What have I done?"

She explained painstakingly, as if she were speaking to an idiot. "Because…of the way…you treat…your sister!"

He was still perplexed. He threw up his hands. "How do I treat my sister? She gets everything she wants, she's grown up in the lap of luxury, and she's getting the best education money can buy. What's wrong with that?"

"Nothing, except that you've left out the one thing every teenager needs."

He folded his arms, mimicking her stance. "And what would that be?"

"A little credit for having some common sense."

"In case you haven't noticed, that's one thing my sister's a bit short on," he responded dryly.

"That's not true!" was her heated response. "She does what

she does for the same reason all teenagers do. To assert their independence."

"And I don't allow her enough independence? Is that what you're saying?"

"No, you don't. You're one step away from being a complete tyrant. You dictate what she is and is not allowed to do every minute of her waking day. You cram these lessons down her throat, *four hours* of lessons I might add, every single weekday—"

"Those are for her own good."

"You admitted for yourself that she's doing well enough. You know she can pass her SATs without much more help!"

He conceded that much. "She probably can."

"So give her a break, Evan! She's on vacation, in case you've forgotten!"

He frowned and rubbed the back of his aching neck. Rissa was making way too much sense, and that irritated him. So he got back at her by asking sarcastically, "Anything else you want to add to your list of my wrongdoings?"

She fielded his sarcasm adroitly and lobbed back at him. "Well, for one thing, you hired a spy to keep watch on her, as though she's some sort of juvenile delinquent."

That was unfair, he thought. Maybe the terms of their employment had been unorthodox, but he'd been offering her a way out of her troubles, and she'd taken it. "I didn't twist your arm, Rissa."

"No. Not exactly. But you had me over a barrel, and you know it. I didn't have much of a choice. It was that or starve."

"And now you're having second thoughts," he guessed.

"Second, third…I feel like a rat. Your sister likes me, and I like her. If she ever finds out, she'll feel so betrayed."

A hardness entered his voice. "Are you planning on telling her?"

"No."

"Then there's not going to be a problem." His tone was one of finality. As far as he was concerned, that was that.

She grunted in frustration. "Evan, it's still wrong."

Perhaps it was his unwillingness to acknowledge her point that made him callous. "You can back out, if you like. I'm not holding you prisoner here." He knew it was a mean thing to say, but he said it anyway.

She recoiled as if slapped, even lifting her hand to her cheek as though gingerly touching a physical bruise. "You know I can't do that, Evan. You know I need this…job."

Shame overcame him. She looked so hurt that he longed to rush over to her and pull her into his arms and apologize. He didn't know what stayed him. Instead, he walked past her to the bay window that looked out onto the rapidly darkening back garden, and stared into the void for several moments. Then he turned to her. "I'm sorry. That was mean."

"Yes, it was," she said quietly.

"I'm sorry," he said again.

She shook her head, dismissing him, but said nothing.

What could he do? He knew she was right, about everything she had said. It seemed as though, no matter where he turned, or what passed between them, they always ended up arguing, and Frankie was always at the center of that argument. He vowed not to let that happen again. The least he could do was be man enough to back down. "I can cut Frankie some slack on those lessons," he offered, more to appease Rissa than to make life easier for Frankie.

"How noble of you."

He ignored her barb. "Three days a week. The rest of the time she has free."

She wasn't settling for that. "Try again."

He struggled against his better judgment, almost breaking

a resolution that was only seconds old, but gave in gracefully. "Twice a week. And that's my final offer."

"Done." Her victory made her better disposed toward him and she gave him something approaching a smile. That gave him the confidence to say, "And I promise not to be so hard on her all the time. She's right. I'm not her father—as she keeps reminding me."

Now that the subject had been brought up, she ventured to ask, "What she said out there, about your parents coming back...doesn't she...?"

"Doesn't she believe they're dead? She knows they are. She's not stupid. It's just that when she's under stress, she retreats into this fantasy where they're alive somewhere, and trying their hardest to work their way back to us. It's just her way of coping."

"Okay. As long as she isn't..."

"Delusional?"

"Fooling herself."

"No. She knows the reality of the situation, and she's accepted it."

She still looked doubtful, but let go of the subject gracefully. She came over to the window and touched him for the first time, letting her hand close upon his forearm and squeezing gently.

Zing.

The hair on the backs of his arms snapped to attention, and once again, he fought this overwhelming urge to hold her. He hadn't forgotten the pleasures of the night before, and wondered what would be the best way to steer her back to the point where they had left off—that is if she wasn't still fixing to bite his head off.

The gentleness in her voice told him that she was losing some of the spit and vinegar she had stormed in with. "You're doing an excellent job taking care of her, you know."

He couldn't resist asking, "In spite of being a despot?"

Now a genuine smile spread across her face. "In spite of that. I know you're trying. She knows you're trying. You just need to stop and listen to her every now and then, that's all. And trust her. She wasn't up to any mischief today, you know. All she wanted to do was go shopping for a new outfit for your party."

"My...?"

She waved her arm, searching for the foreign term that did not come easily to mind. "Your barbecue thing on Saturday. Your cargo-whatever." She added with an impish grin, "*She* got invited."

He slapped his forehead. "Oh, God, the *cargolade*. It completely slipped my mind! I forgot to tell you about it, didn't I?"

"You did," she said solemnly. "But don't worry—Frankie took care of that oversight."

He was genuinely embarrassed. "Oh, I'm such a pig. A total oaf. You're living under my own roof, and I neglected to invite you to a party taking place right here. Forgive me. The only excuse I can offer is that I've had a lot on my mind recently."

Her lips curved seductively. "What were you thinking of?"

Her sudden change of gears, and the huskiness in her voice almost threw him. "I...uh..."

She spotted her advantage and pushed it home. "Was I one of the things on your mind? Or was it all boats, boats, boats, like Frankie says?" The touch on his arm grew lighter, just a brush of her fingertips, but they burned.

"You know I've had you on my mind. All day, and all of what was left of last night. I lost a good few hours' sleep, thank you very much."

She grinned. "Good. Now we're even."

He ventured to ask, "So, you were...thinking of me, too?"

She punished him by denying him vehemently, "About you? All day? Uh-uh. I was too busy shopping…getting spoiled at a spa…"

He could have let her swipe at his ego get him down, but instead he chose to play her game. "What'd you buy?"

Her response was too elaborately casual to be credible. "Oh, this and that." She jerked a thumb in the direction of the shopping bags she had thrown onto the floor. "I got a new dress for your party. Frankie helped me pick it out."

"Is it pretty?"

"Very." Then she added, "What little there is of it."

He thought of her smooth skin being just barely covered by an artful piece of fabric, and longed to find out if reality would live up to his imagination. "Can I see it?" he asked hopefully.

"You'll see it at the party," she answered briskly.

"What if I can't wait?"

Her brows lifted. "You'll just have to."

He gave in with a gusty sigh. "Okay, you win." Then he decided that her little game was giving her too much of an upper hand, so he took it upon himself to shift the balance of control. Both his hands came down upon her hips. The light, pleated, schoolgirlish skirt that she wore felt surprisingly thin. He pulled her to him roughly, so that they were pelvis to pelvis, and held her in such a manner that she would be hard-pressed to escape, should she take it into her head to do so. "So, you say you went to a spa?"

She was more breathless than cocky now. "Yes."

"Enjoyed it?"

"It was…sensual."

"Mmm. Sensual is good." He lifted a few tendrils of her curly, dark hair. It felt like spun silk under his fingers. He lifted the lock to his neck and inhaled. "You smell like a field of flowers."

Her hand came up to cover his, entwining the lock of hair around their fingers so that they were entangled. "Aromatics. Hand-pressed by a bunch of nuns at a cloister a little way down the coast."

"God bless 'em," he said vehemently. "What else did you do?"

"Facial. Sea salt and kelp."

"Is that why you're glowing? Or is it…" he let his other hand slip lower, from her hip to the point on her thigh where her skirt gave way to bare skin "…me?"

"You think too highly of yourself, sir," she retorted, but the quivering muscle in her thigh was like a seismograph to his fingers, transmitting more information about her state than she cared to admit.

He pressed for more. "What else?"

"Massage." Her voice was like chocolate and champagne. "A long, slow one. Warm, sweet oil, all over."

"You could have asked me to do that for you. Saved your money."

"Maybe I needed a professional job done."

"There are some jobs where a professional is no substitute for an amateur with the right motivation."

The very tip of her tongue popped out from between her lips like a bud at the first hint of rain. "What would you consider the right motivation?"

He stared at the pink bud for several seconds, listening to the sound of his own racing blood, howling in his ears, and then let her go abruptly and turned on his heel. Before the shocked look had left her face, he had crossed the study, locked the door securely, checked it, and returned to face her. "Enough with the wordplay," he grunted, and swept her up as though she weighed nothing. He tossed her without ceremony onto the enormous couch, which he had always thought was too cumbersome, but was glad now for its size. It would accommodate the two of them nicely.

He straddled her hips, his thighs like steel bars on either side of her, holding her prisoner, and leaned forward and inflicted a rough, hungry kiss upon her. "I'm done playing," he reiterated. "I'm not standing around for the rest of the night, letting you drive me crazy like this. I want you." He kissed her again, just as hard, and felt her shiver. Then the little, taunting bud opened; her lips parted and she kissed him back ardently.

"Evan," she breathed.

"Yes?"

"Oh, God, I…."

"Want me back?"

She showed no shame in confessing it. "Yes!"

His tongue flicked upward along her throat. "And you *were* thinking about me."

"Yes."

"All day."

She hedged, still clinging to a fragment of her pride. "Most of it."

"That's good enough for me," he grunted.

For a long time the only sounds that filled the room were their soft, breathless whispers and the rustle of Rissa's cotton peasant top as Evan pulled it up over her head and threw it onto the floor. She might just as well not have bothered to put on a bra, so thin and insubstantial was the one she was wearing, but he was glad for its fragility; it came off with a tug and a snap, and joined the crumpled heap of her shirt. Her breasts were high and jutting, pointing straight at him, their nipples plum-dark against her dusky skin. She made him hungry.

"You, too," she begged him.

His fuzzy mind was barely able to decipher her words, much less their meaning. "What?"

"Your shirt. Take it off. I need to look at you."

"Gladly." In a single, fluid movement he stripped to the waist and tossed his shirt out of sight. He loved the way she looked at him then, staring at his bare chest with a hunger equal to his. He felt his own nipples pucker under her gaze. She reached out with one hand to draw her thumb across one of the hard, pebbled buttons of skin, and he had to bite down on his lip to stifle a curse. "You're killing me," he gasped.

"What a way to go." Mischief glittered in her eyes.

The last remnant of his bantering mood left him. He shifted so that he no longer straddled her, and instead they were lying face-to-face on their side, and then renewed their kiss. As his mouth drew all the sweetness he could from her, they each explored the other, hands eager and curious. Skin drawing heat from skin. His desire for her grew from an impatient hunger into a physical ache.

She was the one to eventually break apart from him. She leaned away, and the mere two inches of space this created between them felt like a cold draft. His instincts cried out for him to close it again, but he refrained. "So sudden," she murmured.

He knew that she still had misgivings about the unexpectedness of the intimacy between them, and sought to allay her fears. "But wonderful, don't you think?"

"Yes. It's just that it never crossed my mind when I left home for Europe that I would...meet someone. And when I agreed to stay here, with you, I never really thought that anything like this would come of it. So I'm just a little...overwhelmed."

He could sympathize with that. And as badly as he wanted her, he wasn't prepared to push her into anything further until she was as certain as he that this was real and right. "Do you want me to slow down, then?" He could feel the tension in his muscles as he braced for her answer.

"No," she said. He was glad that she did not hesitate.

He ventured to ask, "Do you want me to…go forward?"

This time, she did hesitate, but he perceived it to be more out of shyness than trepidation. "Yes."

His relief was palpable, but still he sought clarification. "All the way? No holding back?"

"Yes." Her vehemence told him all he needed to know.

"Thank you," he said sincerely. He let his hand trace the shape of her body, from her shoulder, down along the side of her breast, to her waist, and then to her hip, where it settled. *Steady now,* he told himself. *Steady.* He wondered if there was any way to convey his excitement, his anticipation, without scaring her. He wanted her so badly that he even scared himself. He longed to plunge into her as a boy longed to jump off a pier on a blistering summer day. He fought against the urge to strip the rest of her clothing off of her and make good on her invitation right here and now, but Rissa was different. She was no ordinary woman, and the kind of trauma she had been through would require not greedy self-indulgence, but patience, gentleness and understanding. Her illness brought to mind a real concern, and he voiced it.

"What about this?" He let one finger outline the scar that just barely peeked out above the waistband of her skirt. "Would I hurt you? With this?"

To his surprise, she frowned slightly, as though for a moment she had forgotten what he was referring to. That was a good sign. It meant that she was becoming comfortable enough about it to forget it, even when it was bare to him. When she understood the meaning of his question she shook her head in bewilderment. "I don't know."

It was his turn to frown. "What do you mean, you don't know? Has sex been painful for you since your surgery? Is there anything I need to know? Like what I should or shouldn't do?"

She laughed almost ruefully. "Evan, I literally have no idea. I haven't had sex since the surgery."

"Oh."

"As a matter of fact, I haven't been with anyone since my mother died—and that was three years ago. I don't think I even remember how to *date!*"

"Oh," he repeated. He didn't know how he should feel about that. On the one hand, it made him feel honored—almost exultant—that he would be the first man to be offered access to her body in such a long time, but on the other hand, it pained him that her life had been so difficult of late that she had denied herself the solace of male companionship. He himself could not imagine enduring celibacy for such a long time. "Have you missed it?" He was both curious and concerned.

Her shoulders lifted. "I don't know. A little, maybe. But so many things have been going on in my life, that even if I did, there would be nothing I could do about it."

"I'm sorry things have been so hard for you."

She shrugged again, but he knew that she was nowhere near as casual as she tried to convey. "You learn to live with it. I'm doing okay." She lifted her dark, almond-shaped eyes to his, and he longed to ease away the hurt there.

He had to ask, "Are you scared, then? Nervous?"

"Maybe."

"I'd never hurt you. Believe that."

"I believe it."

He wanted to make his point absolutely clear. "We'll choose a time and place when we can be alone, and take our time. Enjoy each other, and not rush. I haven't got anything you can catch, but I promise you that I'll use proper protection, for your own peace of mind."

"Lord knows, it won't be to avoid a pregnancy." Her bitterness took even her by surprise; she drew a hand up to cover her lips, too late to prevent the words from escaping.

Again, he felt overwhelmed by sadness at what her terrible illness had done to her young life. "Oh, Rissa..." he began to commiserate.

"No," she said hastily. "Don't let's spoil the mood. I shouldn't have said anything like that. I know you'll take good care of me. I know you'll be careful. That's good enough for me."

"And I promise you, I'll do everything in my power to make sure that it will be everything you need it to be."

She slid her arms around his waist and pressed her face against his chest. Her words were muffled. "You've already begun to do that."

Together, they listened to the quiet around them. He tried not to think about the fact that they would soon have to disentangle their limbs, rise up, and put in an appearance outside; if Frankie was still speaking to him, she would be expecting them to join her for dinner. He was loath to even suggest it.

"Evan?"

"Mmm?"

"I need to ask you something."

"Anything." All was right with the world; he was willing to share anything with her, right now.

"What did Frankie mean, that you wanted to have children, but your wife wouldn't...let you?"

Anything but that. There were details about what had happened between himself and Jeanine, and the child that had turned out to be more of a fervent fantasy of his than real flesh and blood, that Frankie was not privy to. The barb she had tossed at him in anger had been calculated to hurt, and it had. But Frankie didn't know—and never would know—the half of it. If he had his way, neither would anyone else. It was too agonizing, humiliating, and infuriating to share.

He sat up abruptly and reached for his shirt. Game *definitely* over.

Rissa looked nonplussed at his reaction. "Evan?"

"She meant what she said," he said gruffly. "I wanted children, and Jeanine didn't. It's not all that uncommon."

"Was that the reason the marriage ended?"

"One of them." He really didn't want to talk about it. He gathered up Rissa's clothes and held them out to her. "We really should be going."

"I'm sorry. If I was out of line, I apologize."

He wished her face wouldn't crumple so. He relented, ashamed of his abruptness. "You weren't. It's just that I…" He sighed. "It's getting late. Frankie'll be waiting for us to have dinner." Gently, he helped her into her clothes, and inspected her critically for any tell-tale evidence that she had been rolling around on the couch. She looked exactly like that. Her hair was tousled, her skirt crushed, and her lips looked very, very much kissed. He tried to stroke her hair into place, but she yanked her head out of his reach.

"Don't worry, I'll take care of it. I'll go straight to my room and spruce up and try to look less of a slut. God forbid Frankie even suspect that anything *shameful* was going on between us."

He knew she was still bristling from his sudden withdrawal, so he was patient. "It's not about shame, you know that. It's about circumspection. There is a minor in the house, and she's awake. I already explained my position on that to you, and I thought you understood."

"As you wish, Evan," she said, but didn't look half as upset anymore. That made him feel better. They had too much at stake for them to risk it over a silly spat. She accompanied him to the door without a further word, but before she could unlock it, he grabbed her wrist and spun her around.

His lips brushed hers in a peacemaking gesture. "Soon," he promised.

Her smile told him all was forgiven. "Soon," she whispered back.

How To Shout Silently Across a Crowded Room—and Have Him Hear You

"I look okay, right? This dress is all right, right?" Frankie asked Rissa for the hundredth time for the afternoon. The teenager paced Rissa's bathroom floor, anxiously adjusting and re-adjusting the brief white outfit that she had bought for the *cargolade*. Broad linen straps crisscrossed her slender back, startlingly bright against her skin. A lace panel separating top from skirt only hinted at the navel ring beneath. The outfit was perhaps just a little mature for Rissa's taste, but it truly was a lovely creation. Frankie's blond hair shone from a touch-up and vigorous brushing, and her make-up looked as though she had spent an hour on it. Gem-studded bracelets nestled cheerily among half a dozen colored plastic charity wristbands, and she had managed to scale down her plethora of earrings to a mere two pairs. But no matter how many times she reassured Frankie that the ensemble was not only just fine, but it was gorgeous, the youngster still fretted.

"It's awful. I should never have bought it. People are already turning up, and I look just awful! What I have on *stinks!*" With the drama only a teenager could muster, she threw herself down onto the toilet seat and let her head flop into her hands.

Rissa came and wound her arms loosely around the hunched, despairing shoulders. "Frankie, sweetheart, you're lovely. You're a beautiful girl, and it's a stunning dress. You have the best taste in clothes. Look at me…" She pointed at the mint-green cotton dress that Frankie had picked out for her. It was equally brief, equally strappy, and made Rissa feel more feminine and alluring than she had felt in a long time. She shivered at the thought of the look on Evan's face when he saw her in it, especially since she had taunted him with the prospect the day she had bought it. She knew she looked good; she just wanted to see it reflected in his eyes.

"You picked this out, and it's perfect. I love it. I feel wonderful just wearing it, and I'm not half as pretty as you are. I promise you: it'll be a killer party, and you'll have the phattest outfit there. So let's go on out and greet your brother's guests, okay? Everyone's having fun without us."

Frankie smiled tremulously. "Think so?"

"I know so," she answered confidently, and was rewarded when the teenager got to her feet, hugged her enthusiastically, and kissed her on both cheeks.

"I love you, Rissa! You're the only person who really believes in me!"

The thread of loneliness and need to belong made Rissa sad. "I love you, too, Frankie," she responded honestly. She held out her hand. "Coming?"

"Coming." Frankie was beaming, but her palm was damp.

The music hit them even before they stepped out onto the patio, washing down from speakers hidden in the mimosa trees overhead. Someone with a sense of humor or a mean nostalgia streak was manning the DJ's station, and had decided to treat the party to a round of old French tunes that were so kitschy that they were almost comic: breathy Edith Piaf, crooning Charles Aznavour, and the raw, aggressive sexuality of Serge Gainsbourg. It set the tone nicely for the traditional event.

Many of the guests were already there, and others were arriving in steady streams, hugging and kissing each other in true Gallic style, chatting excitedly in English, Catalan, and French. Most of them were Evan's staff and their spouses, while a few were trusted suppliers and even valued clients. The patio looked like a cocktail party at a United Nations conference: American, British, French, and Spanish guests blended with North Africans of both Black and Arabic heritage, swarthy Mediterraneans, and even guests from as far as Australia and New Zealand.

Everyone seemed to have a glass in his hand. A quick glance at the bar revealed not only innocuous fruity concoctions, but a range of Southern wines, especially local Banyuls and hearty Rivesaltes, Rissa's personal favorites. On the harder end of the spectrum, there was scotch, vodka, gin, and cognac on offer, as well as the suicidal-looking absinthe, which Rissa could not yet dredge up the courage to try.

She couldn't help herself; her eyes flitted across the crowd, searching for a dark head that would stand above the rest. She spotted him easily. As if her glance had telegraphed a greeting, Evan lifted his head in mid-conversation, and waved, motioning them over. He looked incredibly good. For the first time since she'd known him, he had set aside his customary jeans for more formal dress pants in the same shade of midnight as his shirt. He hadn't gone as far as wearing a tie, but his concession to the occasion included wearing his sleeves neatly held together at the wrist by silver cufflinks. He looked smooth, urbane, and relaxed—and he hadn't taken his eyes off her since the moment he'd spotted her.

Suddenly, she was assailed by the same brand of anxiety that had seized Frankie moments before. What if she didn't look as good as she thought? What if her revealing dress did not whisper *sexy,* but instead screeched *trashy?* Suppose, to use Frankie's terminology, her dress *stank?*

Evan's face put her fears to rest at once. As they reached his side, he excused himself from the conversation and embraced them both. "You look good enough to eat," he managed to whisper slyly as he hugged her.

"Hope you're hungry," she whispered back, before Frankie piped up, "Evan, how do I look? Do I look okay?"

Her brother assessed her carefully, toying with her, dragging out the pause before his response, and Rissa prayed fervently that he would not go into older-brother mode and chide her for the amount of skin she was baring. She needn't have worried. "You look like…Mom," he told her. He sounded almost taken aback, as though he hadn't noticed before just how fast his sister was growing up.

Frankie beamed. "Do I? Do I really?"

"You do. You look beautiful. I'm very proud of you."

Before Frankie could bask any further in her brother's admiration, there was a ripple of conversation among the crowd, and they all turned to see what had caused it.

Corbin had arrived. Rissa watched, incredulous, as the birthday boy swept toward them. He was dressed in a three-piece Italian suit that was so white that it almost hurt to look at him. Gold gleamed at his neck and both wrists, in the single stud at his ear, and from the nugget on his tie-pin. His get-up was topped, unbelievably, by a white fedora that was tipped at a foppish, self-conscious angle. He looked as though he had sauntered off a catwalk.

He greeted them all with his characteristic charm, shaking hands with Evan before elaborately kissing both Rissa and Frankie. "Mademoiselle Nerissa," he gushed. "You look absolutely stunning this evening. Later, we will dance, yes?"

"Of course," Rissa managed, thinking that, if nothing else, the experience would certainly be worth a tale or two in time to come.

Corbin turned toward Frankie, who was all but quivering expectantly at her side. "And you, Francesca, are a ray of sunlight." He lifted her hand to his lips and took his own sweet time kissing it. "Never have I seen you look so lovely. With you, I will have *three* dances!"

Frankie flushed inanely, and burst into a fit of giggles, unable to say anything in response. Rissa, who was still holding on to Frankie's other hand, felt her palm flooded with sweat, as though a tap had been opened. Two of Frankie's fingernails jerked erratically against her skin, digging deep. She could both sense and hear the sudden increase in Frankie's respiration. That was when the penny dropped.

Frankie had an awful, no-holds-barred, schoolgirl crush on Corbin.

Why hadn't she seen it before? Now that the scales had been ripped from her eyes, it was painfully obvious. The birthday cake she had insisted on ordering for him for the party, her almost pathological desire to look good tonight, and her dressing up in sexy clothes that were more suited to an older woman. These had all the hallmarks of a young girl who wanted to impress a man.

That understanding led to further questions. Corbin couldn't possibly be the person Frankie had been spending so much time chatting with online and on the phone, could he? Surely no grown man would cruelly lead on a young girl in that way. What could the two of them possibly have to say?

She didn't dare hope that she was chatting with a girlfriend, perhaps, *about* Corbin, rather than talking to him. Frankie was, by nature, secretive. It wasn't her style.

Rissa glanced hastily up at Evan. As far as she could see, he was clueless, and that made her just a bit angry. He lived with one of the parties, and worked with the other. Had he really sensed nothing untoward, in all this time? She'd have to say something to him; that was her job. It was also her responsibility as an adult. And yet, she was reluctant. She remembered what it was like to be seventeen and in the throes of puppy love. The worst fate that could befall you in that state was for your condition to be made known to someone else. Could she really betray this young girl's trust?

Oblivious to her dilemma, Evan was asking Corbin good-naturedly, "So, Corbin, how's the birthday going so far?"

"It has been perfect. Just perfect." He seized the cuff of his jacket and pulled it back a little, revealing the elaborate threadwork on the edge of his white linen shirt. "This shirt, your sister sent it for me, as a present. It is an original, from Milan. See this? This is hand-stitched. Very beautiful. She has excellent taste, *non?*"

"She does," Evan agreed.

Corbin went on, "I tell her, she has a better eye for clothes than half of the fashionistas in Paris, but she doesn't believe me. I tell her, she could be a great designer one day. Or at least, a very fine looking lady."

Beside her, Frankie burst into yet another fit of giggles, but Evan still didn't seem to notice. "So how old are you today?" he asked.

Rissa wanted to kick him. *Open your eyes,* she wanted to yell. *Are you blind?*

Corbin sighed elaborately. "Unhappily, *mon copain,* I have left my twenties behind. I am now thirty years old.

Soon, I will have to go searching for a walking stick. Soon, I will no longer be of any interest to any of the beautiful ladies at this party, as old as I am becoming." He twinkled at Frankie.

She rose to the bait. "You aren't old! You aren't!" She turned to Rissa anxiously. "Tell him he's not!"

Rissa managed to murmur something that sounded reassuring.

Having received the affirmation that he desired, Corbin grinned at them all, and kissed Frankie's hand once again. "Thank you, *belle*. You are too kind." He bowed extravagantly, and took his leave.

"Wow," was the only comment Evan could make.

"Wow, indeed," Rissa said, but for entirely different reasons. She wasn't amused. There was a nasty feeling deep down inside her, and she didn't like it one bit.

Frankie withdrew her slippery hand from Rissa's. Her eyes glittered as though she had a fever. "It's going to be a great party!" she declared. "I'm going to see who else is here."

"Be careful," Rissa warned softly. Frankie didn't pay her the slightest bit of attention. She disappeared into the crowd.

Once alone, Evan slid his arm around her waist. "Hungry?" he asked. "How about a visit to the grill?"

"That depends," she said archly.

His brows shot up. "On what?"

"On what's on the menu. Frankie told me you were serving snips and snails and puppy dogs' tails." She wrinkled her nose. "Not too sure if creepy-crawlies were really meant to be eaten."

With one hand on the small of her back, he guided her toward the spot where all the grilling action was taking place before answering. "Not a good sign, I'm afraid," he said regretfully.

"What isn't?"

His response was so low that only she could hear it. "They

say that people who aren't adventurous eaters aren't very adventurous lovers, either."

"They say wrong," she asserted. "It's just that I prefer my food to have four legs."

He smiled indulgently. "I know. Frankie made sure I had you covered. There'll be burgers, done however you like. One hundred percent Angus ground beef. Will that do you?"

"That'll do me just fine." People were crowding around the tables, eager for the treats that awaited them. They arrived at the melee, and Rissa looked on, simultaneously curious and appalled, as the escargots were prepared by the catering crew. The fat brown snails were being dumped alive onto a tabletop from net bags, where they were ruthlessly seized, had their undersides smeared with herbed butter, and placed on their backs onto slotted grilling trays. Before they could be caught, some of the more determined creatures broke rank and began heading off toward the edges of the table, even making it halfway down the legs before they were nabbed.

"Some of them are making a dash for it!" she exclaimed.

"Insofar as snails can dash, I guess." Evan was amused by her excitement. "Come." He led her to the broad metal grills and pointed into the glowing belly of the beast. "Those are filled with grape branches. It gives the most delicious flavor you ever tasted. And here come the snails."

A caterer's aide placed the trays directly onto the hot coals, and then lifted a long, heavy-looking wooden pole that had a hunk of fat, weighing at least two or three pounds, bound to it with wire. "Bacon fat," Evan explained. "What comes next is bizarre, but fascinating."

As they watched, the man set the fat ablaze and in long, sweeping motions, let the sizzling grease fall onto the unfortunate, upended snails. There was a collective hiss, and a cloud of aromatic steam arose from the grill.

Rissa cringed. "I don't suppose you have any vegan friends here."

"If I do," he responded, "I don't know if they'll want to be my friends much longer. But don't worry. It think it was all over in seconds. They probably didn't feel a thing."

"Probably," she said dubiously. "Anything else being cooked alive tonight?"

"Nope. From here on in, everything else is as dead as a doornail." He scooped up a plate. "Shrimp, calamari, lamb, goat, blood pudding. Half a dozen kinds of sausages: French, German, Spanish, Catalan." He waved toward some long, coiled up strips of brown meat. "You'll want to avoid those. Those aren't sausages."

"Eels," she guessed.

"Right."

"Ugh."

"I'll make a gourmet out of you eventually. I promise you that."

"Knock yourself out trying," she responded to his threat. "In the meantime, where's the beef?"

He made sure she was served, and then helped her to generous servings of salads, French bread, and a hand-whisked, garlic flavored mayonnaise called *aioli*. It all smelled so good. Then he let her down. "I'm going to have to leave you now," he apologized. "Host duty. I have to make sure that everyone's happy. But I'll be back soon to make sure you're okay. Save me a dance or two, will you?"

All yours, she surprised herself by thinking. She nodded mutely. After he was gone, she found herself a seat that offered a great vantage point, and watched the evening unfold around her as she ate. People seemed to be having a great time; the wine flowed and the food kept coming in endless waves. To her amusement, a few men, the kind that turn up at every barbecue full of tips and good advice on how a grill *really* should be run, had waylaid the catering staff and were now handling the grilling themselves, formal clothes be damned. These self-appointed grillmasters busied themselves shifting things around, arguing amongst themselves, pressing oversized portions of meat onto everyone foolish enough to wander within range, and liberally lubricating their evening with much of the fine liquor available.

The music played on. As Rissa watched, Corbin sailed from lady to lady, dancing with many, and flirting with all. And Frankie hovered, always on the periphery, except for the frequent intervals where he passed by to speak to her, tweak her cheek or ruffle her hair. Each time, Frankie's face lit up as though Corbin had her personal dimmer switch in his possession. It almost hurt to watch.

She saw Evan just as often, assiduously working the gathering, bringing drinks, shaking hands and kissing cheeks, laughing with his guests, and generally being a marvelous host. It hurt to watch him, too, but for entirely different reasons. How she had let herself get sucked into his thrall so irrevocably was anyone's guess. Maybe her intense attraction to him was all an illusion fed by years of self-denial and loneliness. Maybe it was a purely physical reaction to the most dynamic and striking man she had ever met. Whatever it was, he left her with the sensation that she was speeding out of control, unable to apply brakes or even guide the path of her mad descent. Without even trying, Evan had snagged her and held her fast.

That, in itself, was frightening.

When the sun sank, the party lights came on. Citronella torches flared throughout the garden, fairy lights winked in the trees, and Chinese lanterns swayed in the boughs, casting a warm, sensual orange light upon them. When Evan finally returned, the music had shifted gears downward to something more sultry.

"I've come to collect on those dances you promised me," he told her.

She mimed resignation. "Got to dance with the one what brung me, huh?"

"More like, dance with the one what's been longing to hold you all evening," he responded seriously.

"Didn't seem so from here. From here, it looked to me as if I'm about twentieth in line," she retorted before she could stop herself.

"Jealous?"

"Perish the thought."

He shrugged. "That's just cocktail party protocol. I have to keep my guests happy."

"Even if it means bestowing on them the privilege of dancing with the great Evan Maynard."

"If that's what it takes." He ended that thread of the conversation right there, taking her wineglass from her hand and tasting it. "Muscat. Ugh. Way too sweet for me."

Rissa loved the fragrant white wine and the tiny, freckled grapes it was made from. She tried to snatch her glass back. "I was drinking that!"

He lifted it high out of her reach, and set it down on a passing tray together with his half-finished scotch. "Not anymore. You're booked." With that, he escorted her onto the deck where most of the dancing was taking place, and drew her against him. Instantly, she forgot all about the wine. Instead, she let her body soak in the sensation of being held against his as he set their rhythm, swaying with him, but not daring to look up into his face.

She tried to make conversation, in an attempt to stop her mind from drifting into places it had no business going. "Great party, Evan. Everything's just perfect. Everyone's having a good time."

"Corbin certainly is," he replied. "He seems determined to turn it into his own, personal birthday bash. He's danced with every woman on the floor at least once."

Rissa wondered how Frankie felt about that. She wondered, too, if now was the time to say something. Perhaps it wasn't, but she'd give it the old college try anyway. "Frankie…" she began.

"Looks amazing. She looks so grown up. It's as if I looked away, and when I turned back, she's transformed into our mother—minus the nose ring and the blond hair, of course. But she's getting to look so much like her, and I hadn't even noticed it happening."

There's much more you haven't noticed, she should have said. But Evan was slowly stroking his thumb along the base of her spine, and she could say nothing more. All she could hear was the music, and all she could feel was him. Now was *definitely* not the time!

A new song began, heralded by slow, penetrating instrumentals and the intense moans of a woman being pleasured. Rissa immediately recognized Gainsbourg's *Je T'Aime, Moi Non Plus* and her skin grew warm. The combination of the music, Gainsbourg's deep, masculine rasp, and the breathy female groans made this scandalous track the most intense that she had ever heard; it certainly had no competitor in English. She was almost embarrassed to be listening to it in Evan's presence.

He must have sensed it, because he commented lightly, "Maybe it's just me, but I always have to fight the urge to light up a cigarette by the time those two are done singing."

She laughed, and a little of her tension oozed out. "It's not just you. They aren't exactly abashed about it."

Then he chose to torment her by asking, "Do you know enough French to understand what they're doing in that song?"

"I don't think you need to know *any* French to understand what they're doing in that song," she replied as the moans and sighs grew even louder.

He clarified. "No, I mean *exactly* what they're doing."

"No," she confessed, but was afraid that she'd explode with embarrassment if he chose to translate.

"Think Bob Dylan's *Lay, Lady, Lay.*"

"Oh." She exhaled. "God." If her skin grew any hotter she'd have to go splash some water on herself.

He peered into her face. "Miss Young, I believe you're blushing!"

"I am not!" she retorted hotly.

"Don't fib. You're lit up like a chandelier. I'm beginning to suspect that you're a whole lot shyer than you make yourself out to be."

"I'm not shy!" she protested, but as the stirring lyrics segued into wave upon wave of ecstatic sighs, she sought to steer him clear of his accusation, if only to spare herself the anguish of further teasing. "Why's it called *I Love You, Neither Do I?* It doesn't make any sense."

Mercifully, he let her off the hook and explained, "Gainsbourg once said that while there are thousands of songs dedicated to romantic love and sentimentality, he wanted to do one about eroticism, a song strictly about sex in its undiluted form. The woman in the song whispers that she loves him while they're making love, and he doesn't believe her. He replies, 'Neither do I.' He thinks that women are so incapable of indulging in sex for its own sake, that they need to profess love for the man they're with in order to justify their enjoyment. He, on the other hand, thinks that sexual pleasure is its own reward. That eroticism triumphs over sentimentality."

Rissa listened, and mulled over his response until the song faded away and another began. Love and sex. At the same time separate and inseparable. She d had sex for pleasure, she would not deny that, and she'd had sex within the framework of a romantic relationship. The confusion started when she tried to pin down exactly where this pervasive desire for Evan ended, and the stirrings of romantic feelings began. Because make no bones about it; they were there. Sitting alone tonight, watching him from a distance, she had become painfully aware that her longing was not just physical, but emotional. What if, in giving in to him physically, she was laying herself so emotionally open to him that she walked away with more hurt inside her than she had when she arrived?

"Do you believe that?" she finally asked tentatively.

"What, exactly?"

"That eroticism triumphs over sentimentality. That sex can trump love."

"Sometimes." He paused for a moment. "But not always."

"Oh." She wondered what she could possibly say next. Even if she knew, she wouldn't know *how* to say it.

He made her musing unnecessary. "Can I ask you something?"

"Anything," she said weakly, and braced herself.

"Do I scare you?"

"What?" That one had come totally out of left field. It was the last question she had been expecting.

"I need to know if I'm intimidating you in anyway. If there's anything about us that makes you feel pressured."

"Like?"

"Like our business relationship. Because I promise you that the conditions under which you chose to stay have nothing to do with what's going on between you and me. You are welcome to be a guest in my home for as long as you feel the need. There are no strings attached to that."

"I know." She was confident in that.

"Good. Because I want this to be purely voluntary. I want you so badly I can smell you even when you're not around…"

At that, Rissa felt a bolt of raw electricity shoot down her spine.

"…but not if you feel as though you owe me anything."

"I don't."

"Good," he said again. He brushed his lips lightly across the top of her head. Then, after a long pause, he said, "I wish everyone would just go home."

Surprised laughter flew from her lips. "What?"

"I want to be alone with you, but everyone's having a whale of a time. If it wasn't such bad manners, I'd leave them all to it and whisk you away to my room."

She wished he could, too. "Serves you right for throwing such a good party," she said tartly.

He sounded repentant. "Mea culpa."

"Maybe you could shut down the music and turn off the lights. That'd be a big hint."

"I damn well should," he growled. "But my mama raised me better than that. We'll just have to wait them out." The last song of the set ended, and he withdrew from her reluctantly, but not before whispering in her ear, "I have to go play host again, but let me tell you this. I've waited long enough. I intend to have you—tonight. Are you okay with that?"

Her throat was so painfully dry that she could only nod.

"Then stick around," he told her huskily as he turned away.

"I'll be here," she mouthed. Then she was alone, shaking, and desperate for a glass of something stronger than her unfinished Muscat.

First-Time Moves That Let Him Know He's Special

As it turned out, Evan was, indeed, a victim of his own success. The first guest didn't leave until midnight, and it took a further two hours for the very last stragglers to drift off. All the while, he kept throwing anxious glances in Rissa's direction, hoping that she wouldn't get too tired, or worse, decide that she was fed up waiting, and retire before he could seize the opportunity to have her to himself. Fortunately, each time she caught his eye, she gave him an encouraging smile, and that was enough to bolster him through the rest of the party. He was glad when she found herself hemmed in by his banker, an American from Chicago, and his wife, a wannabe romance writer, who he was sure would have her talking enough shop to keep her occupied. He hoped that, for her, the time would not drag as much as it did for him.

When he went to her eventually, she had stationed herself pretty much where he had left her after their dance, as though she had taken his admonition to stick around quite literally. That put an anticipatory smile on his face. "Alone at last," he commented unnecessarily as he drew near. "I've sent the catering staff home. They can come and clean up in the morning."

She rose to meet him. "It'll stink out here by then," she commented, observing the clutter of glasses and used plates that the staff had not had the time to recover before they had been dismissed. The grills, though cooling off by now, still gave off the pungent odor of warm grease and carbonized meats. The remains of decimated salads, fruit platters, and cheeses sat forlornly on the main table.

"Let it. We've got fatter fish to fry, and I'm certainly not letting that get in my way."

She pressed her hand to her tummy. "Evan, please! No food metaphors! I don't think I can eat for the rest of the week!"

"I know what you mean."

By unspoken consent, they began walking toward the house—around to the side that led to his room. As though needing something to say to fill any silence that might befall them, Rissa told him, "I tried some of your eels."

He was genuinely surprised and admiring. "You didn't!"

"Sure did."

"What did you think?"

She pulled a face. "That was the first and last time. They tasted like old shoes. Shoes that had been fished out of a river, no less."

He shrugged. "That's one way of looking at it. But at least you had the courage to try something new."

"Bring on my medal," she murmured.

They arrived at his external door, and the banter stopped. Her face was serious again. He had to ask, "You sure you're okay with this?"

He would have preferred if she had not hesitated, but it was only for a second, so that was okay, he guessed. "I'm fine. I want this, too."

He unlocked the door. He had to battle the strange urge to sweep her into his arms and carry her across the threshold. Instead, he stood aside to let her pass. She had been in there just a few days before, also on a late-night visit, but as he turned on just one dim light, she looked around as if she were seeing it all for the first time. He locked the door behind them, and went to sit on the bed. "Come, sit with me," he invited.

She sat without hesitation or protest. Then, she asked suddenly, "What about Frankie?"

"She turned in half an hour ago. Kissed me goodnight and disappeared."

"Oh. Okay." She looked about to say something else, but then bit her lower lip, and whatever it was was banished.

He sought to put her at ease. "There are several rooms and a hundred feet of corridor between us," he told her. "Unless we plan to raise the roof, we should have all the privacy we need."

He wasn't sure if that appeased her, but she let the matter drop. She twisted her body slightly so that she was facing him, and then she blew him away by reaching up, pulling his head down to meet hers, and kissing him full on the mouth. *She* kissed *him!* He responded ardently, both flattered and surprised that she would choose to make the first move. When she pulled away, she was breathless, but smiling as though she had issued herself a challenge and won.

"That was so sweet," he said throatily. "You are so delicious."

Instead of answering, she slipped from the bed to the floor, onto her knees, and before he could fully realize her intent, she was gently lifting one of his feet and removing his shoe. "You don't have to do that," he began, but she shushed him.

"Let me." She removed the other shoe, and then both socks.

Holding one foot in each palm, she bent down and kissed them, one after the other.

It was an unbearably erotic gesture, but he refused to allow himself to be selfish enough to give in to it. Tonight was for her. By her own admission, it had been years since she had had any sexual contact with a man. His intent was to ease her slowly back into it by making it all about her pleasure, reassuring her with his words and his body, as she rediscovered her sexual self. So he withdrew his feet from her light grasp and slid to the floor next to her.

"You're being very brave," he commended her, "but don't focus on me. Focus on yourself."

"I'm almost afraid to," she admitted.

"You don't have to be afraid. I'd never deliberately hurt you. And if I do anything that makes you the slightest bit uncomfortable, you just tell me, and I'll stop right away." He cursed himself for not taking the time to find out more about her medical situation. He had doctor friends, and there were terabytes of information available to him on the Internet. Why hadn't he done some research? What if he hurt her? How much difficulty would she have becoming aroused? Would her orgasm be painful? Would it even be possible? Then he remembered their encounter by the pool; she had found her release easily enough, but even that did little to stop him from kicking himself. He was an idiot. He'd let the opportunity to learn more, to prepare himself, slip him by.

"That's not what I'm afraid of," she told him.

"What, then?"

"I don't know… I'm not sure if I'll remember how to…" She looked away briefly, too embarrassed to go on, and tried again. "I'm afraid that you'll think I'm a dud. That I won't know how to…satisfy you."

He was aghast. "Why?"

"Because, you've had so much more experience than me. And it's been so many years, I don't even think I'll remember which way is up." She laughed nervously.

"*Any* way is up," he told her, "as long as we're both game." He kept his tone light, but sincerely regretted that crack he had made earlier on about poor epicureans being poor lovers. He even wondered if that had prompted her to taste the damned eels. Him and his big mouth. He pulled gently on the bows that held her dress up on her shoulders, and they gave way with ease. Her top grew slack, but, held up by a zipper at the back, stayed put. He added soothingly, still cajoling, "Don't worry about it, sweetheart. It's just like falling off a bicycle— or something. Forget whatever rules you've made up in your mind about should and shouldn't. Just let it happen."

In the semi-darkness, her eyes shone like moonstones. "Okay," she whispered.

He'd had enough conversation. He brought it to an end by kissing her longingly, and, at the same time, taught that zipper of hers some manners. As it came down, the beautiful cotton concoction she was wearing fell around her waist, leaving her breasts bare to his gaze. Her hands twitched involuntarily, as though fighting the urge to cover herself, but she kept them resolutely in her lap. She smiled in triumph over her own fear.

"Good girl," he said softly against her lips. "Brave girl."

Floor games were great, when you were in the mood for them, but that wasn't where he wanted their first experience to be. He half rose, and held out his hand to help her up. This time, he did lift her into his arms, and the bed sank under their combined weight. The crisp, fresh sheets smelled invitingly of lemons.

They kissed, ardently and hungrily for a long time, until he was so painfully hard his whole body hurt, but he bided his time and maintained his focus on her. In a single, precise movement, her panties slid off in his hands, and now all she was wearing was the dress, half on and half off, the top part in a bundle around her belly. He rolled over onto his back, guiding her upward over him until the edges of her skirt fell around his face like a curtain, and the sweet aroma of her wafted down to him.

She didn't protest as he half expected her to; instead, she leaned forward slightly, sighing audibly as her body came into contact with his eager mouth. As he pressed into the folds of her flesh a shudder ran through her, causing the muscles of her bottom to quiver under his hands.

He was a great lover of wine, and considered himself quite experienced in the art of wine-tasting, but for the life of him he could not think of a single wine he had ever savored, in all his travels, that tasted as fine as she. She was all moist warmth, all natural perfume, and he gorged himself until they were both dizzy.

"No more," she pleaded eventually.

Like an alcoholic locked in a wine cellar, he was reluctant to comply. His thirst was unquenchable. But he released her, drawing away and allowing her to flop beside him. Her breasts rose and fell as she struggled to regain control. "Oh," she panted. "My."

He turned onto his side and kissed her softly, allowing her to experience for herself her own heady taste. She ran her tongue along his lips. "Mmm."

"Mmm, indeed." He nuzzled her neck. "That alone was almost enough to send me over the edge."

"Don't you dare!" she cried in mock alarm. "I want more! Much more!"

"More you shall have," he promised fervently. He allowed her to help him out of his clothes, and when he was naked, he removed the only thing still coming between them—her now crushed and rumpled dress. Then they were side by side, facing each other, shamelessly naked. They stroked each other, teaching themselves about the other's hollows and curves, ridges and indentations. She slid her hand downward over his taut, hard belly, past his navel, and stroked him, grasping him in one soft, inquisitive hand.

She looked down between them, scrutinizing him with open curiosity. He felt the color rush into his face; as good as God had been to him in physical terms, he was sure that no man could endure a woman's erotic examination without suffering some sort of apprehension. He felt like a rookie at muster on the first day of boot camp.

"Very nice," she murmured. Her delicate fingers ran the length of him, up, and down again, before skittering through the nest of curly hair she found there. "I like."

Relief ran through him, and was immediately replaced by the thrill of her rhythmic stroking. She pressed her belly and thighs against him so that her hand was sandwiched between them, and persisted in her torture. If he didn't put a stop to it right now, something was going to give. It was his turn to beg for her to stop. She obeyed at once, but her wicked grin told him she knew exactly how much torment she was inflicting.

It was time to get very, very serious. "Ready?" he inquired.

"Been ready for a long time," she assured him.

He left her just long enough to fulfill his promise to keep her safe by extracting a condom from his nightstand and putting it on, and was back beside her almost before she noticed he was gone. She leaned back, waiting for him, and although her skin was heated to his touch, her nipples erect, and her thighs slicked with moisture, he was sure he saw her bite down on her lower lip in apprehension. His nerve almost failed him. "Remember, if I hurt you...."

"You won't," she asserted, to herself and to him, and then reached out, pulled him against her and drew him in.

There are times when pleasure is so sharp, it shares borders with pain. This was one of those times. He remembered how his fantasy of sinking into her was one of diving off a pier into the sea on a hot day. How he had underestimated the experience! It was so much more than that. Rather than soothing and quenching, she lit a fire in him so intense that in an insane moment he was sure he felt his skin bubble. He felt sweat prickle on his scalp, felt it break out on his back under her hands. And as much as he drew upon his resources to steel his self-control, as much as he longed for this to go on forever, he had to give in and allow his release to wash him away far sooner than he had wanted. He had to. The alternative was madness.

He must have cried out, or groaned from deep within himself, because her fingers were on his lips, and she was shushing him, whispering in his ear. His body went limp against her, and he closed his eyes.

"Evan," she called him softly after God only knew how long. "Are you okay?"

It took effort not to slur. "I'm okay," he understated.

"Good." Her fingers were still stroking his face.

"You?"

"More than okay." She pressed her cheek against his. "Thank you."

She was *thanking* him! She who had given so much of herself tonight. He wanted to laugh, but it wasn't funny. "Thank *you*," he countered. As they snuggled in each other's arms, he almost allowed the pleasant, soporific lethargy to claim him, but something told him to look up at her.

Her eyes were upon him, warm, liquid, and full of the same sleepy satisfaction as his—filled with that, and more.

Knowledge, instinct, and a sixth sense let him see beyond her sated sensuality to the depth of emotion welling up beyond, and realization came fast.

Rissa had fallen for him. Hard. He wondered if it had been there before tonight, percolating, growing slowly beneath the surface until it had grown into what it was now. If it had been, he hadn't noticed. He'd sensed the attraction from the start, and had willingly gone along with it, as his attraction easily equaled hers. He enjoyed her company tremendously, even going as far as to adjust his schedule to make sure that his breakfast time coincided with hers, just so that he could steal away an idle hour with her before he went off to work. For her, he felt a mixture of deep affection, genuine admiration, compassion, and masculine appreciation. But shining from her eyes, he could see much more.

He didn't know what to say. For that matter, he didn't know what to *think*. It was a scary situation, and a delicate one. He'd gone into this worrying about the physical harm he could inflict upon her. The possibility of causing emotional pain had, unfortunately, not crossed his mind. Maybe that made him an insensitive pig. For that, he was justifiably ashamed. But here she was, looking at him with love, and he was not in a position to reciprocate. What now? "Rissa," he began tentatively.

She halted him before he could say any more. "It's okay. Really, it is." Her voice was soothing, as though she was more concerned about comforting him than anything else. "It's my problem. I'll deal with it."

He wouldn't have thought that falling in love with him was something that a woman would consider a problem, although, to be fair, if was not returned in kind, he supposed a problem was exactly what it was. At a loss for anything else to say, he called her name again, and watched, disconcerted, as she made a move to get up. "Where are you going?"

She faltered. "I thought you'd want me to go."

"Go? Why?"

"Because… I just thought…."

His hand encircled her upper arm. "Please, no. Stay with me." He shuddered to imagine how cold and empty his bed would feel if she left. He wanted her to stay until morning, wrapped in his arms. He wanted to make love to her at least one more time before the sun came up. He was prepared to beg, if that would make her stay. "Don't go."

She looked about to leave anyway, but hesitated. "I thought you'd run screaming, now that you know."

He shook his head. "I'm not running anywhere. You shouldn't, either."

She gave in, settling against him once again, and letting her head fall onto his shoulder. As she relaxed, her body grew heavy. That was a good sign. "I only just found out," she told him. "I didn't know until just now."

"I'm flattered," he told her sincerely. "I don't deserve it, but thank you." Then, out of regret, embarrassment, even, for not returning her emotions with equal intensity, "I'm sorry."

"Don't be. I told you, it's my problem. It doesn't mean this has to stop. I still want us to…." She laughed self-consciously, at her own inability to be explicit. "You know."

He urgently wanted them to continue, too, but how fair would that be? A one-sided affair, in which one party carried a greater emotional burden than the other, could be disastrous. If there was anyone who knew that from experience, it would be he. Having loved Jeanine for all those years, and receiving nothing but her sham version of it in return, had almost killed him. The difference with Rissa, perhaps, lay in his own compassion. Maybe, if he handled the matter with the respect and caring that she was entitled to, when the time came for them to part she could leave him without too much heartache. Maybe, if he tried hard enough, he could shore up something close enough to love to offer her in return, at least for as long as they would be together. She deserved that much.

"I don't want it to stop, either," he admitted. "But I don't know how fair that is to you."

She dismissed his hesitancy. "I'm a grown-up. I do what I want. And this is what I want. And I promise you I won't get clingy, or weepy, or make you feel uncomfortable. I can handle this." As if to illustrate her control over the situation, she swung a leg over his hips, and hoisted herself up to look down into his face. "Okay?"

It was certainly an offer he had no desire to refuse. "Okay."

"Then it's settled," she said firmly. She bent down to kiss him again, but before their lips made contact, the stillness of the night was broken by a bump, a thud, and the sound of breaking glass.

They both stiffened. "What was that?" she whispered.

"I don't know." Whatever it was, he didn't like it. He half hoisted himself onto his elbows, straining his ears in case the sound should come again. It didn't. If anything, the silence was even deeper.

"A critter outside, maybe? Coming after the leftover food? Maybe a badger or a weasel or something. I don't know what kind of animal they might have in this region, but…."

A reasonable assumption, but it didn't sit right. He eased her off of him and sat up. "That didn't come from outside. It came from in here…somewhere."

Rissa still tried to be rational. "Maybe Frankie just went out to the kitchen for a drink, and knocked something over."

Frankie! His every warning signal was on red. He got up and hastily searched for his pants, pulling them on so quickly he almost tore them. "I'm going to see what it is. You stay here."

"Like hell," she shot back, also searching for her clothes. She found her dress and dragged it roughly on, wriggling her hips to make it fit, not even bothering to hunt for her underwear. By the time she was fumbling with the shoulder straps, he had already torn open his bedroom door and was trotting up the corridor. He had this sick, nasty feeling in his gut that they were not alone, and he hated the idea. Whoever or whatever had invaded his home tonight was in big trouble.

Outside, crickets chirped and owls hooted. Inside, the house breathed and settled as all houses did. But from the direction of Frankie's room came a deliberate stillness that was almost eerie. The silence itself was like a trail of breadcrumbs, leading him to her door. Beyond it, nothing made a sound. Nothing moved. But beneath the door, there was the faintest glow, not much more than a candle's worth.

He sensed Rissa arrive behind him. She was breathing heavily from tension and the effort to catch up. "It's late," she hissed in his ear. "Are you sure—?"

Without a care for the hour, he rapped on the door. "Frankie?"

On the other side, there was a horrified gasp, and a stifled cry. "Evan!"

The door handle turned in his hand. This surprised him; he had expected it to be locked. That wouldn't have daunted him anyway; he'd have kicked it in if he had to. Generally, he rarely entered his sister's room out of respect for her personal space. But not tonight. In a single gesture he threw the door wide open and flicked the switch, flooding the room with light. Then that sick, nasty feeling in his stomach escalated into roiling nausea.

On the far side of the bed, his sister stood, transfixed in horror, hands slapped over her wide-open mouth. She didn't have much on. On the other side, nearer to the door, half squatting in an effort to pick up the remains of the smashed bottle of Swedish vodka that had sounded the alarm that had brought him running, was Corbin. He didn't have much on, either.

First Time Disasters: How To Stay Sane When It All Comes Crashing Down

Rissa had to stand on tiptoe to see around Evan's broad shoulder. What she saw made her heart sink. Frankie frantically floundered for something to cover herself with, eyes so filled with shock that they were almost popping out of her head. Corbin straightened up to face Evan, pushing aside the upturned bedside table that had made the noise that summoned them, and letting the shards of glass fall from his hands. He was clad only in an obscenely small pair of underwear, his olive skin gleaming in the pale light, long hair in disarray, an arrogant smirk on his face. Between the pair, a rumpled bed told its own story.

A bellow of rage exploded from Evan's lips and he uttered something in Catalan which Rissa presumed was a demand for an explanation. Corbin's sneering reply obviously did not satisfy him, because he said in English, "What the hell are you doing here, Corbin?"

Corbin looked at him as if he were an idiot. "I think you

see what I am doing here. It's evident, no?" Then, to add insult to injury, he turned to Frankie, "I thought I told you to lock the door!"

Having gotten over her shock, and having succeeded in covering her nakedness, Frankie was angry and defiant. "This is my room, Evan! You have no right coming in here. No right!" She sought Rissa's eyes with her own, anxious for support. "Tell him, Rissa! Tell him he can't come in here!"

All Rissa could feel was a lump of lead settling in the center of her chest. So much had happened tonight, she could barely string her thoughts together coherently. But it was plain that her observation about Frankie's feelings for Corbin had vastly been underestimated, as was her perception of his hold over her. It was all too evident that in the throes of her infatuation she had made herself an easy target for a predator. And she, Rissa, who could have, should have, said something earlier, had said nothing. Not out of concern for Frankie's privacy, but for her own selfish reasons. Because she had been reluctant to ruin the mood between herself and Evan. She'd dropped the ball, and failed Frankie. What had been lost here tonight could not be regained.

She would dearly have loved to have taken Frankie's side in this, but as an adult, she couldn't. Her tongue stuck to the roof of her mouth.

"Rissa!" Frankie pleaded again, hands outstretched, palms open in supplication. *"Tell him!"*

Beside her, Evan didn't even spare his sister a glance. His venom was focused on the still-smirking man before him. "You disrespect my home, betray my friendship, and impose yourself upon my sister right under my nose?" He was as incredulous as he was angry.

Corbin was taunting, unafraid, arrogant, even faced with the ire of a man who stood a full head taller than he did, and who outweighed him by fifty pounds. In Rissa's opinion, that made him a fool. "I impose nothing. Frankie, she want this as much as I. She ask for this. She ask for this a long, long time now."

"She is a child! She doesn't know what she wants. She can't even begin to understand the kind of animal you are!"

Frankie protested. "I am not a child! I am not a kid. I know what I want! I want Corbin! I love him!"

Evan spoke to her for the first time, too angry to soften his words. "You don't know what that word means. Not yet. You can't."

Frankie's hands came up over her face again, this time, in a failed effort to hide the tears that sprung there. "I do! I do! Why don't you believe me? You never listen to anything I say!"

Compassion propelled Rissa into the room. She picked her way past the broken glass, making sure not to accidentally brush against the loathsome Corbin as she did, and on the other side, she tried to put her arms around Frankie, but the teenager shrugged her off. "You have to tell him, Rissa!"

Rissa tried her best to at least minimize the damage. "Evan, can't the two of you take this outside?"

Evan threw her a look, and, to her relief, complied. "Corbin, get dressed. You and me—outside." He jerked his thumb to illustrate his command.

Corbin was incredulous. "You joke!"

"I'm not kidding. You can do this clothed, or you can do this in that ridiculous thing you've got on, but I'm calling you out. Now."

A fight wasn't exactly what Rissa had had in mind by urging him outside, but right now, all she wanted to do was put an end to this unpleasant scenario and spare Frankie any further trauma, so she said nothing. *Whatever must be done,* she thought, *let it be done quickly.*

Corbin at least had the common sense to put his pants and shirt on, but bravado made him taunt, "You think you're such a big man. You know I have done nothing wrong, but you, you moralistic American, think you must fight for something your sister give freely."

Frankie shrieked, "You're going to fight him?"

"How freely, Corbin? You flatter her with your nonsense, like I've seen you do with a hundred other women." He pointed at the remains of the bottle on the floor. The smell of its volatile contents filled their nostrils. "You ply her with alcohol…"

Corbin snorted. "I give her nothing! It was her idea. She bring it in from your party. *She* give some to *me*."

"And you were in a position to know that she shouldn't have."

Frankie had had enough of being discussed as though she were not even there. "I'm not a baby! I'll drink when I want, what I want. You think I go to parties with my friends and drink soda pop? You think we don't drink between classes at school? You can't be so naive. And you know what? You're a hypocrite, Evan. You keep going on and on about me being too young for this and too young for that, but don't tell me—don't even try to make me believe—that you weren't doing it with girls when *you* were seventeen! I know all about you. I heard all about you from your *wife*."

Evan didn't deny the charge. "That was different, Frankie."

She snorted. "How? Because you were a boy?"

"No, because the girls I was with were also seventeen. That's a far cry from getting ensnared by someone who's thirty. That's not only immoral, it's illegal."

Frankie folded her arms stubbornly. "I don't see any difference."

By now, Corbin had put his shirt on, and still seemed hell-bent on baiting Evan. "Speaking of hypocrites, you talk about morality, but…" he tilted his chin in Rissa's direction, "from what I see, you and your pretty little houseguest don't look as though you were the model of behavior tonight. The buttons on your jeans not done, her hair is a mess, and that dress… It's only ready for the trash can. So don't talk to me about what's good, what's proper."

Evan flinched, and hastily sought Rissa's eyes. Her face was hot with embarrassment. To have such an intimate, special encounter sneered at by this odious man was a humiliation she wasn't prepared to deal with.

For the first time, Frankie seemed to notice their appearance. She understood the implications, and gasped. "You slept with him? My brother? Why?"

There was no sense in denying it. "It's…complicated," was all she could manage. She was ashamed by the inadequacy of her explanation and her inability to say any more.

Evan cut across them. "What I do in my home is my own affair, Corbin. And there is a great difference between my conduct and yours. Rissa is an adult; she's free to make her own decisions. My sister is a minor. In my country, we call that rape."

Corbin snorted. "In my country, we call it seduction."

Rissa could tell by the tension in Evan's jaw and the pounding of a vein in his temple that he was at the very end of his tether. "She is a young girl!" he raged.

Unable to contain his own cockiness, like a rooster that had just had the run of the henhouse, Corbin crowed, "She's a woman, now."

That sealed his doom. Evan hit the sneering man so hard that he went flying backward onto the dressing table, sending perfume and makeup bottles crashing to the floor. Without giving him any chance to recover, he dragged him to his feet, and hit him again.

Frankie screamed and lunged forward in an effort to separate them. "Don't! I love him!" It was all Rissa could do to physically restrain her.

The altercation didn't take long. It was not a fight so much as a beating, as Evan, holding the multiple advantages of weight, height, fitness, and outrage, lit into him again and again, dodging Corbin's efforts at retaliation with such ease that the interloper barely managed a few feeble blows. It ended as abruptly as it had begun, with Corbin struggling to regain his feet and toppling backward onto the pile of glass splinters. He yelped in pain, but had the good sense to stay down.

Evan came to stand over him. Rissa half expected him to place one foot onto his chest and grind him against the glass, much as one would crush a bug under his heel, but she should have known that Evan would not fight dirty. All he said was, "Get up. Get out."

Corbin rose gingerly, shaking himself free of glass shards. The back of his splendid white linen shirt, Frankie's birthday present, was flecked with red. He was too ashamed to lift his head. He managed one parting curse, and walked toward the door without another look at anyone.

Frankie sobbed brokenheartedly in Rissa's arms.

Standing hesitantly in the doorway, Evan asked hopefully, "Is she okay?"

What a stupid question! While part of her understood why he had been driven to violence, part of her was impatient with his male inability to come to a more peaceful solution. Her response was curt. "No, Evan, she is not okay. Go away."

Corbin was already leaving. Evan glanced at his receding back and then back at his sister. "I need to make sure he gets off my property. His car must be around somewhere. I'll be back. Frankie..."

"You heard her. Go away! I hate you. Don't speak to me again!"

Evan gave Rissa a worried, pleading look, but she dismissed him as well. "Leave us, Evan. I'll handle it."

Reluctantly, he left them.

As the door closed, there was a sense of release, like a balloon deflating. Rissa waited until Frankie's sobs subsided, and then sat on the bed, letting Frankie sit beside her and pulling her down so that her head lay in her lap. She stroked the short, disheveled blond hair that framed the wan, tear-streaked face.

"I'm sorry," Rissa told her. She wished her words weren't so powerless.

"I hate him," Frankie reiterated.

"He was only trying…" Rissa began to reason.

"To do what? Ruin my whole life?"

"To protect you."

"I don't need his protection. I'm not a little girl. I knew what I was doing. This was supposed to be a special night, and he ruined it. Tonight was supposed to be the most special night in my whole life, and my brother comes and spoils the whole thing. If it wasn't for him and his interfering, it would have been perfect!"

Rissa felt her heart sink even lower. Who was responsible for teaching this nonsense to young girls? Why were they still buying wholesale the myth of the perfect first time? It was heartbreaking; generation after generation of girls allowed themselves to be set up to anticipate a perfect night with a perfect prince, and created expectations that were so high that the majority of them suffered heartache and bewilderment when the chasm between their fantasy and reality opened up before them. She was quite certain that even the magazines she wrote for had to claim some portion of the blame, and hoped that her own writing was levelheaded enough not to have ever contributed to the mess. She had to say something.

"Frankie, I have to tell you something. Will you listen?"

Frankie lifted her wet lashes and nodded.

Rissa wondered where to begin. "Sweetheart, I know tonight was important to you. Believe me, I understand. And your brother understands, too. I'm sure that when he calms down, he'll tell you so—"

"I'm not speaking to him," Frankie interrupted.

Rissa went purposefully on. "You read all these books and magazines and watch teen movies that paint the whole issue all rosy, and sprinkle it with gold dust, but a whole lot of that is just a fantasy. This perfect first time, it just doesn't happen. At least, not for most of us. It's a doorway we all have to go through, but most of the time, it's disappointing, or painful, or uncomfortable, or embarrassing, or, sometimes, tragic. But you'll get over it."

"I won't. I never will."

"You will. I did."

Frankie squinted skeptically. "What, did your brother beat up your boyfriend?"

"No. I don't have a brother. I wish I did. But I suffered humiliation just like you did. I wanted to die. I wanted to dig a hole and bury myself. But you know what? Time passed, and I got over it. I can almost laugh about it, if you get me in the right mood."

At least, Frankie was interested. That was a start. "What happened?"

It wasn't a story that she relished sharing with anyone, in spite of her own assertions that she had, in fact, gotten over it, but if it would help Frankie, she was game. "It was my freshman year at college. My first time away from home. I grew up fairly sheltered, and I was really young, and easily influenced. I remember getting a terrible crush on a junior. He was one of the popular boys—a great dancer, a hard partier, unbelievably good looking. He did everything—swimming, tennis, basketball, soccer."

"What was his name?"

"Keron."

"Okay. Go ahead."

Rissa inhaled sharply and gathered up her courage. "Well, stupid me, I managed to convince myself I was in love with him, almost at first sight. I did everything I could to be near him. I went to all his games, even though I was never much for sports. I found out what bars or parties he would be going to over the weekends, and turned up, just so that I could 'accidentally' bump into him. I gate-crashed if I had to. It was as close to stalking as I'd ever like to get. I must have been really annoying."

"And…?"

"And either he decided to give in as a means of getting rid of me, or he simply availed himself of what I so foolishly put on offer. But after months of brushing me off, he asked me out. It was to this big party on campus, one of those rowdy ones that spread out all over, with some people partying, some lighting barbecues, and some couples wandering off to cars or corners to make out. I was over the moon. I couldn't believe that he had finally noticed me, and I was delusional enough to have convinced myself that just because he had asked me out, it meant that he was as much in love with me as I was with him. I made up my mind that my virginity, my heart, and my soul were his for the asking. Somebody should have given me a good shaking.

"Anyway, I spent a whole week preparing for my big moment. I crash dieted to get into a new outfit I bought. I did my hair, even though I could hardly afford a hairdresser at the time. I bought makeup, perfume, and an assortment of birth control devices I hadn't a clue how to use."

Rissa stopped and laughed self-deprecatingly. "God, I was a mess. I was a bundle of nerves. The whole night, I hung on to everything that he said—when he chose to talk to me, that is. He spent most of the time joking with his soccer buddies. I even had to get my own drinks. But I hung around. And then the moment came. He took me away from the site of the party, to an empty classroom…" She paused. As anxious as she was to help her young friend by sharing her own experience, and as much as she had sworn that enough time had passed for her to be unaffected by it, she discovered that there was still pain there.

"And you did it?" Frankie asked, totally engrossed in the story.

"I guess you could say that. The only positive thing I can say about the entire experience is that it was mercifully fast. It was over without any preliminaries, painful, and as far from romance as you can possibly imagine. Keron, he was casual, almost matter of fact about the whole thing. He got up and walked away when he was done as though he had just washed his hands or brushed his teeth. He flicked the lights off as he left, as though I was another piece of furniture in the classroom. He left me there, alone, in the dark, crying. I was shocked, devastated, and spent a long time lying there on the dirty wooden floor, blaming myself. Wondering what I had done wrong, to make my fairy tale night turn into a nightmare."

"That's awful."

"Not as awful as what came after. He never spoke to me again, never even looked in my direction. Now that he was done with me, I didn't exist. I was like a used tissue thrown onto the floor, and kicked into a corner. At the end of the semester, he and his soccer team thought it would be hilarious to do up a poster of their picks for the 'Ten Worst in Bed,' with photos and names of the girls. I was on the list. They made photocopies and plastered them all over campus. They became a collectors' item. I, and the other girls on the list, became a laughingstock. It was a whole year before I even ventured out on another date." As she finished her story, she felt suddenly tired.

Frankie shifted in her lap, but made no move to sit up. "I'm sorry to hear that, Rissa. I truly, truly am. But there's a difference between you and me."

"What's that?"

"Corbin didn't do anything wrong. This was all Evan's fault. If it wasn't for him—"

God, so much innocence. She still had so much more to learn. "If it was a good experience for you, Frankie, I'm happy, honestly. I was merely trying to illustrate how sometimes, things don't turn out the way you planned them. But your brother reacted the way he did because you still have so much to learn. There are so many things you don't understand yet, and so many ways to get hurt."

"I know all about AIDS and STDs and pregnancy and stuff," Frankie countered hotly. "I learned all about it in school. And I took care. I made him use one of those…things. I'm not stupid."

"Good girl," Rissa said sincerely. "But there are more risks to sex than disease. Emotional risks. Hurt feelings, broken hearts."

"Corbin loves me, too," she said earnestly. "I know—he told me. And I love him right back."

What did you say to that? Surely, even in a bid to protect her, it was unfair to belittle the extent of her emotions. Unlike Evan, Rissa was quite sure that even at seventeen Frankie was perfectly capable of loving, and loving deeply, even if that love was misplaced, and put her in great jeopardy. She refused to discount the legitimacy of the young girl's feelings.

But Frankie must have read doubt on her face nonetheless, because she said passionately, "I do! I can't understand why

you don't believe me. You know what it's like to love someone, don't you? Haven't you ever been in love? And I'm not
talking about stupid Keron. I'm talking about true love, the
real thing."

Rissa closed her eyes involuntarily. The excitement of the
last half hour or so had all but chased from her consciousness
the startling, daunting discovery she had made in Evan's arms
tonight. Or, to be fair, it had not been so much a discovery as
much as it had been a concretization of a suspicion that she
had been holding for some time. It had been as though their
lovemaking had acted as a gelling agent, bringing everything
together so that it held a recognizable shape.

She'd fallen in love with Evan. This hadn't been the pleasant summer interlude she had bargained for, encouraged by
the gorgeousness of their surroundings, the inherent romance
of the French countryside, and his own dynamic personality.
This was real, and concrete, and scary. She hoped her reaction
did not show on her face.

Her hope was wasted. Frankie, with the sharp-eyed astute-
ness of a perspicacious teen, gasped. "Oh, my God! You're in
love with my brother!"

Rissa considered denying the accusation, even if only to
buy herself time to think of a suitable response. "I…"

Frankie wrinkled her nose. "You're kidding! Ugh!"

"Ugh?" Little sisters were notorious for being incapable of
recognizing the charms of their siblings, but even so, the
"ugh" took her by surprise.

"Why? He's horrible. He's mean and bossy."

Rissa had to step to Evan's defense. "He's also a kind and
loving brother to you. He makes a point of spending time with
you every night after dinner, watching movies you want to
watch, and playing video games you want to play. He takes
you wherever you want to go on weekends. He buys you

anything you want to have, and works his tail off so you can go to the best school you can, live in the nicest house I have ever seen. Admit it—you like being with him. You enjoy his company—when you're not fighting."

"I guess," she begrudged.

"He loves you enough to fight for you, even when you don't think you need fighting for."

To her surprised relief, Frankie didn't even counter that. Instead, she regarded Rissa intently. "So, you love him."

"Yes."

"You tell him?"

"No, but I think he guessed."

"What'd he say?"

She shook her head. "Not very much."

"He love you back?"

"I don't think so." That admission hurt.

"He's not gonna," Frankie asserted with the casual cruelty of youth.

"Why not?" Rissa asked, even though it cost her much to ask the question.

"She screwed him up good."

"Who did?"

"His wife. Jeanine."

"Ex-wife," Rissa corrected automatically.

"Whatever. She killed him. She's been gone years, and he still hasn't gotten over her. I'll never know exactly what she did to him, but whatever it was, it cut him up. He's never been the same person. Even when they were still together, and they were living in a bad marriage, he wasn't the way he is now. Not like this."

"Like what?"

She shrugged. "I don't know. Dark. Sad. Longing."

Rissa mulled this over. If what Frankie was saying was

true, she would have to be even more on her guard than she had thought. If Evan's ex, whatever she had done, had wounded him so deeply that she or any other woman who came after would never stand a chance of being loved, then she never had a prayer of seeing even a glimmer of her own feelings reflected in his eyes. She'd need to be careful.

Suddenly, she felt tired. Her head drooped, and her shoulders sagged. Frankie spotted it at once. "You need some sleep."

"Yes."

Frankie sat up. "Me, too, I guess. Maybe if I go to sleep now, I'll wake up in the morning and find out that all this never happened. At least, the second half of the night."

Rissa knew that there was little chance of that happening, but she didn't bother to reply. Instead, she got up slowly, shaking out the cramps in her thighs. "I'd better get going, then."

Frankie gave her a wild-eyed look. "No!"

"It's almost dawn," she said patiently. "We both need—"

Frankie clung to her arm. "Stay here! You can sleep here. Don't leave me, Rissa. I need you."

Rissa glanced at the large, rumpled bed, and thought of all that poor Frankie had been through for the evening, and her heart softened. It wouldn't kill her to stay here for a few hours, if it was the only comfort she could offer. In response, she sat down, and Frankie hurriedly turned off the lights and crawled in next to her, fluffing out her pillows and stretching out like a little girl waiting for her bedtime story. "Thanks."

"Don't mention it." Rissa tilted back next to her, and willed her exhausted body to relax. She tried not to think of the irony of the trick played on her tonight by some mischievous deity. This wasn't exactly the Maynard whose bed she had hoped to share. But she was tired, and a bed was a bed. To be honest, she wasn't so keen on being alone right now, either. She closed her eyes. She wondered if in the morning, as

Frankie had suggested, she'd wake up and find that none of this had really happened after all.

And if so, would that be a good thing or a bad thing?

"Sorry, Rissa." Frankie's voice was muffled behind her.

"About what?"

"About Evan." Then she was quiet.

How To Pick Things Up Again When He Thinks You've Let Him Down

The night was unusually dark. A coastal breeze sent clouds inland, obscuring the moon and blotting out the light by which Rissa and Evan habitually swam, so they had to rely on the lamps scattered throughout the garden to find their way around the pool. Evan sat at the shallow end, his legs dangling into the water. Rissa stood between his knees, facing away from him, her back against his chest. She was glad for his arms around her; they provided warmth as well as comfort. The dogs snored loudly nearby.

"Think she'll ever speak to me again?" Evan asked mournfully. "It's been days."

"She will." Rissa was sure. "But young girls can hold a grudge for a very long time. You'll just have to wait her out."

"I'm not a patient man. And she's my sister, for Pete's sake. We shouldn't be like this. I've tried everything I can think of. I've stood outside her door and pleaded for her to listen to me.

I've apologized in every way I know how. I've even tried to meet her on her own turf: I've e-mailed in several apologies. But nothing. She won't even come out of her room. She must be going crazy in there, staring at four walls."

"She comes out when you go to work," Rissa reminded him.

"Well, at least there's that. But I'm driving myself insane, wondering if I did the right thing. Asking myself if I was right to be that mad. I'm not a prude, but my sister is all I have." He waited, as though afraid to ask, and then, tentatively, "Do you think I did the right thing?"

He was pleading for her affirmation, but she wasn't too sure she could give it. She wondered how she could answer that question tactfully. "I understand why you did what you did. Corbin was being very provocative, and the whole scenario took us both by surprise. But maybe…" She hesitated. "Maybe there was a better way to handle it."

He groaned. "A better way to react to a near-naked man in my sister's bedroom? Like what?"

She had to honestly say, "I don't know."

He brooded. "There you go. No way of telling, right now. Maybe history will vindicate me; maybe it won't." He suddenly had a thought. "Is she eating okay?"

"She's eating just fine. Her behavior is almost normal. We have a swim together every day. We watch movies. We play tennis. She hasn't said a word about Corbin."

"Thank God you're here," he said fervently. "At least I know she's in safe hands." He leaned forward to press a kiss upon the center of her head.

She wished he was glad of her presence for reasons other than his sister's well-being, but since the night of the *cargolade,* Evan had not so much as approached her for a kiss. She wondered if his reasons for that had more to do with his discomfort over her unrequited feelings for him than they did for his perturbation over the impasse with his sister.

Uncannily, he seemed to sense her unspoken question. His arms tightened around her. "I'd love to take you somewhere special, just you and me. You deserve it. I'd like to take you to a nice place and share a special meal with you, book a booth in the corner of some quiet restaurant, order champagne and strawberries, and kiss the taste of strawberries off your lips. I wish I could take you shopping, shower you with special things. Earrings to frame that beautiful face of yours. A dress to bring out the color of your eyes. But I can't. Not with Frankie like this. It's just not right, leaving her alone."

"I understand." Her words had a hard time making it out of her throat.

"And the reason I haven't come to you, or asked you back to my room, is that it's just too uncomfortable. Believe me, I spend many hours alone, wrestling with the devil, trying to talk myself out of coming over and knocking on your door. I can't stop thinking about how good it was between us that night, and how much I want you again." He spun her around in the water so that she was still standing between his knees, but looking up into his face. "But Frankie's presence, her anger, just radiates out at me from her room, like a malignant force. And I feel ashamed. I lie there, wanting you, with that crack about hypocrisy just ringing in my ears, and I'm paralyzed."

"You're not a hypocrite," she hastened to assure him.

"That's what logic tells me. But between Frankie and Corbin, and the comments they threw at me—at us—I feel ashamed. I want to be with you so badly, but under the present circumstances, even if I made it to your door, and took you to bed again…" He half smiled. "Let's just say it might end in humiliation for me, and frustration for you."

"You're not a performing seal," she said quickly. "I'd understand. We don't have to do anything more than lie together. Kiss. Hold hands."

"I know. Maybe soon. Maybe even tomorrow. But not now."

"Okay." She couldn't hold his gaze anymore, so she looked down at his reflection on the rippling surface of the water, like Perseus able to look upon the face of the Gorgon only as a reflection in his shield. She was afraid to let him see the relief there. It was far, far better to know that his avoidance of her was due to his own inner struggle, and not born out of a reluctance to reprise their intimacy, now that he knew she loved him.

He understood her reason for looking away, and coaxed her chin upward with one hand. "It wasn't about that. I thought you knew that."

"About what?" she stalled.

"How you feel," he said delicately. "As I told you, I'm flattered. I'm honored, and touched. But I'm not afraid. I won't let it scare me away. As a matter of fact…" He paused, as though wondering whether he should say anything or not. "If I were ever to fall in love again, I'd wish it was with someone as sweet and smart and beautiful as you." His caramel eyes were dark with longing and regret, and Rissa found herself mesmerized by them. "But it won't happen. Please, don't… pin your hopes on me."

"Why not?" Her voice was hoarse.

It was his turn to look away. "Been there, done that," he said a little too flippantly. "Doesn't work. And I don't need to be bitten twice to know that love is not for me."

How could someone so young, she wondered, and who had so much to offer, become so embittered that he could assert that love was not for him? With the pool of good, honest, attractive, available men dwindling every day, that alone was tragic. Whatever could this woman, this Jeanine, have done to him to have caused so much damage? She found herself hating the faceless woman; wherever she was, she hoped she was miserable.

She longed to ask him about it, plead with him to share even a little information about the woman who, though long absent, was still both competition and stumbling block. But she'd asked before and been brusquely rebuffed. Lord knew, she'd bite off her own tongue rather than ask again.

But the question hung in the air between them like a mist. Evan sensed it, and was still as reluctant as ever to answer, because he clumsily redirected the course of their conversation. "Corbin seems to have abandoned the job."

Personally, Rissa didn't give a rat's tail about Corbin's whereabouts, but she feigned interest, resigning herself to his red herring with good grace. "Really?"

"And it seems as though he's left town, too. I passed by his apartment, and his neighbor says she hasn't seen him in a few days. His boat's gone from its mooring at the marina. The harbormaster hasn't seen him in a while, either."

"You went looking for him? Why?"

"To hammer out a severance deal. Things haven't been going all that well between us professionally anyway, with his business philosophy diverging so sharply from mine recently, and I don't think our personal beef is going to help any. So it's best we part company."

"Where do you think he's gone?"

He shrugged. "No idea. He's an excellent sailor, so maybe he just put out to sea for a while. Maybe he moored at one of the smaller marinas along the coast, just to avoid me, and the situation, for a bit. Good riddance, either way. I'll let my lawyers get in touch with his, and we'll handle it that way. With any luck, I'll never have to see him again."

Rissa shook her head sadly. "Poor Frankie."

"Still thinks she's in love?" he asked rhetorically.

"*Thinks?* Don't belittle her feelings, Evan. As much as you have an adult perspective on the whole scenario, don't treat her as though she's too young and too dumb to have any genuine feelings. What she feels is real. It hurts." *Love always hurts,* she thought, but did not voice, *when the object of that love is not available to you.*

"I know it's genuine," he said gently. "And I know that it hurts. I just wish it had happened with someone more suitable. Less dangerous. You know…" He paused thoughtfully. "If we'd rushed into that room and discovered some young boy from the village, someone her own age, I probably would have shown him the door with little more than a lecture to be careful. I certainly wouldn't have stood in the way of her seeing him again. As I said, I'm not a prude. And as Frankie so pertinently pointed out, I had my own teenage shenanigans. I know what it's like to be seventeen. At that age, they have needs and drives that are probably more potent than ours, because at least we've learned to control and handle them. I might not have relished the idea of my sister in a physical relationship with a boy, but I certainly would have understood. I'd have gritted my teeth and acknowledged her right to make her own choices."

"Instead, it was Corbin." Her regret was as great as his.

"Instead, it was Corbin," he echoed. "As harmless as a serpent in a hatchery. If only I'd known. If I'd had the slightest inkling that it was brewing, I might have been able to head it off. God, if only…." He must have caught the mad flush of guilt that sprang to her face, because he trailed off and stared, incredulous. Then he gasped, "You knew?"

The water around her became suddenly cold. Only her face was flaming hot. She floundered, "I had an idea. I just guessed…."

Evan leaped out of the water as though it were full of

stinging jellyfish and stood at the edge of the pool, looking down at her. "You knew?" he repeated, incredulous. "And you didn't say a word?"

She scrambled out of the pool, unwilling to allow him such an unfair height advantage, babbling as she did so. "I didn't *know,* not really. At the *cargolade,* I saw them together, and I saw the way she was looking at him. I saw the look in her eyes, and I guessed. And he was toying with her, flirting, and she was blushing and hanging on to his every word."

He picked up his towel and scraped it angrily across his chest as though rubbing away a dirty smudge. "And yet you said nothing."

"Honestly, Evan, I just thought it was a crush. I had no idea it would come to this. I hadn't a clue what they were planning. All I saw was a young girl who was sweet on an older man. I made up my mind to talk to her about it, at another time, when we were alone. Just me and her."

The eyes that had held hers so warmly while he had made his passionate declarations of desire for her were now hard, and cold, blazing forth a frigid fire. "And yet you didn't see fit to inform me of your suspicions. Even though this was expressly what I'd hired you for."

The reminder of their employer/employee relationship, just moments after they were cuddled against each other with the casual intimacy of lovers, was like a harsh slap. Her ire rose to meet his. "I'm sorry to have failed so miserably in my duties, *boss,* but I was thinking like a woman, not a spy. I saw a young girl facing a potentially hurtful situation, and I resolved to talk to her about it at an appropriate time. A party thronging with people is not an appropriate time. If you are unsatisfied with my performance, feel free to dock my pay for the night in question."

By now, even the dogs had become aware of the rising

tension, and had shaken themselves from their slumber, and were eyeing them curiously, wondering at the cause of it.

"You know it's not about that!" Evan snapped.

"No? Then why'd you bring it up?"

He brushed away the question. "All I'm saying is that you could have mentioned it…."

"While you were sailing around entertaining the old gang? Being charming and funny and dancing with half the women there?"

"I was busy, maybe, but not too busy for my sister. I'm never too busy for my family."

"Well, I thought it could wait until morning. As it turned out, I was wrong. Besides, I didn't want to say anything that might have upset you. I was scared that if I did, it would have—" She bit off the rest of what she was about to say, embarrassed to admit that she had been so eager to spend their promised night together that she had been loath to do anything that might have derailed it. She hid her confusion by making a big show of toweling her hair.

He understood immediately, and his anger softened. "You were afraid to ruin the mood."

"Yes," she snapped. "I was afraid to ruin the mood. I was afraid that if I so much as hinted that your nemesis was flirting with your sister, and that she was head over heels in *crush* with him, you'd have gone storming about like a mad bull, and whatever chance you and I had of…*doing it,*" she used the expression with bitter condescension, masking her shame with sarcasm, "would be shot. I wanted what you were offering, and I was afraid to throw a spanner in the works. I put my needs first. I thought I'd have had more time to handle the situation with Frankie. I gambled, and we all lost. Okay?"

"Calm down." He tried to lay his hand on her shoulder but she wrenched away. "I think I understand—"

"No, you don't. There's a whole lot you don't understand."

"Like what?"

"Like, I wouldn't waste my breath trying to explain." She hated that he'd thrown their business relationship in her face. She hated that there was a business relationship in the first place, and was ashamed of what it entailed, not to mention that he'd made it quite obvious that the first chance she'd had to earn her keep, she'd blown it. And why? Because she was so bent of having sex with her employer that she'd neglected her duties. That made her feel cheap, and her desire for him felt tawdry.

She expected him to plead again for an explanation, but he did no such thing, sorely disappointing her. Instead, he tried to say, "I'm not angry—"

She didn't let him finish. "Don't start that again! You keep saying over and over again that you're not angry with me, but you are. Why bother to deny it?"

"I was, but you've explained yourself. Now that I understand, it's over."

"It's over because you say it is, huh?"

He sighed from deep within. "If you'd like to keep the matter open, then it's still open."

"Don't patronize me!"

His patience was stretching thin. "I'm not. I'm just trying to give you what you want."

"Don't. I don't want anything." She knew she was being childish, but she didn't want to stop. "I don't want to talk about it anymore." This, she realized, effectively closed the matter, which is what she was protesting against in the first place, but she was beyond caring.

He stared at her for several moments, and then said, "It's late. We should go inside. I think all I need right now is my bed. Are you coming?"

"Where? To your bed?"

"No," he answered slowly, "inside."

"I'm fine right here."

"It's going to get cold soon."

She dropped to her knees and put her arms around Dante and Plato. "Dogs'll keep me warm. Don't worry about me."

"I won't," he said shortly. "Have it your way." He left without a backward glance.

It was getting cold, and Rissa wondered how long her bravado would keep her out here before she would put her tail between her legs and slink back in. What had made her behave like that? She'd been downright aggravating; she knew that. He'd said what was on his mind, and then tried to make amends, but she'd been infantile and willful and slapped him down. Why?

It was facile to think that she had become that angry over his chastisement of her. She'd made a mistake, and Frankie had paid for it. But she'd offered an explanation, and Evan had accepted it.

So why was she still so mad?

Honesty took her further back in the conversation, past the issue with Frankie and Corbin, and past the issue of her employment, until she got to the kernel of the problem.

And the problem was Evan and his ability, or lack thereof, to fall in love. *Don't pin your hopes on me,* he'd cautioned her. *Once bitten, twice shy.*

He'd sounded a warning bell, loudly and clearly, setting the terms and limitations of their relationship. They were non-negotiable, and laid plainly on the table for her to accept or refuse. If the situation in the house were ever to return to a place where they could resume their relationship, it would have to be on his terms or none at all. She was free to love him, as long as she understood that he was not prepared to love her back.

Ah, there was the rub.

* * *

"I've been thinking," Frankie yelled across at Rissa from her florescent pink inflatable chair in the center of the pool.

On her towel near the edge, Rissa rolled over to face her. "Yeah? That'd be a first," she kidded.

Frankie let the ribbing wash over her as though she were the proverbial duck's back. She pushed her sunglasses up onto her forehead and straightened up gingerly, so as not to tip over into the blue water that lapped all around her. "Yeah."

"Okay, I'll bite. What you been thinking about?"

"I've been real mean to my brother," she said soberly.

You aren't the only one, Rissa thought guiltily. Three whole days had passed since she had behaved so badly with Evan on this very spot, next to the pool. Since then, her interaction with him, what little there was, had been polite and strained. He left long before she was up for breakfast, and she found herself sharing dinner with Frankie alone. It was an uncomfortable situation, with each person in the house mad at someone else, and she felt guilty about the part she played in it all. Even the housekeeper, Madame Soler, noticed that something was wrong, and crept silently from room to room as though the floor were studded with land mines. Something would have to come to a head soon, before the tension in the house exploded outward like a firebomb.

"I realize it was really childish of me, not speaking to him all this time," Frankie added with a grown-up air. "And I want to make it up to him."

Rissa was both surprised and pleased. "Really?"

"Yeah." Frankie slipped from her perch into the water, and splashed to the edge, where she clambered up onto the tiles and shook herself all over. "I want to have a surprise waiting for him when he gets home tonight. I want to get him some presents, something really nice, and cook him dinner."

"You? Dinner?" Rissa asked dubiously. "Making it up to him sounds like a great idea, but…."

"Oh, I can cook! Really, I can. You'll see!" She slipped her hand around Rissa's wrist and tugged on it. "Come."

"Where?"

"Town. I've got a menu made up, and there are things we need to get. I want to go to the market, so we can buy fresh stuff, and flowers. And we can pop into one of the chic stores and you can pick out a sexy cologne for him. Something *you'd* like to smell on him…" She rolled her eyes ostentatiously, as though still getting used to the idea of Rissa and Evan was still a task.

Rissa wondered privately whether she would be getting close enough to smell Evan anytime soon, considering the state of their relationship, but instead she just said, "I think that's just great. Evan would like that. I'll just give him a call and let him know where we'll be—"

"If you call him, how will it be a surprise?"

"Well, you have a point, but I still think it's only polite to let him know we'll be out."

Frankie pouted. "What, I need his permission to go to town now? All of a sudden I'm five years old? You're acting as though he hired you to baby-sit me or something."

Rissa hoped she didn't wince. The last thing Frankie needed now was another betrayal. She struggled with her better judgment for just a moment, and then gave in. "All right, but we'll leave a message with Madame Soler, just in case he calls."

Frankie snapped her fingers. "That's it! But just tell her we're going shopping. Let's not tell her what for. It'll ruin the surprise."

"What about that dinner she's preparing? Shouldn't we get her to stop?"

"Nope. That'll let the cat out of the bag. We'll just put her stuff in the fridge and have it tomorrow." She clapped her hands. "He'll be so surprised!"

He would, indeed, Rissa thought. But much happier just to have the love of his sister once again. He had been pining for her, and if there was anything she could do to return the harmony that once existed between the two siblings, she was only too glad to help.

"How 'bout some cheesecake?" Frankie suggested.

"You're kidding, right?" Rissa puffed. They had been pounding the streets for almost three hours now, darting into and out of stores, and rushing from stall to stall at the open-air market that Evan had taken her to on her first day. Their arms were full of the spoils of their quest: fresh crabs, fruit and vegetables, cut flowers, preserves, and Evan's favorite olives. They toted shopping bags from some of the ritziest boutiques, holding a bottle of cologne that Rissa honestly did wish she'd be able to smell on Evan, as well as a set of hand-kerchiefs Frankie insisted he needed, and a new linen shirt that was, fortunately, nothing like the one she had chosen for Corbin. Rissa was all shopped out, and she told her so. "I don't think I could hold another package. My arms are falling off. Besides, what do we need cheesecake for? We've got profiteroles *and* Florentines. And a whole bunch of marzipan fruit. How much dessert do you think we can eat tonight? I don't want to waddle onto that plane at the end of the summer!"

Frankie laughed. "I don't mean to carry, I mean for now. Aren't you hungry?"

Come to think of it, shopping did whet the appetite. "Good idea," she enthused. "I wouldn't mind a nibble. And I wouldn't mind the chance to put these bags down for a few minutes, either. Where'd you have in mind?"

Frankie pointed across the way to the Café de la Colombe,

one of her favorite watering holes. "There." She headed in that direction without even waiting to see if Rissa would follow. "Come on!"

They found a seat outside on the *terrasse*, where they could enjoy the rest of the warm summer afternoon and watch people passing by. They piled their shopping onto two of the chairs and slumped gratefully into the other two. No sooner had Frankie sat down, though, did she pop up again like a Jack-in-the-box. "Oh…"

"What?"

"Nothing," Frankie answered cheerily. "Bathroom break, is all. I'll be right back."

"Now that you mention it, I could do with a pit-stop myself." She half rose, but Frankie waved at their shopping. "What? Leave all our parcels out here? What about all our stuff? No. You watch the parcels, and I'll be back in a sec. Then you can go. If the waiter comes while I'm gone, I'll have a mocha cheesecake and a hazelnut latte. Tell him heavy on the whipped cream, 'kay?"

"Okay." She watched as Frankie hurried into the café, and then closed her eyes, tilting her head backward and drinking in the sunshine. Things would be better soon; it looked as though the crisis between brother and sister was finally about to come to an end. Maybe once that tension died down, she and Evan could concentrate on the task of mending their own fences.

The smiling waiter came over, and waited patiently as Rissa made her order in her halting French. A full ten minutes had passed before he returned with Frankie's order, as well as her plain old black coffee and strawberry cheesecake, and there was still no sign of Frankie.

Rissa frowned, uneasy but not worried. Maybe there was a long line in the ladies' room. But the café wasn't even half full; it was still quite early, and even the after-work crowd wouldn't be out yet. Another five minutes passed, and then five more, and the fingers of dread began slowly to take hold of Rissa's heart. Maybe Frankie was sick in there. Maybe… something had happened.

She glanced at the parcels she had been admonished to watch over, and then glanced back at the entrance of the café. *Something's wrong. Something's definitely, definitely amiss.* Parcels be damned, she decided. She swept up only her purse, and hurried in through the main doorways and toward the bathrooms. There were only three stalls, and two were empty. "Frankie?" she called softly. There was movement behind the locked door, but no answer.

Discreetly, she tilted her head just low enough to catch a glimpse of the pair of feet under the doorway, but the beefy, gray-clad ankles were certainly not Frankie's. Rissa stood before the sinks, heart thumping, a cold mist of sweat breaking out all over her body. Frankie was not in the bathroom. She hadn't exited the café through the front doors, either, as Rissa had been facing them the whole time. There were only two explanations for this: either something awful had happened to the teenager, or Rissa had been had again. The more likely, and more palatable explanation was that Frankie had found a way to get past her, to pursue whatever adolescent agenda she had in mind. As worrisome as that was, it was preferable to the idea that something ugly had befallen her.

It was even more likely that the entire story about wanting to buy Evan presents and cook him a meal was simply a ruse to divert Rissa's attention long enough for Frankie to get away. And Rissa had fallen for it wholesale.

"You fool!" Rissa chastised herself aloud. "You stupid, trusting, gullible, addle-brained…." She passed her hand across her forehead and it came away damp. Her breathing was erratic, sharp and burning in her lungs. If Frankie had given her the slip—and she fervently hoped that was all it was—how had she done it?

The heavy-set, middle-aged woman in the bathroom flushed and exited the stall, nodding vaguely in Rissa's direction as she left. Rissa examined each stall in turn. The one formerly occupied by the woman had the only window in the room. Rissa wrenched it open to discover that it was covered by rusting but solid burglar-proofing. She hadn't left via the window.

Rissa dashed outside into the main café, eyes darting left and right, in the faint hope that Frankie had encountered someone she knew and had stopped by their table to chat, but there was no sign of her. Panicked now, she grabbed the arm of a passing waitress, and desperately tried in mangled French to describe Frankie and ask if she had seen her. The girl frowned in concentration, understanding what she was asking more through Rissa's pantomime and the English she eventually fell into. The young woman shook her head. "No, no, I have not see her."

"Is there anybody else I can ask?"

The girl looked at her curiously. "*Si vous voulez, Mademoiselle,* you ask everyone here." She balanced her tray and walked off.

Ask everyone in the room? She didn't think she had the courage or linguistic skills for that. She twisted, looking around again...and then she spotted her answer. There was a side door, almost hidden from view by ornate pillars and loops of strung garlic and dried peppers. From its position, and the chairs and tables pressed close to it, she surmised that it was not often in use. She crossed over to it. The table closest the small door was askew, as though someone had squeezed past it. She tried the handle. It was unlocked.

Rissa shoved the door open; it struggled on its hinges, unaccustomed to being used, but let her through. It opened onto a cobbled side alley that slanted up for several yards before angling sharply to the right. She rushed out and up along the path. She could smell the accumulated garbage from the café and other nearby restaurants, as well as the dank, moldy smell that alleys just seemed to have. The cobbles under her feet were rough from age and misuse. Buildings leaned in on her, going only a few levels up, but noise emanated from every one of them: women shouting, children laughing, radios blaring. As she rushed around the corner, she had to pull up sharply to avoid slamming into a wall that came out of nowhere. It was a dead end. The only way out of there was over the wall.

She turned back, dejected, but did not re-enter through the side door. Instead, she followed the narrow alley to its end in the other direction: it led right back to the huddled tables and chairs where she had been sitting. Could Frankie have managed to slip past her, behind her back, without being seen?

Rissa dropped into her chair and let her head fall into her hands. She'd messed up. She'd let down her guard, walked blithely into Frankie's trap, and now her charge was missing. But why had Frankie done it? Maybe she just needed be on her own for a while, or wanted to go to a party or head off to the beach. Maybe it was just a stunt to get back at Evan. She was sure that Frankie was too smart to truly endanger herself. But jump high or jump low, Rissa had been the responsible adult in the scenario, and she'd well and truly screwed things up.

Whatever would Evan say?

The prospect of his reaction was even more frightening than whatever high-jinks Frankie could take it in her mind to get up to. How would she break the news to him? Should she call him? It didn't feel like the kind of thing one should tell someone on the phone. Maybe she should take a taxi to his office.

Maybe she should just shoot herself now, and save him the trouble.

What should she do? It would be idiotic to stay in town and look for Frankie; she didn't know the place half as well as the girl did, and she didn't have a clue where she could possibly have headed. The more sensible option would be to go back to the house, and wait. With luck, Frankie would turn up in a couple of hours, after she was through perpetrating whatever mischief she had in mind, gleeful that her prank had worked. She'd have to tell Evan what had happened, of course, and then withstand the firestorm that would certainly follow, but after that, it would be over, and then all would be well again.

Her head hanging low, she stood and tried to gather up as many of the packages as she could. She would have to sacrifice some of them: there was no way that she could hold them all. She almost smiled at the sneaky strategy on Frankie's part, ensuring that she would be too bogged down by parcels to follow her.

As she turned toward the roadway in search of a taxi, a shout rang out behind her. She spun around hopefully, but it was only the waiter hurrying forward, a frown replacing the smile with which he had greeted her earlier. *"Mademoiselle, l'addition!"* He waved the check under her nose, and then pointed at the untouched desserts on the table. *"Il faut payer."* He rubbed his fingers together in the universal sign for paper money, just in case she had not understood his request.

Now her confusion had made her a thief. Apologizing profusely, and trying to balance her parcels while rummaging through her purse, she pulled out more than enough euros, and pressed them into his hand. He fished into the capacious pockets of his apron, fumbling for change, but she breathlessly told him to keep it, and hurried away to look for the taxi that would take her to the house. That took courage. Evan would not be happy.

A glimpse of his stunning blue car parked carelessly in the driveway as her taxi pulled up in front of the house dashed any hopes she might have had of a few moments alone in which to gather her thoughts before she called him. He was home several hours before he was due, and that alone filled her with dread.

The main doors were shut but not locked. Madame Soler did not come to greet her, and that was unusual. The taxi driver assisted her with her parcels as far as the hallway, but then, either reading her tension or spooked by the uncanny pall of silence upon the house, fled. She was to face the music alone.

"Evan?" she called timidly, but not as loud as she should have, if she were really expecting a reply. The main hall and sitting room were empty, as were the kitchen and dining area. In the family room…nothing. She persevered, heading further in toward the bedrooms, calling his name again. She noticed almost absently that she was still clutching the paper-wrapped cut flowers, and thought that she should put them down, but there was no vase nearby, and setting them down on the floor seemed like such an odd thing to do, so she kept her grip on them.

She passed her room and Frankie's not bothering to look there, but went straight to Evan's room and knocked. Receiving no reply, she opened the door and stuck her head in. It was neat, untouched, and empty. Maybe she should try around the back of the house? But intuition and logic made her check one last place, a room that she had only been to once: Evan's study.

The door was ajar, and Evan's voice could clearly be heard. She slid in as unobtrusively as she knew how. He was talking rapidly in Catalan into the phone, his back partially turned to her. Upon her entry, he turned to her, but did not acknowledge her presence in any way, unless she counted the cold, hard, fleeting look that slid across his features and then went away. She was forced to remain there, idiotically holding the flowers, feeling, like Alice in Wonderland, like she was shrinking slowly, getting smaller and smaller as his voice and presence filled the room.

When his conversation was over, he slammed the phone down with such violence that she jumped. The stems of the flowers crunched under her nervous fingers. He remained with his back to her for several moments, both hands clutching his desk to steady himself, and she heard him take a long, deep breath.

Oh, God, she groaned inside.

When he spun around there was a fire in him that she had never seen, even when he was pounding into Corbin. And in a tone of voice she had never heard, he bellowed, "Where the hell have you been?"

She was so afraid in the face of his ire that she was shaking. She wanted to cry. She wanted to run. She laid the poor, abused flowers down on his desk, buying herself a few seconds to screw up her courage, but even so, when she spoke she sounded like a lost little girl. "Evan…what happened?"

The question threw him. He gave her an incredulous stare. "That's what I want you to tell me. *What happened?*"

"Frankie and I, we went into town. It was her idea. She told me…she said…that she wanted to surprise you. To buy you presents to say she was sorry. So we went into town."

"And…?"

"And then…" Where could she start? What could she say? That she had allowed a seventeen-year-old to drag the wool down over her eyes and disappear into thin air? "Then…" In the face of his cold fury, her courage failed.

"Where…is…my…sister?" It was a lion's roar, and it all but shook the house.

Her battle against the threatening tears was hard-fought. There was no sense in stalling any longer. He obviously knew

that something was amiss. It seemed, too, that he knew more
than she did about the whole situation. She threw up her hands
helplessly and confessed. "I don't know." She repeated her
question, even though she knew the answer would be dreadful.
"What happened, Evan?"

In response, Evan whipped his cellular phone from its customary place on his belt and skated it forcefully across the
desk at her. She tried but failed to catch it, and it clattered to
the floor. With fumbling fingers she retrieved it. It was opened
to a short text message, silent black letters against a glowing
background of blue, but the words swam before her eyes. She
squinted at them, trying earnestly to decipher their meaning,
but gave up. Holding it out to him in her shaking hand, she
pleaded. "It's in French, Evan. Please...I can't...I don't know
what it says."

Instead of taking the phone back, he came slowly around
the desk to tower over her. Her pale, terrified face and wide
eyes did not serve to diminish his wrath one iota.

Hands on his hips, face close to hers, he told her in words
that fell like hammer blows. "What it says is that my sister
has been kidnapped."

Reluctant Partners: Fighting Your Way on Board When He Wants To Fly Solo

Rissa's rubbery legs took her to the couch, but no further. There was pounding, blinding pressure behind her eyes, and stark terror in her heart. As she sat, the nightmare, and all its implications, crowded in on her. Wrong again. She'd been presented with the possibilities that either Frankie had gone off on a lark, or that something had happened to her, and for her own peace of mind, she had chosen the less lethal option. She'd been wrong. And now it seemed that she was guilty of much more than simple negligence. If anything bad happened to the girl, how would she be able to live with herself?

Evan stood above her, his face a mask. "Tell me everything that happened today."

Her words spilled out with the relief that only confession brings. She explained to him how she and Frankie had been lounging at the pool when the girl had suddenly suggested that they go into town.

"You could at least have let me know where you were going," he interrupted.

"She wanted to surprise you. She said it was all for you. Besides, we've been into town several times before without having to inform you. How was I to know that this time was anything different?"

He nodded curtly. "Go on."

She described their route, from market to boutiques, told him about their purchases, and explained what had happened at the café.

"And you let her go?"

In spite of her guilt and trauma, Rissa began to get irritated. "She wanted to go to the *bathroom,* Evan. She's not a toddler. She can go to the bathroom on her own, can't she?"

"You women always go in pairs."

"We *don't* always go in pairs. And besides, we had all those parcels. Who was going to stay behind and watch over the parcels? She went to the bathroom, and I ordered for us. When she didn't come back, I got worried, and I went looking for her. She wasn't anywhere." Rissa put her hands up over her face to hide her shame. "And I'm sorry. I've done a lousy job watching her from the start. Every time I've had a chance to prove myself, I've failed. When I saw she was gone, I thought she'd just run off to have some fun on her own. I thought I'd just come back to the house, and then she'd be home in a couple of hours. I'm sorry, Evan, I had no idea… I never dreamed, I never imagined that anything this horrible could ever have happened."

The storm clouds that had been forming ever since those first, sinking moments of realization at the cafeteria finally broke, and tears spilled out between her fingers, hot and bitter. "I'm sorry," she said again. "Who took her, and what do they want?"

Evan stared at her incredulously, and then said, "Relax, Rissa."

Relax? Was he mad? She stared up at him with huge, confounded eyes. "What?"

He must have decided that looming above her was too intimidating, because he came to sit next to her, on the very couch on which they had lain wrapped in each other's arms not too long ago. She wondered if this change of position was preferable. Having to crane her neck backward to look at him was uncomfortable, but having him sit next to her, in the mood he was in, was downright unnerving.

When he spoke again, his voice was slightly less aggressive, perhaps as a concession to her tears. "Nobody's snatched my sister, Rissa."

He was making no sense. Her mouth hung open, but her bemused questions could not leave her lips.

He explained. "That message was not written by a native French speaker. It has an error in it that a careless person, someone who never bothered to work on their grammar, would make. The kind of error my sister would make, if she was in a hurry. And the figure it asks for, fifty thousand euros, is laughable, as far as ransoms go. At current exchange rates, the euro is just higher than the American dollar. Who asks for a fifty thousand dollar ransom? Especially if you consider that a true professional, a genuine kidnapper, would have taken the time to find out the state of my finances, and if he had, he would have asked for ten or twenty times that. Fifty thousand euros is the kind of money a teenager would think is a lot."

Rissa was still baffled, still staring up at Evan's face through watery eyes. "I don't understand."

His anger waned just enough for him to explain, "Rissa, my sister has staged this whole thing. The whole setup, from the trip into town to the disappearance in the bathroom, smacks of just the stunt she would pull. My guess is she's still very mad at me, and that this is payback. It's also a sort of declaration of independence for her, her way of telling me that she's a grown-up and that she can handle herself. There's enough money on that credit card of hers, and in her savings account, to keep her comfortable in a little hotel somewhere for several weeks. And if I pay the so-called ransom, better yet. She'll be able to upgrade her hotel and shop her heart out. It's the perfect plan."

It took a long time to process this information; it was all just too uncanny to be true. But at least, if Evan was right, and this was all just an elaborate charade, she was back to Option One, that Frankie had simply run away. So much better than that second, awful option! This in no way reduced her unwitting complicity, however. "And I fell for it," she muttered regretfully.

"I told you before, my sister is slippery," he responded dryly.

"I'm sorry," she said once more.

He dismissed her apology. "Being sorry doesn't help. What I need to do is find her, and find her fast. Because there's another element in this scenario that you obviously haven't thought of yet, and that's the element that worries me most."

She tried to guess what he meant, but her confused brain would let nothing through its tangle of questions. "What element?"

He pursed his lips, and the single word he spat out was tainted with distaste. "Corbin."

Understanding was quick in coming. "She's gone to look for him?"

"Either that, or they're in this together." He made a face. "I wouldn't put it past him."

"Why would he—"

"For the same reasons Frankie would—revenge, and to prove a point. He knows that just having her gone would send me half out of my mind with worry, but the idea of being with her again, and knowing that I know exactly what he's doing, is just too tempting to resist. He knows that just thinking of her with him, allowing him to do whatever he wants to her, is killing me."

Now that much of his anger was deflected away from her, she wondered if she had the courage to touch him, just to offer comfort. She didn't. "What do we do now?"

"What *I* need to do is track her down," he responded, explicitly excluding her.

"How?"

"I'm working on that. A good place to start is electronically."

She gestured toward the cellular phone that sat between them on the couch. "The message?"

He shook his head. "That message was web-based. It could have come from anywhere, any phone, computer, or cyber café in town. It could have come from Timbuktu, for all we know."

"What, then?"

"Hack Frankie's computer, and her cell phone, and see what information I can glean from that."

"You can do that?"

He gave her a self-deprecating half-smile. "That's not one of my strengths. I have someone working on that for me. Valentin, my IT man, is in Frankie's room, working his way through her hard disk, trying to break into her chat logs, and see if he can find anything I can work with."

Rissa started, looking around as though she expected the man to appear in the doorway right before her. "Now?"

"Now."

"Hacking. Is that…you know…."

"Legal? Probably not. But given the situation, I think it's justified. And considering the fact that I paid for the computer, the phone, and the airtime, I think I would at least have some rights."

"You probably do," she agreed.

"I've also put the word out for information on his boat. I've got friends in the boating business up and down the coast, from Spain to Syria, and a good deal of Northern Africa as well. If he goes international, he'll have to get clearance from his port of departure, and I'll know about it. If he stays in France, he'll have to berth somewhere, and the harbormaster will let me know. What I've found out so far is that since he left Perpignan a week ago, he's been moored at Collioure. That's a tiny village just a few miles south-west of us."

"So, he's nearby."

"Nearby, and, unfortunately, very much part of the equation." Evan got up. "While I'm waiting on Valentin to come back with his report, I have some calls to make."

She knew she had been dismissed, but she wasn't letting him do that, not this time. "What can I do?"

"Nothing." He headed for the phone, but stopped when he saw the flowers. He picked them up and turned them over, examining them curiously.

"We got those for you," she told him, feeling foolish. "They're a little battered, but…."

He sniffed them experimentally, and then held them in both hands as though cradling a baby, and gave her a strange look. "Thank you."

She wondered whether he was pleased. "There's more. A shirt, and some cologne, and—"

"As soon as we get my sister back, I promise I'll be happy to see them," he told her carefully. "Could you put these in some water?"

She did as he asked, and returned hastily to his study, where she hovered until he pointed at the couch with the pen in his hand. She sat down, feeling foolish as the minutes went by and he went from phone call to phone call with very little further acknowledgment of her presence. Almost an hour later there was a knock on the door, and a bright-eyed young Frenchman entered with a sheaf of papers in his hand. She assumed that this was Valentin. The young man bowed briefly in her direction before hurrying over to Evan's desk, whereupon he spread the papers out before him. The two were engaged in earnest discussion of their contents while Rissa watched, alternately fretting and fuming at his deliberate exclusion of her.

After a while Evan stood, and the two men shook hands. When he deigned to address her again, he said, "I'll just see Valentin to the door. I'll be back in a minute."

While alone she toyed with the idea of sneaking a peek at the documents, but in the unpredictable mood that Evan was in, she knew that was far from wise. She should be grateful he hadn't sent her packing for her failure.

When Evan came back, he surprised her by saying, "Come, look at these."

She joined him at the desk. He laid the papers out before her, pointing from one to the other in turn as he explained their contents, even though they were almost entirely in English. "I had Valentin search for everything between Frankie and Corbin, every chat, every e-mail, every text message, and then had him pick out key words, including any mention of you, me, money, boats, etc. This is what we've come up with."

Rissa crooked her head to one side to examine the printouts, at once embarrassed to be eavesdropping on a private conversation, but at the same time anxious for any clues that might lead them to Frankie. Much of the conversation took the form of Frankie's stream-of-consciousness babble, a mixture of flirtation, passionate declarations of endless love, bitter denouncement of Evan's restrictions, and a vow to be with Corbin, whatever it took.

And, slowly, the plan unfolded. Between the two conspirators, they hatched out a plot for Frankie's escape. The ransom was Frankie's idea; it was, just as Evan had suspected, just extra spending money to sweeten the pot. Her means of escape, and the plan to dupe Rissa into being an unknowing accomplice, was also Frankie's idea. Rissa cringed as she read Frankie's gleeful assessment: "Rissa'll fall for anything. She's a total sucker."

At that, she sat back, shame burning, feeling betrayed and foolish. She'd loved that young girl dearly; still did. And Frankie had used her.

"Doesn't mean she doesn't love you," Evan comforted. "Doesn't mean she doesn't love me. It's just that they're a little selfish and insensitive at that age. Don't take it personally."

Don't take it personally? She'd been fool enough to give her heart over to both Maynards, and neither one placed much value on her love, or returned it. She couldn't respond.

"The important thing is, now we know where they're headed." Evan tapped one of the papers, his finger pointing out their destination. "Barcelona."

She tried not to let her heartache get in the way of the importance of the task ahead. She tried to concentrate on Frankie's safety, rather than on her betrayal. "Barcelona's a big city, from what I hear."

"It is. But he's mentioned that his family owns property there, although he hasn't said exactly where. I know that Corbin's mother is from Barcelona, and I know her maiden name because Corbin carries it. Sáenz. He'll most likely head there by boat, because according to my information, his car is in long-term parking. I just need to track him down."

"By boat?"

"No, that makes no sense. He's already got a head start, and I have no idea which marina he's heading to. My car will give me more flexibility. I'll be able to get to the marinas there and ask questions, and I'll also be able to find his family home, once I get the address. If worse come to worst, I just have to wait until I get another text about a drop-off point for the ransom, and that will help pin them down. I'm leaving for Barcelona tonight."

Rissa had had enough of his persistent, deliberate exclusion. "You keep saying 'I.' Why?"

He gave her a direct stare. "What would you like me to say?"

"How about 'we'? I'm in this, too, you know. Frankie is my friend, and I care about her. And part of this is my fault. If you're going to Barcelona, I'm coming, too."

"I'm going alone," he stated firmly. "You'll just slow me down."

She couldn't believe she was hearing this. It was time to stand up for herself. "I've had enough of this, Evan! I won't let you treat me this way. I've stood in your office like a whipped dog, saying over and over again how sorry I am. I made a mistake, and I regret it. I made a mistake and I failed in my mission, and in acknowledgment of that, I remove myself from your employ. I no longer work for you. But that doesn't mean I have no more interest in your sister. She's in way over her head, and as a woman, as her friend, I'm going to do whatever it takes to help her. And I'm not taking no for an answer. If you're going to Barcelona, I'm going, too. If you're going to the gates of *hell*, I'm going, if that's what it takes to get her back. Understand?" By the time her speech was over, she was right up under him, her finger pointed at his face, even her hair bristling with anger. When he didn't answer, she repeated, *"Understand?"*

He gave her a shocked half-smile, as though he'd kicked a sleeping Pekinese and it had rounded on him like a pit bull. *"Whither thou goest, I will go,* huh?" he quoted.

"Something like that."

She waited for him to refuse her again, daring him to, but was almost surprised when he said, "I'm leaving in two hours. Pack yourself a bag with enough clothes for three days or so. And I suggest you get something to eat. It's going to be a long night."

Faint Heart Never Won: When To Stay Put, and When To Go For It

Rissa felt better after a shower and a meal, but only slightly. She packed hastily and lightly, not knowing where she would be spending the night or just how tough the next few days were going to be, and wore a simple polo shirt and the most comfortable pair of jeans she owned. She was ready and waiting when Evan called.

He took her bag wordlessly, and threw it into the car trunk along with his. Sensing that their departure was imminent, the dogs clamored for attention, bumping into their legs and brushing against their hands. He patted them absently. "I sent Madame Soler home early, but I've called her and asked her to pass by every day and take care of the boys. With luck, we won't be long."

Rissa was still uncomfortable with the idea of being with him in such close confines, especially since she was unable to read his mood. He was no longer snarling at her, but he had made it quite plain that he had no desire for her company on this trip, and that he would have preferred to be alone. So she made a big deal of the dogs, hugging them close to her and kissing them on their noses before releasing them and entering the stifling cocoon of the car, where she would be obliged to sit just inches from him for heaven knew how long.

He turned his head slightly as he started the engine. "You sure you want to do this?" he asked. "There's no telling how this is going to end."

"You sure *you* want to do this?" she retorted.

"I don't have a choice."

"Likewise." She deliberately stared out the window, ending the issue there and then.

He didn't push it further, but concentrated on getting their journey under way. The winding coastal road was intriguing enough to hold her attention, veering from lush greenery to arid, almost desert-like conditions, to craggy rock faces with stalwart, spiky succulents clinging to them. The onset of evening bathed the countryside in a mellow glow, and she would almost have enjoyed the trip, had the circumstances—and perhaps the company—been different. She was almost disappointed when he turned off the scenic route and joined the gray, ugly highway.

He knew what she was thinking. "Coastal road is much prettier, I know, but time is of the essence."

She couldn't argue with that. "How long, you think?"

"Five hours, maybe, if I don't get stopped for speeding."

"You planning on speeding?"

"Yes."

True to his word, he put the sleek blue animal through its paces, driving with confidence and efficiency, yet not recklessly enough for Rissa to sense herself in danger. As darkness fell, he put the top down, most likely as a treat for her, and slid a CD into the powerful, sensitive player. The night air filled with bluesy, smoky soul music.

She raised her brows. "Hmm. American music. What a surprise!"

He gave her a genuine smile. "The Sardana isn't the only music in town, you know."

"I know it. I just wasn't sure you did."

"Don't worry. As deeply entrenched as I've become in the wonderful culture of this place, I haven't forgotten who I am. I still read the American papers, watch the American news, and listen to good old soul. I haven't completely sold out."

"Glad to hear that." What she was glad to hear, actually, was the level of normalcy in his voice. She didn't think she could have borne spending several hours in his company with him still furious with her.

She was almost surprised when the French-Spanish border appeared in the distance; he really had eaten up the miles. Late evening traffic was minimal, and border-crossing formalities were dispensed with with characteristic European efficiency. Once on the other side, he commented, "Good thing you got your passport replaced, or I'd have had to stow you away in the trunk."

"He made a joke!" she marveled aloud. "He actually kidded with me."

For the first time in days, Evan touched her. It was just a light, reassuring pat on the knee, but it meant the world to her. "I know I can be a real bastard when I'm angry," he told her, "but the good news is that it doesn't last long. I blow off steam, and then it's over, okay?"

"Okay," she said simply, but she could barely suppress her glee. Maybe things were returning to normal between them. Maybe she would soon be able to breathe easy in his presence once more.

"And for what it's worth," he added, "I'm glad you're here, helping me get through this."

She concentrated on the passing scenery to divert herself from the need to answer, but that statement alone was enough to buoy her through the rest of the trip. Eventually, she nodded off, not even aware of Evan putting the top back up again as the night grew cooler. She awoke briefly for a rest stop at a highway travelers' station, and then the next time she opened her eyes, they were surrounded by bright lights and towering buildings. Barcelona.

"You should have woken me up!" she grumbled. "I wanted to see the city from the start!"

"It's much better in the daylight," he comforted. "And I figured, the more rest you get now, the better. Like I said, we have no way of knowing what's ahead of us."

She craned her neck anyway, taking in the breathtaking juxtaposition of centuries-old buildings such as churches, theaters and museums, with modern, shiny glass structures. He pointed out a few things to her as they passed them, explaining, "The general layout of the city center is very unusual. If you notice, the corners of all the city blocks don't come together at a ninety-degree angle, as they do in most American cities. They're cut off in such a way that each city block is not a square, but an octagon of sorts. It was designed to capture and channel the wind, to keep the city as cool as possible during the summer months, when it can get pretty hot."

"I've never seen that before," she marveled.

"Quite ingenious. It does exactly what it was intended to do—cool the city, create a sense of space, and minimize the sensation of overcrowding, even at rush hour."

Rissa sniffed the air, and there was a hint of salt in it. "I smell the sea."

"The port is nearby, almost within walking distance. The

bay is magnificent. You'll see more of it in the daytime, when we start looking for Corbin's boat."

"We're not going now?"

"No. There's not much left of the night. It's better that we get some sleep, and start off fresh in the morning. I don't expect it to be easy."

The car turned onto a new roadway, and again, she was entranced. They were moving alongside a broad promenade, lit with glowing orange lights, and even at this late hour, it was thronging with people. Some people strolled while others hurried. Couples walked side by side, clasping each other's hands. Youngsters sat on the curb or on benches, smoking, drinking from dark bottles, necking in shadows. Street performers mimed, juggled, blew fire, or went through a variety of bizarre acts as passers-by threw coins. At regular intervals, small kiosks sold newspapers and books, flowers, and, bizarrely, animals such as birds and hamsters.

"Las Ramblas," Evan explained. "Literally, 'The Promenade.' It's the heart and pulse of Barcelona. Almost everything that happens, happens here. The city has gone to great lengths to make sure that it's always a pleasant place to be, and they place heavy restrictions on what can be sold here. It's mainly confined to food items, such as light cafeteria meals, corn nuts and *churros,* reading material, including spurious magazines…"

Rissa laughed.

"You can buy flowers, you can buy a hamster. If you're in the market for a pet tarantula or a baby scorpion, this is pretty much the best place to find one."

"I'll remember that," she said seriously.

"And if you're lonely, and in need of company in the short term, it's a sure bet here, too."

"And you know this…how?" she asked archly.

"So I'm told."

"So you're told."

He took his teasing gracefully, and continued his spiel. "Barcelona has been a trading port since the early Roman times, so it's always filled to the brim with tourists. It's one of the liveliest cities in Europe. As a matter of fact—" he glanced at his watch "—much of the night life doesn't begin until one or two in the morning. See how busy it is?"

"It would be nice…" she began wistfully, and then stopped.

He reached out and stroked her hair gently. "It's a pity that we're here on such unpleasant business. I'd have loved to have taken you around. I love this city. There's art and history on every corner. Some of the most famous artists of modern times have lived here—Dali, Miró, Gaudi, and Picasso—and they've left their fingerprint everywhere. They've left their souls here, like a breath on the wind. There are museums here where you can spend an entire day, and still feel that you want more. There are sculptures, parks, and cathedrals that will leave you trembling. Maybe, when this is over, we can come back again…." He left the rest hanging.

They turned just off the Ramblas, and the architecture changed once again. It became dark and brooding, with craggy façades and heavy iron porches. Hideous gargoyles glared down at them from almost every building. It was like something out of Bram Stoker. "This is the *Barri Gotic,* the Gothic quarter." He pulled into a parking garage before informing her, "This is where we'll be staying."

"Here?" she asked doubtfully as he withdrew their bags from the trunk, locked the car and pocketed his parking stub.

"It takes some getting used to, but it's not really all that scary." They emerged from the garage onto the street. "Don't be intimidated by the gargoyles. They're very important to the Catalans. Their ugly faces are designed to scare away the devil and his minions, so the fiercer the gargoyle, the more protected you are."

"I should feel real safe, then."

He smiled reassuringly. They arrived at a huge, rusting portico, and Rissa could see between the iron bars that there was a tall, narrow building set back from the roadway. Vines crawled over every surface of it, to such an extent that she could not even guess at its original color.

"My favorite *pension*. I'm in Barcelona on business once a month or so, and I always prefer to stay here, where it's cozy and friendly, rather than in a big, impersonal hotel. You'll like it, I promise you." He rang the bell, and after some time an old man, his buckled spine bent almost double, emerged from the door, crossed the courtyard, and opened the tall gates. He looked a hundred years old: he had no hair to speak of, and his liver-spotted skin was a tough mass of deep grooves, but his eyes were a bright, perceptive blue. He offered his trembling hand to Evan. "Señor Maynard," he said in greeting.

Evan grasped his hand warmly, and murmured what Rissa assumed to be apologies for rousing him so late. "I rang in advance," he explained to her. "They normally don't admit guests at this hour, but since I'm a regular...."

"They made an exception just for you." This was a man who always got exactly what he wanted, she noted.

"Yes," he replied without a trace of irony.

They followed the old man into the building. She was immediately struck by the homey, welcoming smell of the place, a mixture of brass, polished wood, and something she was sure was cinnamon. The walls were covered with fading Romanesque friezes, and even indoors, ivy poked out from any crack and crevice that it could find. She had the sensation of being jerked backward in time to some indefinable period.

She expected to be led to the registration desk in the foyer,

but instead they were taken directly up several flights of stairs.
"As it's so late, we'll handle the registration in the morning.
I'm sure that Señor Palazon would prefer to return to his
bed." In support of Evan's declaration, the old man pressed
two jingling bunches of keys into Evan's hand, nodded politely in Rissa's direction, and disappeared more quickly than
Rissa would have imagined him to be capable of.

That left them alone. Evan sorted through the keys in his
palm, checked the doors before them, and then unlocked one
for her. He preceded her, clicked on the light, and placed her
bag on the floor near the entrance. The room was, like the
ground floor, a quaint mixture of decors, with modern amenities mixing with a mish-mash of throw rugs, ornaments and
furniture. They faced each other, a little awkward, unsure of
what to say. He was standing quite close, and his physical
presence was overwhelming.

"I hope you'll be comfortable," he said formally. "Try not
to worry too much. Things will work out."

"They have to," she promised herself fervently.

"They will," he asserted. "Goodnight."

"Goodnight."

He didn't move. He seemed to be debating...or waiting.
"If you need anything," he said softly, "I'm right next door."

She watched him mutely as he gently closed the door behind him.

She busied herself by unpacking the T-shirt she intended
to sleep in and placing it over the back of a chair. It was the
same big, white shirt he had brought her on her first night in
Perpignan, when she had had barely a stitch to wear. He'd
insisted she keep it, and she hadn't minded one bit. Even
washed, it smelled faintly of him, and she wore it almost like
a talisman.

She stripped the bed of its heavy, old-fashioned quilt,

threw back the topsheets, and then began to undress. What a long, hard day! Nothing had gone right; it was one of those days when you regretted even getting out of bed. She slipped the shirt over her head, adjusted the level of her air-conditioner, patted her pillows, and lay back, trying to force her body to relax and welcome sleep. She tossed about, unable to find a comfortable position, but persevered. Sleep would come, eventually. It was purely a case of mind over matter.

But her body wasn't minding. It was far too aware of Evan's presence just beyond the wall. She tried listening out for him, but the old, solid walls were thick. Was he asleep yet? Or was he as wide awake as she? *If you need anything, I'm right next door.* What the heck was that supposed to mean? Was it an invitation, or was he simply being polite? What did he mean by "anything"? Was his offer restricted to an extra tube of toothpaste, or a magazine? Because what she needed, what she desperately wanted, was him.

She got out of bed and stood barefoot on the wooden floor, thinking hard. What to do? She did have the option of going over there, but what if she woke him up? What if she went over there, and all she received was a puzzled stare? Was she quick enough at thinking on her feet to come up with some silly, innocuous excuse to cover up her embarrassment?

Should she, or shouldn't she?

Her love for this man provided an answer. Literature throughout the ages was rife with stories of lovers who proved their courage by crossing oceans, fighting wars, or slaying dragons, just to be near to the object of their desire. All she had to do was step outside and rap softly on his door. With luck—and she laughed at this faint hope—he'd be too deeply asleep to hear her, and she could scoot back to her own sanctuary with her pride intact. The worst that could happen would be that he would be awake, her mission would fail, and she would slink back to her room with egg on her face.

It was better than dragons.

She left her room silently, not even bothering with a dressing gown or bedroom slippers, as the chances of encountering someone else in the hallway at this hour were close to nil. At his door, she inhaled courage through her nostrils, and tapped lightly with just one finger.

The voice inside made her jump. "It's open."

Open? In a strange place, at this hour of the morning? What did that mean? She checked it, and sure enough, it was. Inside, Evan was seated in a huge armchair, his laptop open on his knees. He was wearing only his shorts. He looked up at her and gave her the warmest smile she had received from him in aeons. "I was hoping you'd come. I left it open for you."

That told her all she needed to know. Her nervousness left her like a bothersome ghost returning to its haunt. "You should have been more explicit in your invitation."

"I was afraid you'd turn me down, or worse, slap me."

She crossed over to him quickly. "Coward."

"Guilty." He shut down the computer and set it aside, holding out his arms.

She clambered onto his lap. "What were you doing?"

"Just running a few searches. Telephone directories and the like. Nothing of value, really, just something to keep my mind off…you."

He was so solid under her. He felt so good. She murmured his name as she bent to kiss him. It was a yearning, searching, hungry kiss. They touched each other, hands remembering and rediscovering. "It feels like such a long time," she said into his ear.

"Too long. Touch me."

"I am."

"No, here." He guided her hand to where he wanted it, and then groaned, pulling at her T-shirt. "God, take this thing off. Hurry up and get naked."

"I will if you will," she countered.

They wriggled out of what clothing they were wearing, and he pulled her back onto his lap, where their kiss resumed, deeper and more demanding than before. But the time they had spent apart made her eager for more.

"This is a very big armchair," she observed. "Big enough for both of us."

"And it reclines."

"Show me."

He did.

He reached down between her legs to stroke her, make her ready, but she was way ahead of him. This was not a trip she planned to spend smelling the roses. She wanted all of him—right now. "No delays," she instructed.

"I concur," he managed to say.

She hoped he had come prepared.

He had.

Rissa frowned up at Christopher Columbus. From high atop his pedestal, Christopher Columbus scowled back down at her. She and Evan had spent an hour at Port Vell, asking questions about Corbin's boat, but none of his contacts had seen it, or had any record or knowledge of it's having moored there or planning to do so.

Their disappointment did little to reduce their appreciation of the sheer beauty of the port and its surroundings. Everything around her clamored to be seen, from the bustling ferries and cable cars, to the Aquarium that tried to lure visitors inside with promises of performing orcas, to the Moll D'España, to the old official buildings strung with the same bright red-and-yellow Catalan flags and banners that had festooned the buildings of Perpignan. The spirit of the Catalunya really did span the frontier between both countries.

Evan followed the direction of her gaze. "They're a fiercely independent people, the Catalans. Call a native of Barcelona a Spaniard, and you stand a fairly good chance of getting a punch in the face."

"Think they'll ever become an independent nation?"

"Not likely, considering the state of European politics, and the difficulties involved in seceding from not one but two separate countries, I can't see it ever happening. I'm afraid that they're condemned to live in a state of occupation, a bit like the Basques."

"Pity," she murmured.

"They're coping. As long as you always remember who you are, that's all that matters, right?" He looked down at her and smiled the kind of smile a man gave to a woman when he was completely satiated after spending the night indulging in her. How they had managed to rouse themselves that morning was anyone's guess. He took her hand, engulfed it in his, and squeezed it gently, not needing to say anything.

Rissa basked in his glow. She allowed herself to be led to the car, and to be courteously seated, sighing with contentment. The summer day was brilliant, the azure sky almost cloudless, and the glittering sea was like spangles on a prom dress. Music seemed to come from everywhere, and the walkways were thick with tourists and holiday-makers eagerly seeking out the sunshine. The air smelled of sea-salt, Spanish wine, and suntan oil. And her body…it tingled all over, having been smoothed in his hands like a carefully polished stone. What a perfect, perfect day. Had it not been for the urgency of their mission, she would have been convinced she had died and gone to heaven.

"Where to, now?"

"There are several other marinas nearby. We just have to go through the process of elimination. All it takes is patience."

Patience paid off. At their third stop, they hit paydirt. Waiting outside the harbormaster's office, Rissa knew instantly from the determined look on Evan's face as he exited that he had found the right place. But yet she asked, "They're here, aren't they?"

Instead of answering, Evan took her elbow. His frown was scary enough to prompt her silence. He was walking so fast that she had to trot to keep up. In his hand he held a small yellow sticky note, which, she assumed, held the number or co-ordinates of Corbin's berth, but he didn't consult it. She was quite sure that it was burned into his mind. The marina was fairly small, which was probably one of the reasons that Corbin had chosen it, but even so it took a while to cross it, and Rissa wondered if it would not have been better to drive over. But she guessed it was a good thing that Evan was blowing off steam by walking. Hopefully the few moments of exercise would pre-empt another whaling when Evan got his hands on Corbin, but she wasn't banking on it.

He strode up one pier, with Rissa panting at his heels, and stopped suddenly in front of a gleaming white boat. It was a good deal smaller than the *Sardana,* Evan's boat, but certainly more ostentatious. Brass clashed with chrome, and even from where they stood, the red upholstery shrieked for attention. She didn't know much about boats, but off the bat she could see why Evan's and Corbin's business philosophies would clash.

"Come on." Evan prepared to board, without so much as calling out first.

Rissa hesitated. "Shouldn't you…"

"I've got no time for pleasantries," he answered shortly.

"You can come aboard, or you can wait there." The satisfied lover who had so recently been holding her hand was gone now, replaced by an irate big brother. He didn't even take the time to see which option she would choose, but instead hopped aboard as easily as if he owned the vessel. Rissa scurried behind him, climbing up gingerly, her strict upbringing causing guilt at their trespassing to burn small cigarette holes in her conscience. She reasoned that if it was necessary to get Frankie back, well, so be it.

Once on board, Evan shouted loudly, first Frankie's name, and then Corbin's. The only response was the creaking of boards as the boat lifted on a swell. He ducked into the cabin, and this time, she didn't follow. He emerged a few moments later, holding a small object in one hand, which he held out to her. It was Frankie's MP3 player.

"At least I've confirmed that she's with him," he told her. He didn't sound too pleased with the fact. "There's nothing here, though—no clothes. I assume she didn't have much with her when she left, so I hardly expected to find any of her luggage, but there's very little belonging to him. No bags, no clothes, no shaving implements or toiletries."

"What does that mean?"

"It means they've left the boat and gone on land. And it probably means they won't be back for a while."

Her spirits sank into her feet. "So, what—?"

He brushed past her and began to descend. "We look again. The marine search has now become a land search, unless he's moved from one boat to another, which I doubt. He doesn't have the resources."

She was puffing as she followed him back in the direction they had come from. "Land search? How do you undertake…?"

"We start by finding his family property. I already anticipated that, and searched through the phone directories last night. Zip. The next step is government departments, try to find homes that are likely to be his or his family's. Even if we do succeed, they may not have gone home. Barcelona is one of the most popular tourist destinations in Southern Europe— there are a thousand hotels and *pensions* here. They could have gone to ground in any one of them. Phoning every one would take days, assuming they've registered under their own names. But I'm counting on what I know of the man. Rather than spend his own money on a hotel, he's more likely to stash her away at his family home until such time as I pay this so-called ransom. That would give them enough money to strike out and have fun."

She'd forgotten about the ransom demand for fifty thousand euros. "You're thinking of paying?"

"No, but as far as they're concerned, I still think it's genuine. They have no way of knowing that I've figured out that they're in this together, and that the whole thing is a sham. The message I got yesterday said I was to wait on further instructions to deliver the money. I've already texted back to the account it came from, saying I'm willing to play ball. Hopefully that will smoke them out."

She didn't share his conviction that any of this would work. "Why don't we just go to the police?"

He stopped dead and spun around. "And tell them what? That two lovers have run away to be together? That my sister has a boyfriend I don't like?"

"She's still under the age of—"

"The age of consent in Spain is thirteen."

"Oh, my..." She put her hand over her mouth, barely able to believe it.

He nodded sourly, and unlocked the car with a click, still remembering to hold the door open for her, even in his distracted state. "So, we do this on our own. We go back into town and start searching public records for a property we only have his word exists—even though we can't be sure whose name it's under."

"That's next to impossible."

"Better than waiting around sitting on our thumbs." He started his car so violently that gears grated as they peeled off. Rissa held Frankie's player in her lap, turning it over and over, asking it questions that it could not answer, and hoped against hope that things would work out okay, even in the face of her ever-rising doubt.

For the next four or five hours, Rissa sat by helplessly as Evan pored over electronic and paper records that she couldn't understand because they were in Spanish and Catalan. They moved from government offices to post offices to libraries, where Evan grilled clerical workers and pounded on his laptop. At the end of his quest he had in his hand a daunting list of addresses, some spaced as far as twenty miles apart. Rissa eyed it and groaned inwardly, but Evan seemed re-energized by his achievement.

"Now, we hit the road," he told her. "See how many of these we can visit before sundown." He must have seen her blanch, because he paused and looked concerned. "Are you tired?"

"Hungry, too," she said wistfully. "Breakfast was a long, long time ago."

He was all apologies. "Oh, angel, forgive me. I got so carried away that I let you sit there and starve. I feel so selfish. Come, let's find somewhere nice where you can get some rest and we can refuel. Okay?"

She couldn't have been happier to comply. To her delight, he took her to a small bodega in a courtyard within sight of Las Ramblas, where she could indulge herself in the strange and entrancing parade that passed by, while she allowed him to select a spicy Catalan meal smothered with peppers and mushrooms, with a huge bowl of rosemary olives on the side, and washed down with the house wine served in a red clay carafe. Dessert was a sticky concoction of honey and cream, and although he declined to order anything himself, he didn't refuse her when she spooned some into his mouth.

Just being with him, sharing a ridiculously small wooden table in a courtyard cooled by chipped fountains and hanging ferns, her feet out of their slippers and pressed against the smooth stone tiles, she was overcome by love and contentment. But there was pain there, too. He was so beautiful, and, even with all his flaws, such a wonderful, caring person, that she ached with longing to be with him. Why was it that the last thing that passed through her mind when she went to sleep, and the first thing on it when she woke, was him? Loving Evan was like stumbling into the La Brea tar pits; with every effort to struggle free, she only became more deeply mired.

Where would it end? Summer didn't last forever. With all her insistence that she could handle herself, and that she was mature enough to be in a relationship where one party loved and the other did not, what shape would she be in when the leaves began to fall from the trees, and Frankie—assuming that she returned to them—had to go back to school? Evan would fulfill his promise, and supply her with a one-way ticket back to Philadelphia, whereupon she would find herself home with a gaping hole in her chest, and her heart would remain in Perpignan. Could she stand the pain?

He leaned forward, not sure whether to smile or frown. "I wish I had a movie camera."

"Why?"

"Then I could have filmed that sequence of expressions that just worked their way across your face, and maybe sit down in a quiet place and try to figure out what they all meant." He touched her lips with one finger. She managed to restrain herself from drawing it into her mouth and sucking longingly on the tip of it.

Or you could just ask me, she wanted to say. Instead she was dismissive. "It's nothing. You wouldn't be very interested."

"That's where you're wrong. I'm interested in everything that goes on with you. You'll never know, Rissa, what this past week has been like for me, and I'm not talking about all that drama with Corbin and what's been going on with Frankie and me. You've been on my mind so much that I can barely get through my work day. And even when I'm in bed I can't sleep, because my brain keeps churning, going over and over things that have happened in the past, things I've done, decisions I've made. It's like I'm working my way through this huge storehouse of junk and I need to examine every piece before I decide whether to throw it out, pack it in a box, or keep it to use again."

She listened carefully, trying to understand what he meant by all that. What was he saying?

"It's frustrating. It's futile. Every time I clear away some boxes, I find more boxes. And I keep asking myself if there's a way to either shove enough of them aside to clear a path for you to come in, or throw enough away to find you a comfortable space. You understand what I'm saying?"

She understood perfectly. He was trying to tell her that there was no way that he could love her, because his mental junk just kept getting in the way. She knew without having to ask that many, if not most, of the items that cluttered his storehouse belonged to Jeanine. Why did this woman bedevil him so?

Not that it mattered. All she needed to know was that he was trying, as delicately as possible, to tell her to give it up. Stop hoping. He'd said it before, but she, like a fool, had let Barcelona go to her head and make her giddy enough to allow this love she had for him to pour from her eyes, and it was making him uncomfortable. Maybe if she had a better poker face, she could go on playing this game according to the rules they had agreed upon, but that wasn't working out. She was a lousy poker player. And a poker player who knew she was lousy had only one option: fold.

But he was speaking again. "What I'm trying to ask you... what I want..." A sharp buzzing filled her ears, and she was convinced for a second that her distress had become translated into sound. But Evan had heard it, too, and frowned, unclipping his phone from his belt and peering down at it.

His face turned to stone. He stared at the small blue screen for a long time, reading and re-reading the message, and then abruptly stood up, summoning the waiter and pressing a handful of bills into his hand without even glancing at the check. Rissa got up so fast she knocked over her wine. The deep stain spread across the red-and-white checkered tablecloth like heart's blood.

"What?" she asked anxiously. "What, Evan? Is it from them? What does it say?"

He put his hand at the small of her back, urging her back in the direction of the car as if he was afraid that she would lag behind if he did not help her.

"This one's from Corbin, no doubt. It's in Catalan."

"And...?"

"And the demand has changed. He wants half a million euros for Frankie."

Rissa choked.

"This time, he's serious."

How To Stand Upright When Everything Around You Is Falling Down

Evan felt that if he got any tenser a spring would pop inside him. He knew that Rissa was brimming with questions, but he wasn't in the mood to say anything right now. He needed to focus all of his mental energy on a single goal: getting his sister back. She probably sensed this, because she sat beside him and did not make a peep.

They'd been sitting in the Parc Güell for more than two hours, waiting for Corbin to contact them. He had not identified himself in the brusque communiqué, but both men knew exactly where the other was coming from. It was also interesting that Corbin knew that Evan would already be in Spain—the evidence being his choice of location for their meeting. At least that told him that they were playing on the same field, and there would be no need for either one to bring the other up to speed.

It was just like Corbin to make them wait. It would bring him malicious delight knowing that he was forcing Evan, an impatient man by nature, to cool his heels until such time as he chose to reveal himself. For all he knew, Corbin could be somewhere in the park with them, hidden behind an elaborate topiary, watching him sweat, and loving it.

The park was a masterpiece, the kind of work that could arise only out of genius, madness, or a generous helping of both. It was the brainchild of one of Barcelona's most beloved sons, an artist by the name of Gaudi, who had transformed it into a wonderland of gigantic mosaic animals and twisting pathways lined by pillars in the shape of women and strange creatures, built by hand, stone upon stone. Like many of the city's attractions, it was one of those places that he would have loved to have visited with Rissa under happier circumstances, and seen it all afresh through her wonder-filled eyes. He would have enjoyed holding her hand as they explored the many cool, greenery-draped pathways, or sat near the chattering fountains, or marveled at the eccentric collection of statuary. He would have loved to have taken her to a nearby café and ordered tapas, and introduced her to sweet, milky *chufa de horchata* to wash it down with. But that wasn't going to happen.

He rubbed his forehead, trying to quell the fantasies of homicide that dwelled there. It was uncanny how not once in his lifetime, but twice, he had been called upon to endure the torment of extortion by a callous, unscrupulous person. No man should have to endure that. Twice he'd been forced to make the ugly decision to hand over money for the life of someone he loved, and experience didn't make the second time around any easier. Right now, he didn't feel very much like a man. He felt like a helpless child; he wanted to storm at the Fates that had selected him for a reprise of their cruel joke, years after they'd broken him with it the first time. He wanted to rage at the sky, sob out his anguish in Rissa's arms. He deeply, desperately, missed his parents. If only, like Frankie, he could delude himself into believing that they were alive somewhere out there, and that he could reach across to them psychically to consult their wisdom!

"He wouldn't hurt her," Rissa said beside him. "I mean, Corbin's a lot of things—he's a womanizer, and a poser, he's greedy and sneaky—but he's not the kind of man to truly hurt her, is he?"

"Who knows? You can never tell how far money can drive someone. Greed is the ultimate motivator for some people. And as for not being the type of person to do something, I'm not exactly the type of person to commit murder, but from where I'm sitting, it's beginning to look like a damn attractive option."

She put her arm around his shoulder, and that kindness almost made him fall apart. "We have to stay calm," she told him, "for Frankie's sake."

That "we" was like a dart to the heart. He remembered how emphatically he'd insisted on excluding her from his mission the day before, replacing her "we" with his "I." What a mistake he'd almost made! How horrible this would all have been to endure if he had left her behind!

He wondered what he could say to her, but the necessity to respond was washed away in the wake of Corbin's arrival. The man stepped out of nowhere, appearing in the path near to their bench with almost preternatural stealth, making Evan's skin crawl. He leaped to his feet, heart pounding, adrenaline gushing into his veins as he watched Corbin approach. Next to him, Rissa stood, too.

Corbin was casually dressed with his usual flair: tight slacks and open-necked shirt, gold gleaming at his throat, wrist and fingers, and the ever-present hat cocked at a cheeky angle. He was smiling as a man would smile when meeting an old acquaintance after a long interval. There were a few small, fading bruises and encrusted scabs around his eyes and mouth, the last souvenirs of the beating Evan had delivered, and seeing them gave Evan a small measure of malicious satisfaction.

Corbin addressed himself to Rissa first, grasping her hand without seeking her permission, and kissing it with elaborate flair. "Mademoiselle Rissa, how delightful to see you again. You are as radiant as ever." She scowled and pulled her hand away, looking down at the back of it as though a bug had crawled across her skin, making no secret of her distaste.

Atta girl, Evan thought.

Corbin was unruffled. He went on, still using the dulcet tones that belonged at a polite social gathering, "How do you find Barcelona? I'm sure that Evan must have told you it is the land of my mother's birth. I spent many years of my life here, and I return whenever my oh-so-busy work schedule allows." He threw a hard look at Evan, but returned his attention to Rissa in the next instant. "Every time I come here, it is as though I am seeing it all for the very first time. The city is like a magnificent woman. No matter how often you make love to her, you think only of her when you are away. It is a city for lovers." He threw another look at Evan, even more malevolent than the first.

That does it. This is not a bullfight, and I won't allow any more red flags to be waved before me. "Where's my sister, Corbin?" Evan demanded.

Corbin sighed theatrically. "You will never make a good European if you are unable to control this American impatience of yours. In this country, business begins only when the pleasantries are over."

"I'm good enough at being what I am," he retorted, "and the pleasantries are over. Where is my sister?" He had hideous visions of her being imprisoned somewhere, frightened, maybe even hurt, and certainly devastated by this sudden turn of events, where a schoolgirl prank had ballooned into something ugly and dangerous. "Is she all right? If you hurt her in any way, I'll spend every day of the rest of my life making you pay."

Corbin tut-tutted him mockingly. "Come now, I would have thought that after all these years you would know me better than that. *One* of us here is not a violent man."

Evan chose to ignore the barb, and was about to speak again when Rissa piped up. "Well, where is she?" She had her hands on her hips and had a daunting no-nonsense look on her face that made him proud. "No games, Corbin. Where's Frankie?"

Corbin addressed his response to Evan. "Your sister is happy, well fed, and having the time of her life. I am a businessman, not an animal. I would die rather than hurt a single bleached hair on her beautiful head. She is somewhere out there in this magnificent city—" he indicated the expanse behind him with a sweep of the arm "—in the company of two of my sisters, who are close enough in age to share her all-consuming interest—shopping. In the haste of her departure yesterday, she left with very little to wear, you understand." He directed a mocking smile at Rissa. "So she and my sisters are rectifying that problem. Of course, their interaction is quite comic to observe. My sisters speak very little English, and Frankie's Spanish is weak and her Catalan abysmal, but, you understand, for teenage girls, shopping is the universal language."

His face became serious once more. "So let us not worry unduly about her. She is safe, happy, well, and spending your money. Let us, instead, discuss business, like the gentlemen that we are."

"Kidnapping is a serious crime, Corbin," Evan snarled. He was glad to hear that Frankie was in better shape than he had imagined. He trusted Corbin at least enough to believe that what he said was correct. All it meant was that Frankie was not yet aware of the seriousness of her predicament. If he was able to end this horror quickly and cleanly, she would never have to suffer.

Corbin lifted his eyes to the heavens in mock surprise, holding out his hands as though pleading for guidance from the angels. "Kidnapping? Oh, my friend, how sadly you misunderstand. There has been no crime committed here. There is no kidnapping. Frankie is with me of her own free will. This is her desire. I have treated her well. Very well." He added this last with lascivious emphasis, and Evan's stomach roiled.

"But you've demanded a ransom," Rissa pointed out hotly. "That makes it a kidnapping."

Corbin sobered up quickly, clasping his hands before him. "The problem with those electronic devices, these modern-day phones, is that text messages present so small an opportunity to explain oneself fully. The sum that I require is not a ransom. It is merely a consideration."

"For what?" Evan demanded. He couldn't believe he was hearing this.

"For the great pain that it would cause me to give up your sister's affections. She is a sweet creature, and a most loving one, and while I regret that I am unable to return her affections with the same intensity that she holds for me..." Evan glanced guiltily at Rissa "...I would not be a man if I did not avail myself of the many glorious delights she has to offer."

Evan felt his fingers curl into fists; it was only Rissa's restraining touch on his arm that stopped him from losing control completely and risking time in a Spanish jail by launching an all-out assault.

"Can you imagine that the sweet love of this girl is so great for me that she is prepared to give up her schooling? It is her great desire to forget her education, and instead roam the Riviera with me. She has this fantasy of the two of us, stopping at ports by day, lounging on beaches, and feasting on French bread and cheese, sharing a bottle of wine on the deck of my boat, making love when the sun goes down. What man in his right mind would deny such an exquisite creature this delight?"

"Make your point fast, Corbin."

His response was hard and flat. "My point is that your sister is living in a fantasy. I have no doubt that if I were to indulge her, she would tire of it all in a few months, and return to you and beg for forgiveness. Your first option is to leave her with me, and wait for her return. Within those few months, though, I am sure you can imagine the lifestyle that she will lead. I am a man of the world: I have friends in many ports who will find that exotic little mink most irresistible, and access to... shall we say, chemical preparations which enhance sensation but destroy good judgment. Your sister would be willing to experiment with many things that would not otherwise even have entered her imagination, if I tell her that it would please me."

Evan blanched.

"She is at the age when such experiences would change her for ever. What guarantee do you have, Evan, that the child who has so happily left your home on the adventure of a lifetime, will be the same person who will return? What will she be like, once every last shred of her innocence is stripped from her? Do you think that she will even resemble the sister that you remember?"

Evan felt like throwing up. Corbin was right. He did not need to restrain Frankie in any way. She would go willingly, believing that her love would last forever. And during the time they were together, he would alternate between his trademark seductions and his notorious casual cruelties, wearing away at the personality that Evan knew and loved. He had no idea how Frankie would adapt to these events, whether she would return broken or whether she would develop a hard, protective incrustation around her heart that might last the rest of her life. It was a risk he couldn't take. "And in exchange for the money…?"

"In exchange for that petty sum, I will be kind. I will kiss her gently, and lament the fact that I am unable to continue. I will think of something urgent—a new job abroad, a family illness. Or I may simply explain that my conscience has grown to the point where my guilt is too much to bear. I will tell her that I love her, but that she must return to her family and to her education." He gave them both an ugly grin. "Don't worry. I will think of something. Lying comes easy to me."

"You're forgetting one thing: I can simply call my sister, and ask her to come home with me."

Corbin laughed. "You? Come on, my friend. Has she spoken to you this past week? Has she said a word to you since you put your fists upon the man she *loves?* I would suspect that your influence upon her right now would only serve my purpose. Adolescents are like eggs—you subject them to heat, and it only hardens their resolve. I don't think your tongue is silver enough to change her mind."

Evan felt the weight of defeat upon his shoulders. Corbin had presented him with no other choice but to give in. But at least, it was not as bad as he had thought. Frankie would not be physically harmed; that alone was important. "So, how do we do this? Shall I write you a check?"

Corbin smiled pleasantly, victory upon his lips. "Forgive me for my cautious nature, but I would prefer to see for myself the appearance of the funds in my own account." He lifted his arm and looked at his watch, even though the fading light precluded the need to do so. "Unfortunately, these Spanish banks and their strange hours, they are long closed. Surely this can wait until morning?"

"I'd like to see her, still."

He shook his head. "Ah, I am afraid that is not possible. We will be dining tonight as a family, my mother, my sisters, and Frankie. She is very much looking forward to it. You would not want to spoil that for her, would you?"

"When, then?" Evan grated.

"I suggest that we conduct our business first." He handed Evan a folded slip of paper. "That is the name and address of my bank here in Barcelona. We will meet as it opens, and transact our business like civilized people. Surely a man of your means can make that all happen in half an hour or so?"

Evan nodded curtly.

"Good. Afterward, we will all meet for breakfast—you and your young lady," he smiled benignly at Rissa, "myself, and Frankie. We will share a meal like friends. For your generosity, I will throw in the bonus of telling her that you and I have made peace. That should be sufficient to incline her positively toward you again. Then at the end of the meal, I shall hold her close, and with regret in my eye, bid her farewell. You have my word, as a man of honor, that I will not attempt to contact her again." Corbin looked satisfied with himself. "Are we all agreed?"

Evan glanced at the slip of paper in his palm, and gave Corbin one last glare. The man had him over a barrel, there was no doubt about that. "Very well," he said shortly. "I will meet you in the morning."

Without another word, Corbin bowed in Rissa's direction once more, and with a last, triumphant smile, spun on his heel and left the way he had come.

As it did on almost every night of the year, Las Ramblas teemed with life. Around them, summer tourists clicked away at building façades and monuments, pointing and laughing, mothers pushed their babies in prams, children shot past on scooters, buskers played everything from ragtime to classical violin. A caricature painter approached them, waving his pad and charcoal and saying something in Portuguese, but one look from Evan sent him scurrying. He was not in the mood to enjoy any of it. He and Rissa had made a failed attempt at dinner; it had been a delightful meal served in a café not far from their *pension,* but neither of them could choke down more than a few bites. When he had suggested a walk, she had gladly agreed.

His only concession to her was the conscious effort he made to slow his pace to make it easy for her to keep up. He walked in silence, his face deeply grooved by a frown, fists jammed into the front pockets of his jeans, eyes fixed on his feet as they trampled the colored stone mosaics that paved the promenade. The bustle and noise around him were a mere backdrop to his jumbled, anguished thoughts. He was at once so pained and angry that only exercise provided a measure of respite.

Rissa, her hand on his forearm, was silent for most of the walk, her eyes darting from stall to stall and street performer to beggar, but always returning anxiously to his face. "I wish there was something I could do," she eventually said in frustration.

"I'll be fine," he lied, "once I get my sister back. Then everything will be okay."

"At least he hasn't hurt her."

"Not physically, no. But did you hear what he threatened to do? Turn her on to drugs. Pass her around his friends like a tray of canapés. As though she's just a toy, and who she is means nothing. Her humanity means nothing." His mouth was full of the bitter taste of futility. "And there's not a single, damn thing I can do about it, other than buy her back like a piece of property. Which makes me almost as bad as he is. I'm literally bartering for human flesh again."

She was quick on the uptake. "Again?"

Evan could have bitten his tongue off. There were only two people alive who knew what had happened on the day his marriage had died, and he preferred it that way. It was all too ugly to share, and too humiliating to admit to. But Rissa had stopped walking, forcing him to stop, too.

"What do you mean, 'again'? Has this happened before? Did someone take Frankie?" He couldn't bear the look of concern on her face. "What?"

"It had nothing to do with Frankie."

"Who, then?"

"It's not something I want to talk about," he said tightly. "It's over and done with."

She wasn't letting him off that easily. "No, obviously it's not, if it has you so upset." She was firm, but gentle. "What you were saying to me about that storehouse in your mind... those boxes full of junk...."

"Yes?"

"That sounds like a whole lot of junk right there to me. Maybe if you talked about it...."

"I might be better able to manage my junk?" He was dubious. He didn't believe that pain shared was pain halved.

"Worth a shot. Besides, you told me that that junk was what was getting in the way of you and me. If that's the case, you owe it to me at least to show me the face of my enemy."

"You want me to tell you how my wife punched a hole in my belly, tore out my insides, and left them hanging?" Sarcasm made good armor.

She stood by her guns, not softening as he had half expected her to. "If that's what happened."

They had almost reached the southern end of Las Ramblas;

the statue of Columbus at Port Vell was well within view. It was darker here, slightly sinister, almost, as the black expanse of the water loomed before them. He made an abrupt about face, turning north again, in the direction of the Plaza Catalunya, where their walk had begun. Rissa turned with him, waiting for a response.

Last night, she'd called him a coward, albeit jokingly. There'd been more truth to her words than she knew. Where his personal life was concerned, he had never been a very open person, and preferred to suffer a thousand agonies silently than admit to even one of them. But Rissa was right; he owed her an explanation.

Dumb luck presented them with a vacant bench, and he motioned for her to sit. He sat next to her, elbows on his thighs, hands clasped, and began directing his story toward the tiles at his feet.

"I married Jeanine when I was very young—just twenty-five. Too young to differentiate between style and substance. I'd known her just a year, but I was entranced by her. Everything about her was flawless, from her hair to her toes. She knew about clothes, food and music, and I was happy to let her organize my life, choose our house in San Diego and fill it with furniture and art. My parents were still alive then, and business was doing well, so there was enough money for her to indulge her tastes. She traveled while I worked, collecting whatever caught her fancy in London or Paris or Amsterdam or wherever was 'in' at the time. I didn't mind it because it made her happy. She made me happy.

"Then my parents disappeared, and for months thereafter my only obsession was finding them. I did everything I could, searched everywhere I could imagine they would end up, made every effort, no matter how futile I thought it would be. She was understanding at first but as the months dragged on, she began to resent the time I couldn't be with her. She traveled more, shopped harder.

"Frankie came to live with us. She was just a kid then, very impressionable, and believe me, Jeanine made an impression. She taught my sister everything she knew about style and fashion, and gave her a taste for designer items that she'll probably have for the rest of her life. She impressed upon her values that I didn't like seeing in someone so young, a kind of selfishness and shallowness that people in Jeanine's circle embrace, for some reason. But I was busy searching for my parents, and let a lot slide. I didn't intervene."

"You were still young," Rissa comforted, "and you had a lot on your shoulders. Besides, Frankie is a very determined personality. I doubt there was much you could have done."

"I don't know. But I should have tried. And then Jeanine became more demanding. She wanted a bigger house, she wanted to move to a trendier city. When I opened the *atelier* in Perpignan, she almost had a fit. She didn't mind living in France, but Perpignan is not exactly the bastion of haute couture. She insisted that if I needed to be near the coast, we move at least to Nice, so that she could surround herself with the beautiful people. And, as young as she was, Frankie joined her in her demand. But Perpignan was the best place for my business, and I decided to stay. So Jeanine simply spent less and less time at home, and more and more time traveling. Our marriage began to unravel. She came home only to deposit her latest purchases, book herself another destination, and fly off again. It was a horrible time. Frankie was constantly mad at me because she idolized Jeanine and thought that her departures were all my fault. And I missed Jeanine, too. Desperately. She was my wife, and in spite of everything, I loved her very much."

He stopped, remembered pain being the only thing that circumvented a bitter laugh at his own youthful foolishness.

"I'm sure you did," Rissa said. "I'm sorry you were hurt."

"Not as hurt as I was at the realization that my dreams of raising a family were crumbling along with my marriage. I've always wanted children. There's nothing that would give me pleasure like spending time with my own children the way my parents spent with us. I feel that I have so much to offer a child, and so much to teach. There's a little ego there, too, I have to admit. I'd love to see my name go on, pass my father's genes on to my own son...." He raised his head for the first time and looked across at Rissa—and stalled. The look of anguish on her face bewildered him briefly, and then he remembered. Rissa was incapable of ever having a child. Here he was, moaning self-pityingly about a woman who chose not to ruin her figure and, as she bluntly put it, her whole life, by bearing him a child, when he himself at least retained the biological capacity to do so. Rissa didn't have that luxury.

"I'm sorry," he blustered. "That was clumsy of me."

She was brusque. "Go on."

He persisted. "I was insensitive, Rissa. I'm sorry—"

"Go *on*, Evan!"

To press further unwanted apologies upon her would be equally callous, so he let it rest and reprised his story. "I tried everything I could to convince her otherwise. I was even contemplating giving in to her demands and moving my fledgling business to Nice, even though I knew that to do so would cause it to suffer, maybe even destroy it, if only she would give in and give me at least one child.

"Then, it was as though a miracle happened. Jeanine walked into my study one day and placed a piece of paper on my desk. It was a lab report. It said that she was pregnant. I can't describe to you how happy I was. I threw my arms around her and promised her that she would have everything she desired. But something was dead wrong. Jeanine didn't hug me back, didn't smile, didn't say a word. I felt every drop of blood in my veins go cold. I got very, very scared. I didn't know of what, but I was terrified for the baby, and myself."

Rissa was barely breathing. "What happened?"

"She was calm, cold, and explicit. She laid another set of papers on my table, lawyer's papers. She wanted a divorce."

"And the baby?"

Bitterness twisted his lips. "That was the kicker. I stood there and watched my wife explain that, in addition to the divorce settlement she was demanding, she wanted another payment, several hundred thousand dollars—and this is the exact word she used—as *consideration*." Corbin's term, come back to mock him.

"For what?"

"For the life of my child. If I paid, she agreed to delay the divorce until the baby was born, and to sign over all parental rights to me. She would never see him or her again."

"And if you didn't?"

"She showed me an appointment card to a woman's clinic in town. There was an appointment written on it, for a date a week later. She was brutally clear: either I paid up within seven days, or she was keeping that appointment. My baby would be…" Even after five years, he was unable to even finish the thought.

Rissa finished it for him. "Gone," she whispered.

"Yes."

"What…did you do?"

"My parents' property and their interest in our San Diego factory were all tied up in legalities, and would be for years. My own business was still very young, and I didn't have that much money readily available. I scraped up the money every way I knew how, taking out loans, drawing huge advances, and relying on many of my father's old friendships for leniency. I'm sure that many of them thought I'd gotten into trouble gambling or with drugs, but my father's memory was enough to get my foot into the door. She'd given me a week— I paid up within twenty-four hours. I handed her a cashier's check for all of it, every penny. To me, there was no moral question, nothing to think about. My child's life was worth everything I had, everything I owned. The devil could have taken my soul, for all I cared.

"And fool that I was, after I handed over the money, I *thanked* her. For giving me a child. I promised her that she would have the best medical care available throughout her pregnancy. And she stood there with the check in her hand and laughed."

"Laughed?"

"As you can see, I have no child."

Rissa closed her eyes and bowed her head. "She went ahead and did it anyway." -

"No. There was never any need. I stood in my study that evening and watched my wife laugh in my face. She called me a naive fool. The test was a fake, and a bad one at that. She'd printed it up herself on my own computer. I had just been so swept away by joy that I was incapable of seeing that."

"She was never pregnant?"

"Jeanine? No. She would never have been that careless. I should have known that. But happiness had made me gullible."

"Why didn't she just divorce you, and take the settlement? Why did she need so much money?"

"Payback, as she carefully explained, for all the years of her life I made her waste in the sticks, away from the theaters and parties and fancy stores. Not to mention the fact that when Louis Vuitton is your second home, you're going to need all the money you can get. She informed me that when she had married me, she had known that I would eventually be a rich man. She just never imagined that I'd also be a boring one."

"You're not boring," Rissa said hastily.

He didn't acknowledge her compliment, but instead finished his story. "So, as it turned out, there was no reason to delay. I signed the divorce papers right there, handed them over, and left the room. I had to. I was so furious, so devastated, that I could have torn the house apart, whether she was in it or not. I walked outside, sat on the front steps, and collapsed in tears. I felt as though my child had been murdered, even though it had never even existed. In twenty-four hours that lie had become so alive in my mind that I had fallen in love with it. I felt gutted. I think I cried all night, got hopelessly drunk, and then cried all of the next day."

He felt Rissa's arms around him, and her lips against his cheek. "I'm sorry."

"You don't have to be."

"I am anyway. I can't imagine how deeply you must be hurting. I wish there was some way I could help."

"You helped by listening."

He felt drained. It had been a hideous day, and the only thing that had helped him through it was the fact that Rissa was there with him. He rose painfully; his bones ached like an old man's. "Maybe we should go back in," he suggested.

"We could do that."

She kept her hand on his arm, but maintained the same silence that they had instituted during their descent. The half-mile strip of promenade seemed exhaustingly long, and it was only embarrassment that prevented him from hailing a taxi and cutting out the need to walk entirely. So they walked past the Boqueria market, with its strong smells of fruit, cheese, and pickled pigs' feet, past the human statues and the jugglers, and managed to arrive once again at the *pension* without getting their pockets picked.

She followed him into his room without asking. He was

grateful for her intuition; he needed her desperately. She took her clothes off wordlessly and crawled into his bed and lay on her back, waiting. "You wasted money on that second room," she observed idly when he joined her.

"Could have been worse."

"How?"

"You could have stayed over *there*."

She seemed to know that tonight he needed her to take charge. She made love to him with careful, protective gentleness, as though she were cradling an egg between her hands. But as their sexual intensity deepened she became increasingly sad. He had the feeling that she was drawing his pain and unhappiness from him in an effort to make him feel better, but in so doing taking it into herself. Their coupling gave him an eerie sense of finality, almost as though this was her way of saying goodbye. That terrified him.

A sigh of release escaped her lips, and with it, her first verbal confession. "I love you, Evan."

He hid his face in her neck and answered the only way he knew how. "Thank you, sweetheart."

Stuck in a Hopeless Relationship: When To Stay, and When To Cut Bait and Leave

Rissa knew she was taking a chance, but it was a chance that had to be taken. She'd lain next to Evan for a long time, afraid even to move in case she roused him, until she was sure that he was in the deepest possible sleep, and then she'd eased from his bed as silently as she was able. Her last, stealthy act before she slipped from his room was to unclip his cellular phone from the belt still looped around the waist of the pair of jeans that he had draped over a chair the night before.

But leaving Evan sleeping was not the big risk; calling Frankie was. From the deep silence of her room, she dialed, hoping to God that Corbin, presumably with her, would be asleep at this hour. Conversely, she hoped that Frankie was still up, and able to catch her call before the phone woke anyone. She banked on her knowledge of the girl's night-owl nature to assure her that her target was awake.

She was right. Frankie picked up on the forth ring. Her voice was suspicious. "Yes?"

Thank you, Lord. "Frankie, it's me."

"Rissa!" Frankie squealed.

That was loud enough to wake up Rip Van Winkle. "Shh! Is Corbin nearby? You'll wake him."

"Don't worry. He's not here."

She was surprised. "He's not?"

"Nah. We're in his mother's house, and he said that out of respect for her we should have separate rooms. It's a really nice room."

That was a relief. At least they could speak openly. "Are you okay?"

"I'm having a blast," Frankie enthused. "I've been out all day with Corbin's sisters, and we got our feet done, and I bought this cool pair of sandals—" She halted, and then with typical adolescent abruptness, veered in another direction. "Is Evan really mad?"

"No, not at all. He's just worried about you."

"Huh. Right. He's just upset because I'm not around, doing as he says like a good little girl."

"That couldn't be further from the truth. Evan just wants you to be safe and happy."

"I *am* safe and happy. I'm in love with Corbin, and he's in love with me. And his family adores me. They told me so. And I like where I am and I'm happy here." Frankie's voice hardened. "You're not going to make me come back there, you know, so if he asked you to call me, tell him I said—"

"He doesn't know I'm calling," she answered hastily. She remembered what Corbin had said about teenagers being like eggs, hardening under heat. If she didn't play this right, she'd blow the only chance she had. "And I'm not calling to make you come back."

"Why, then?" She was still wary, still disbelieving.

"I'm calling to say goodbye." At least that much was true. After all that Evan had told her tonight, there wasn't much point in staying. Any hope that she held out that by the end of summer she would have succeeded in making him love her back was dashed by his story. Evan wanted—he deserved—a woman who could give him children. That woman was not she. Every day she spent with him, no matter how filled with pleasure, would only make it more painful to leave him in the end. It was better to cut and run now than live in false hope.

Frankie sounded puzzled. "Huh?"

"I'm leaving. I've decided to go back to Philadelphia as soon as I can, and you're the only real friend I have here. And I want to see you before I go."

"Why are you leaving?"

"I can't tell you that. It hurts too much."

"Was he mean to you?"

"No, nothing like that."

"Because he's real mean. That's the way he is. He's a mean person—"

"He's not mean, and you know it!" Love made her as defensive as if she herself were being attacked. She tried to soften her words, reluctant to let Frankie slip from her hook, now that she had baited her. "Let me see you again, just one more time, before I go. Because I'm leaving today, and I can't go without seeing you."

Frankie hesitated. "Rissa, I'm not in Perpignan any more, you know. Corbin and I—"

"Sailed to Barcelona. We know."

Frankie gasped. "How did you know that?"

"Your brother had a lucky guess," she answered dryly.

"So then, how will I see you? You're miles away!"

"Not exactly. I'm nearer than you think."

"You're in Barcelona? No way!"

Evidently, Corbin had told her nothing about his brother's presence, or even that Evan was aware of her whereabouts. The man really knew how to play his cards close to his chest. "Really. We're in this place off Las Ramblas. In the Gothic Quarter."

"Old man Palazon's place. Yeah, I know it. Stuffy little dump, eh? I could never understand Evan. Five-star hotels all over Barcelona, and he has to hole up in that crumbly old wreck every time we go. Believe me, there's no accounting for taste!" She halted, and veered again. "You came looking for me, didn't you?"

"Yes, we did."

"Well, I'm not coming—"

It was time to take control of the situation before she ruined everything. Rissa said firmly, "Listen, Frankie, it's true we came here looking for you, but I'm not part of that anymore. I'm leaving Evan, and I'm going home. But I can't leave without seeing you. I don't want Evan to know I'm going, and I don't want him to know I'm seeing you. So please, if you can keep my secrets, I'll keep yours."

The prospect of keeping a secret from Evan was attractive enough to capture Frankie's attention. She lowered her voice is if there suddenly was the risk of being overheard. "What do you want us to do?"

"I want you to sneak out and meet me. Nobody has to know. Can you leave the house and get around the city on your own?"

"Now?" she asked dubiously.

"No, it's not safe. It's way too late. I meant early in the morning, before breakfast. Before anyone's up."

"They sleep late in Spain you know. It doesn't have to be that early."

"Evan doesn't ever sleep late. If I'm to get away without

him knowing, I'll have to leave here before six. Can you manage that?"

Frankie yawned. "Oh, man, I only get up at six for school."

"So pretend it's school time. Please, do it for me. Besides, there's something I want to give you before you go." She hoped that last bit sweetened the pot enough.

It did. "What do you have to give me?"

"A farewell present. Something I hope you'll accept."

"Where, then?"

"At the statue of Columbus."

"What, that old thing? I know a lot of ritzy places you'll like better—"

"I've only been here a day. It's the only place I can find on my own. Please," she pleaded, "come meet me there. Six-thirty. Can you do that?"

"I can do that," Frankie said.

Frankie might be good at all this cloak and dagger stuff, Rissa thought, but she wasn't. By the time she had slipped from the *pension* at first light, she was a bundle of nerves, and now, standing near the *Monument a Colom*, in the shadow of great palms, she was sure that she was a second away from snapping into two. Frankie was already twenty minutes late. What if Evan woke up and discovered her missing, and through some magical means, figured out where she'd gone? She half expected him to turn up at any second. And what if Frankie didn't show?

It was true that in a matter of hours, Evan and Corbin would meet to execute their "gentleman's agreement", and Frankie would, one way or the other, soon be removed from the ambit of Corbin's toxic influence, but at what cost? Even if Evan was able to sustain the financial blow of this ludicrous "consideration," paying it would strike at his manhood and skewer his conscience, and after what he had told her last night, she was uncertain whether he would be able to survive the experience intact. So if there was one thing she could do for Evan, and for Frankie, before she left, this was it.

Rissa paced nervously, trying to distract herself by focusing on the elaborate sculpting at the base of the towering monument. Around her, traffic was sluggish, as the parade of the tour buses was still a long way off, and the morning rush hour ritual had not yet begun. Where was Frankie?

She got her answer fifteen minutes later, when a taxi drew up and Frankie hopped out, bleary-eyed but grinning. The two fell into each other's arms, hugging tightly for a long time before letting go. Rissa was surprised at how happy she was to see the girl. She'd missed her more than she'd thought.

"You look wonderful, Frankie." She touched her cheek.

Frankie beamed. "Thanks. You look…tired. Didn't you sleep?"

"No. I was afraid to, in case I overslept. So I sat on the window box in my room and looked out onto the street until it was time to leave."

"And Evan?"

She shrugged. "I don't know. Awake by now, maybe. Hopefully he thinks I'm in the bath, or gone for a walk or something."

"He'll come looking for you," Frankie said darkly. "He's like that."

Then I'd better make this quick, Rissa thought. The two faced each other, both hands outstretched between them, warmly clasped. She wondered where to begin.

"No hard feelings on the restaurant thing, right? Leaving you like that?" Frankie was a little abashed, anxious for forgiveness but still reluctant to apologize.

"No hard feelings."

"You know why I had to do it. I knew you'd understand. You know what it's like to be in love, don't you?"

"I know," Rissa said sadly.

"Then you understand."

"I understand." Of one accord, they sat on a low stone pedestal, unmindful of the decades of smog and grime that encrusted it.

"So," Frankie began, with the directness of youth, "why are you leaving him?"

"I just have to."

"But why?"

As uncomfortable as it was having such an intimate discussion with Evan's own relative, she thought she owed Frankie a straight answer. "Because I love him too much."

"That doesn't make any sense," Frankie snorted.

"It does, if you consider that he can't love me back."

"Can't or won't?"

"Either one is just as bad."

"I know why he won't," Frankie asserted. "I told you already—Jeanine. He's still sore that she dumped him. And he still wants her back. I kept telling him, if only he'd moved to Nice…"

There was so much that Frankie didn't know about that marriage! But the things that she didn't know, Rissa was not at liberty to tell her. "I don't think he wants her back," she said delicately. "But she's done things, bad things, enough to make it impossible for me to ever feel that I have a chance with him. I can either leave now, or leave at the end of summer, like we agreed…."

"Like you agreed?"

Rissa almost slapped her forehead at her slip-up. The contract between Evan and Rissa was one thing Frankie need never know about: it had been wrong from the start, and they had both known it. If she could spare the youngster the pain of knowing that her brother had hired a spy—a particularly inept spy, but a spy nonetheless—to watch over her, then all the better. She explained lamely. "His invitation to stay expires at the end of summer, when you go back to school."

Surprisingly, Frankie accepted this without question. "Okay."

"So I can leave now, and end this, or stay with him for another few weeks or so, and go home even worse for wear, because no matter how long I stay, that won't change things. And the way I see it, there's no sense in my staying around, hoping, and letting myself get hurt."

"So you're leaving."

"Yes."

"Today?"

"Yes."

"Are you going to tell him anything?"

She shook her head. "I don't think I can. If I look into his eyes, I'll crack. I'll be lost."

Frankie didn't seem to find the deception or sudden flight the least bit questionable. Her bigger concern was, "Will I see you again?"

"I hope so. Maybe I can come visit you in San Diego."

"That would be nice." She smiled genuinely. "You flying out of Barcelona?"

"I guess so."

"Got a ticket yet?"

"No. Hope I can get one at the airport."

"Good luck with that."

"Thanks." Rissa realized that leaving Frankie would hurt almost as much as leaving her brother would.

Now that all the formalities were over, Frankie swept her from head to toe with sharp eyes. "So, what was it you bought for me?"

"Huh?" Rissa was momentarily nonplussed.

"You said you got me a present. What is it?"

"Oh." Nerves assailed her once again, and her mouth grew dry. This was the second, perhaps more important motive for their meeting, and the more delicate one by far. If she let this chance slip her by, she would never forgive herself. The fallout would be devastating. But she owed it both to Evan and to Frankie at least to try. "It's not something I bought, actually," she began.

Frankie's curiosity was aroused. "Did you make it?"

"Not exactly."

Frankie bounced in her seat, like a child at a birthday party. "Well, what, then? Show me!"

Wishing she could back out now, but aware that it was too late, Rissa reluctantly drew Evan's phone from her pocket and clicked it open. "It's this."

Frankie scowled in puzzlement. "That's Evan's phone," she said dubiously, not understanding.

"I know. There's something I want to show you." Rissa frowned at the phone, scrolling through until she found the message she wanted, and then turned the screen to face Frankie. "Look."

Frankie still didn't get it. "At what?" She read the message anyway, and Rissa watched her face anxiously as the expression on it changed from puzzled curiosity to stark disbelief. "What's this?"

"It's a message Corbin sent to your brother yesterday, demanding a meeting."

"Corbin knew you and Evan were here?"

"Yes."

"And he didn't say anything to me?"

"Apparently not. Do you see what else he demanded?"

Frankie looked at the phone again. "Half a million? I don't understand. For what?"

"For you."

Frankie laughed weakly. "No, that's not right. That first message, for the fifty thousand euros, I sent that, from a cyber café in Perpignan. It was a joke, sort of. We figured if we could get bit of money to play with, then fine. If not, we'd get by. It was a joke."

"This message wasn't. Corbin was serious. I know. Evan and I met him yesterday."

"You didn't!"

"We did. At the Parc Guëll, while you were out shopping with his sisters. He made it very clear; Evan was to hand over half a million euros, and he was going to let you come home."

"He wouldn't do that!" Frankie was becoming agitated, her chest rising and falling, her eyes wide with disbelief.

Rissa placed her hand on Frankie's head and stroked the short hair. "I'm sorry, sweetheart, but he did."

Frankie bounded out of her seat and started to walk off. "This is a trap! You and Evan set this up, didn't you! You faked that message, didn't you!"

Rissa ran after her. "We didn't. We couldn't have. Look and see who sent the message. Do you recognize the number?"

Frankie stopped running, but didn't look at the phone again. "Please," Rissa pleaded, "look and see who sent it."

Still suspicious, Frankie checked the origins of the message, and then her arm fell to her side. "I don't believe you."

But she did, Rissa saw. She was just unwilling to accept what she was reading. She said gently, "Frankie, I know you love Corbin, but he doesn't deserve that love. There's no easy way to tell you this, but you need to understand. He doesn't love you back."

Frankie clung mulishly to hope. "Yes, he does. He told me so."

"Sometimes people say things they don't mean."

"You mean, like luring them out to a bogus early-morning meeting and feeding them a bunch of lies?"

"I mean, like telling you things you want to hear, because it suits their purpose."

"But he *told* me...." Frankie faltered.

It was now or never. Rissa would have to be cruel in order to make this work. "He told your brother that he was willing to use you for as long as it was convenient, and then he would send you, or whatever was left of you, back home. He threatened to get you drunk, get you high, whatever it took, and pass you around to his friends for them to use as they wanted."

Frankie gasped. "But I never would have done *any* such thing!"

"Love and drugs are a powerful combination, and Corbin can be very persuasive."

"I *never* would!"

"I'm glad to hear that. But that was his plan. Still is his plan. Use your love to his own advantage, abuse your trust, and leave you a broken wreck when he was done. And as you can see, he also offered to sell you back to your brother, like a slave on an auction block."

Frankie's jaw worked frantically as she struggled to come to terms with this information. She looked at the phone in her hand again, thinking hard. "And was Evan going to pay?"

"He and Corbin have agreed to meet at the bank as soon as it opens, this morning. That's why I had to see you so early."

"To pay to get me back."

"To pay to save your life. Tell me, Frankie, if Corbin had succeeded in doing all these things to you, what kind of person do you think you'd be, in a few months time? Would you even recognize yourself?"

"I don't believe..." Frankie began, and faltered. Her head

dipped in resignation. Her next words were almost too soft to hear. "How could he?"

What ran through Rissa's head was *because he's a vain, cruel, self-indulgent bastard who's interested in nobody's welfare but his own.* She was, however, prudent enough to temper what actually came out of her mouth. "I don't know. But whatever it is, you have to understand that it has nothing to do with who you are, or how much you're worth. It doesn't mean you're not loveable. It just means that you loved the wrong person."

Frankie looked so forlorn that Rissa felt sorry for her. "What do I do now?"

"Get out while you can. Leave while you still recognize yourself, and while you still like who you are."

She wilted visibly. "This was supposed to be a dream. My adventure."

"Finish school first. After that, you have all the time in the world to have adventures. Trust me. I've had lots, and there are a lot more waiting for me. It's just that there's a time for everything, and your time hasn't come yet." She closed her hand around Frankie's wrist. "You've got to go home."

"Evan will hate me."

"Evan will never hate you. He loves you more than anything in the world."

"But I'm so ashamed…."

"You don't have to be. Believe me, he understands. He told me so. Just go home, and you'll see. All he wants is to have you back."

In an uncanny confirmation of her words, there was a loud shout and a frantic honking from across the street, and a squeal of brakes as Evan's shiny blue car surged up out of the traffic like a leaping dolphin, skating to an awkward stop in an even more awkward place. Rissa's heart leaped.

"What's he doing? He'll get towed!" Frankie said irrelevantly.

Evan didn't look as though he cared about that, or about the now growing stream of cars that separated him from them. He dashed across the road, deftly weaving between bumpers, not even reacting to the curses hurled at him by startled drivers. He arrived unscathed at the base of the statue and grasped Frankie by the shoulders. "Are you all right?"

She looked bewildered by his sudden arrival and unsure of the reception she could expect. "Okay," she mumbled.

"You sure?"

"I'm fine, Evan!" She was still defensive, a little wary.

"Thank God!" Evan turned to Rissa. "Where did you find her?"

"I called her and asked her to meet me."

He was incredulous. "You called her? You just picked up the phone and called?"

"Yes."

He looked as though he didn't know what to say. He mumbled to himself, dazed. "That's all it took." He shook his head, and added a fervent, "Thank you. From the bottom of my heart, thank you."

She never had the time to acknowledge his gratitude. "I told you he'd come looking for you," Frankie said.

Evan was still out of breath, his face still ashen with anxiety. "You scared me half to death, Rissa, disappearing like that. I found you gone and I didn't know what to think. At first I thought you'd gone for a walk, but something was just gnawing away at me. It didn't feel right. So I looked the only place you know—Las Ramblas. I went up to the Plaza, and then I headed in this direction." He stopped abruptly, realizing how ludicrous the conversation was when there was so much more important at hand. He turned to his sister. "Francesca," he began.

"You only call me that when you're mad at me. You see, Rissa? I told you he'd be mad at me!"

Before Rissa could even think of a response, Evan said gently, "I don't call you that because I'm mad at you. I call you that because that's what Dad used to call you. Remember?"

Her mouth moved convulsively. "You're not Dad."

"I know." As Rissa watched, feeling more and more like an intruder every second, tears gathered in Evan's eyes, and spilled down his cheeks. He fell to his knees before his sister, taking both of her hands, and pressing his face into them. "I know I'm not Dad. I tried to be, God knows. Maybe I was wrong in that, but it was the only way I knew how to protect you. I'm sorry for every time I hurt you. I know I was bossy, and sometimes I didn't listen hard enough to what you had to say. I meant well. That's my only excuse."

Frankie looked down at the top of her brother's bowed head, nonplussed, not knowing how to deal with this sudden outpouring of emotion from a man who was always so stoic in her presence. She eased one of her hands from his grasp and laid it on the back of his head.

Not waiting for an answer, Evan went on. "I promise it will be better from now on. You'll have more of a say in the way things work. From now on, we won't do anything about your life unless we both agree on it. All I want is for you to forgive me and come home. I love you, Frankie. You're all I have. Please, come back home."

Rissa felt tears stinging at her own eyes, partly out of pure joy at seeing brother and sister reunited, and, she was ashamed to admit even to herself, partly out of scalding jealousy. *I love you. You're all I have.* Evan was a family man, and she would never, could never be what he needed to make that family complete. She looked around frantically, wishing she could escape.

"Get up. You're getting your jeans dirty," Frankie told him. "And you are so gonna get towed!"

Evan laughed at her typically prosaic response. He did rise, but still held her hand. He had to have an answer. "Forgiven?"

Frankie smiled at him, and her indomitable spirit shone through it. "Yeah, okay."

"Home, then?"

"All right." They hugged tightly.

When they parted, Evan was beaming. "Come on, Rissa. Let's get out of here before I don't have a car anymore."

How she wanted to go back with them! Oh, how her resolve began to melt! It wasn't so bad, being with Evan. He was affectionate and generous and kind, and the sex blew her mind. The end of summer was only a few weeks away. Why couldn't she just go back with him, gather her rosebuds while she might, and then, when it came time to go, kiss him goodbye and leave with dignity?

Because her pain would double every day, and at the end of it all she would just be one huge bundle of hurt and loss, and if there was one thing she had already had more of her fair share of in life, it was loss. Leaving him now wasn't just the right thing to do. It was the *only* thing to do.

The simplest gesture, shaking her head, took enormous strength. "You two go on ahead. I won't be coming."

Evan frowned, not understanding. "What?"

"She's leaving you, Evan," Frankie explained helpfully.

Rissa hoisted her knapsack to show him. "This was a one-way trip. Whether or not I managed to meet Frankie, and whether or not I was able to convince her to go home to you, I wasn't planning on going back to the *pension*." She was unable to use the truer phrase, *I wasn't planning on going back to you.*

Evan was incredulous. "What were you planning to do?"

"I was, uh, going to take a taxi to the airport, and see if I could get a flight, any flight, back to the United States. Then I'd make my way back to Philly, and—"

"How were you hoping to get to the airport? You don't even know your way around!"

"I know what a taxi looks like, and I know enough Spanish to ask for the airport. I can take care of myself, you know. I'm not an idiot."

Evan didn't contest her assertion, but instead said accusingly, "You were leaving without saying anything?"

"I left you a note at the front desk. I just asked them to give it to you after lunch. And I'd have called you, you know."

"When?"

"From the airport, or as soon as I got home." *As soon as I was able to talk to you without breaking down.*

His expression was a mixture of hurt and perplexity. He actually put his hand over his chest, as though she'd stuck him there with a small, sharp blade. "But why? I thought—"

Frankie intervened. "What about your stuff? The clothes we bought. Aren't they back in Perpignan?"

It was easier to answer Frankie's question than Evan's. "They're just clothes, and it's not as if I had a lot. I've got my laptop, my passport, and my bank cards. I'll be okay."

Evan repeated himself, cutting across the nonsense. "*Why,* Rissa?"

"It's too hard…"

"What's too hard?"

"Too hard to explain."

"Hard or not, you *owe* me an explanation."

This wasn't how she had anticipated her next conversation with him to be. She had hoped that there would at least be many miles between them, rather than being mere inches from his aghast face, in the midst of swirling traffic, with his sister near enough to hear every word.

Seemingly reading her thoughts, Frankie stepped away, veering around and heading toward the road. "I'm going to sit in the car—at least that might protect it, seeing as it's parked practically on the sidewalk and all. You two sort yourselves out."

They watched until she was safely on the other side, and then Evan's attention returned to her. "Rissa?"

"I don't have an explanation."

"But last night, we were in bed together, and it was so good. And now, this morning... Did something happen? Did Corbin get to you?"

That was ludicrous. "No."

"Did Frankie say something?"

"No."

"Is it me?"

Not in any way that he might think. The stock answer to that, *no, it's me,* was such a cliché that she refused to insult him with it, even though it held an element of truth. The shock and hurt in his clear, caramel eyes were more than she could stand. One more minute of this, and she would relent, melt in a puddle of weakened resolve, and that would be the death of her. She had to be strong, for her own survival. "It just wasn't working out. That's all. There's no other explanation I can give. It was nice, but now it's over."

"Nice?" he echoed in incredulity. "Ice cream is 'nice.' What we have—"

"Had," she corrected. "We don't have it anymore. It's over now, so take your sister home, okay? She needs you."

"She needs you, too."

Her ego wondered why he didn't say that *he* needed her, but her weakening resolve was glad that he hadn't. "Not anymore. You don't need a spy for her anymore."

"She doesn't need a spy. She needs a friend."

"You be her friend. Be her brother." This wasn't getting

them anywhere. She had to sever this tie once and for all. She swung her bag over her shoulder and said gruffly, "I've made up my mind, Evan. We can stand here and argue all day, but I've made up my mind. Go!"

His puzzlement was overcome by anger and frustration. "Just like that, huh?"

She turned away, unable to bear looking at him anymore. "Just like that. Go, Evan!"

She half expected a reply, half hoped that he would try to restrain her, but she took several steps and no response was forthcoming. Piqued, she looked back, just in time to see his straight, stiff back as he stepped onto the pavement on the other side of the road and threw open the car door. There was rage in that swift, simple gesture. He hurled the car off the edge of the sidewalk as abruptly as he had arrived, causing other drivers to swerve to avoid him. Behind the tinted glass, she couldn't see his face, but knew that it would be an angry mask.

As the car drove away from her, she saw just the faintest shadow of Frankie's hand, waving at her, from the passenger's side window.

Cleaning Out Your Closets—How To Make Room for That Special Someone

Once Frankie returned to San Diego, back to school, a pall of quiet descended upon the house that threatened to send Evan nuts. He hated the fact that there was no Frankie blasting music from her room or splashing in the pool, and no one to watch movies with. He hated the quiet, the dead air that filled every room. Even more, he hated the fact that Rissa was gone.

In the weeks since her abrupt, almost bizarre rejection of him he had spent many of his empty hours puzzling over her departure. There was no rhyme or reason to it, or, at least, none that he could fathom. One night he'd fallen asleep naked, pressed against her satiny skin, and the next morning he was standing in the road asking himself whether he was hearing her right, whether she was really going to walk away, hop on any available flight home, and exit his life just like that. Just like that?

That night on Las Ramblas, he'd poured out his pain to her, hoping that she would understand why it was so difficult for him to allow her in. He'd started that conversation at lunch, trying to explain his conflict with an analogy about the storehouse in his head, intending to plead for time. He wanted her, and wanted to be with her so much that for the first time he was motivated enough to confront his mental junk. All he had needed from her was time to sort it through. Why hadn't she given him that time?

Love didn't leap upon him without warning like a leopard from a tree; he just wasn't that kind of man. He was a farmer, who nurtured it from a seedling, watering it and caring for it until it grew into something wonderful. If only she had waited. If only she had stayed. Now, his seedling had sprouted into a plant that was bearing bitter fruit, and as much as he tried he was unable to stop himself from gorging upon them, even though each bite, each memory of Rissa, was agony.

He had had Madame Soler neaten up her room, but couldn't even bring himself to send her things to her. In the past few weeks, he'd received a short note, written on generic paper, letting him know that she was safely back in Philadelphia, had found a new apartment, and was on the verge of finishing her children's novel and preparing to shop it around. Her return address was duly written in her scrawling hand on the envelope, and he could not count the number of times that he had placed that envelope on his desk and picked up the phone, half-ready to call his travel agent and book himself a flight to Philly. Maybe, after enough time had elapsed and she saw him in person, she might be prepared to hear him out, listen to his plea for another chance. But pride stopped him. Fear stopped him.

So he rattled around his now too-large house every evening after work, followed dutifully by Dante and Plato, picking up the TV remote and putting it down, booting up his computer and then letting it go to sleep again, searching for something to fill his hours. Nothing satisfied him.

He was standing in his kitchen, hands upon his hips, staring down with pursed lips at the meal Madame Soler had prepared for him, wondering whether he should eat it or not, when the phone rang. He took his time answering it. Hardly anyone of interest called him at home anymore; ex-girlfriends who, aware of his usual self-imposed hiatus during Frankie's visits, were trying to re-establish contact now that she was certain to be gone, friends extending casual invitations to parties he wouldn't attend, and the occasional business call that was always redirected to his office.

He barely had the receiver in hand when he heard the shrill yell on the other end. "Evan! Oh, man, tell me it's you!"

"Frankie!" A smile came immediately to his face. Since they had repaired their fences in Barcelona, the time they had spent together had been wonderfully relaxed, filled with happy days on his boat or wandering through town. He was always glad to hear her voice, and she never failed to lift his spirits. "How are you, honey?"

Her reply was a moan. "Oh, man, Evan, it's awful. I'm in big, big, trouble. You've got to help me!"

He almost choked on the air that he sucked in. "What happened?"

"I didn't mean anything," she began. "I mean, we were just playing around…."

That sounded bad. He tried to be patient with her usual meandering mode of conversation. "What happened, Frankie?"

"My friends and I…just girls being girls, you know?"

"Frankie, please, just tell me."

Her pause drew on for far too long, and then she answered in a rush, "We were planning to have a party in the dorm, okay? A secret thing after lights-out. For fun. And me and another girl, we got picked to go and get, you know, stuff for the party…."

He didn't like the sound of that one bit. "What kind of stuff?"

"You know, like pretzels and stuff."

"Uh-huh."

"And maybe a few beers. And some wine. And just one bottle, *one bottle* of vodka. Not a whole lot, understand?"

Then he got the picture. "You got caught buying alcohol?"

"Sort of, yeah."

"How did you manage to buy alcohol? Didn't you get carded?"

"There was this guy, right? That one of the girls put me on to? Well, he sold us some fake IDs…."

"Oh, God," he groaned.

"He said they were foolproof."

"And they weren't."

"Not exactly."

"So, what happened?"

"Well this store clerk, he got all prissy on us and called the police. We begged him to just take the booze back, but he refused, and the cops called the sisters at school, and handed us over."

"And now?"

"And now the principal is mad. You should have seen her, Evan. She had a fit. She started screaming and ranting and saying she wanted to see our folks, and…" To say that the pause that followed was pregnant would be to understate its duration and intensity.

He tensed himself for what was to follow that "and."
"And…?"

"And I'm gonna be expelled."

He couldn't stop the roar that burst from him. "Expelled? For buying alcohol? Isn't that a little harsh?"

"Not really. Zero tolerance and all. You know…"

"But that's ridiculous. You made one mistake…" It was then that he realized that he was making a huge and, most likely, erroneous, assumption. He sought to confirm or negate it. "That was the first time, wasn't it?"

"Um…not really."

He had to bear in mind the promise he had made to her not to be so overbearing, and that was the only thing that restrained him from blowing the roof. He steadied himself, and when he was calm again, said patiently, "Don't worry about it. You aren't going anywhere. I'll just call the principal and clear this up, okay?"

"Don't do that!" she said hastily.

"Why not?"

"Cause that was the first thing I said, that you'd call, and she went into this whole speech about how she was tired of absentee guardians and people who weren't even interested enough in their families to handle things personally, and that she wasn't going to let herself get pushed around over the phone."

"That's ludicrous!"

"Well, that's what she *said!*" He could almost see Frankie pout. "Don't blame me for what she said, Evan." Her voice softened. "If you call her, that'll just be the last nail in my coffin. You have to come. Please. Pretty please, Evan. I need you."

His protective instincts overrode his urge to balk at the petty stance taken by Frankie's principal. If a face-to-face encounter was what it required, that was what they would have. "I'll be on the first flight I can catch," he promised softly. "Don't worry about it."

"I knew you'd come through," Frankie crowed.

That made him feel all warm inside.

The best Evan could manage as far as flights were concerned was a series of exhausting hops that took up the rest of that night and most of the following day, but at least his seats were, for the most part, comfortable enough to allow him some sleep. Upon his arrival in San Diego, he immediately drove to the house he had there. For the past few years, he had only used it on his regular business visits to the U.S., whenever he needed to drop in on his factory to chat with his managers and foremen and see how things were going, so the house was normally shut tight. He had an arrangement with a caretaker to ensure that the place was thoroughly cleaned, opened up, and aired once a week, so at least it was not musty.

He lingered just long enough to shower, shave, and change his clothes before setting off to meet Frankie. She'd insisted that she wanted to meet him away from the school, so that he and she could come up with the best strategy for handling her situation. She had therefore suggested Balboa Park, a convenient drive for him and easy enough for her to get to and still make it back to school in time for curfew.

He'd agreed without much fuss. At least this way, he could find out exactly what had happened. He couldn't believe that, less than a month after hugging him goodbye and promising to be more careful in her choices, Frankie was in trouble again. He felt guilty about not having accompanied her back to school, as he usually did, and ensuring that she was settled before returning to France, but in the spirit of their newfound trust in each other, he had acceded to her request to travel alone. He supposed that that wouldn't have helped, anyway.

He sat down in the shadow of the Natural History Museum, enjoying watching people stroll by. The September evening was mild, and people seemed happy simply to be out in the open air. Uncharacteristically, Frankie was less than ten minutes late. She threw herself at him with her usual aplomb, peppering him with kisses, and then sat next to him, beaming. "You came!"

"Did you think I wouldn't?"

"No, I knew you would. Are you okay?"

"A little travel-worn, but fine, otherwise. More importantly, how are you?" He surveyed her critically, trying to assess her emotional state. For someone in a serious crisis, she seemed to be holding up remarkably well.

"Great."

"Glad to hear that." He wondered how to approach the subject at hand without coming across as parental. He decided it would be better to just allow her to bring it up herself. This turned out to be an unwise decision: Frankie proceeded to prattle on about a series of irrelevancies, and all the while her eyes darted around them, looking for what, he couldn't imagine. Eventually, after fifteen minutes had dragged on, he interrupted. "Aren't you going to tell me what happened?"

She looked momentarily blank. "With what?"

"With the alcohol and the fake ID? With your principal?"

"Oh, that."

He felt his lips twitch. "That."

"In a minute. I'm waiting."

He frowned, puzzled. "Waiting on what?"

"Oh, just waiting...." she answered vaguely, not even looking at him.

He drew on his patience and cooled his heels, forbidding himself to become irritated, until, several minutes later, Frankie leaped up onto the bench and waved her arms frantically in the air, yelling, "Over here! Over here!"

Who was she yelling at? He turned in the direction of her gaze—and his heart stopped beating. Rissa was hurrying across the tiled walkway, the same knapsack over her shoulder that she had held on the day she had walked out of his life. He did a cartoonish double take, his brain unable to process the information that was unexpectedly being thrown at it. What the hell was going on?

When Rissa drew near, her expression was as confused as

his. "What's happening?" she puffed as she let her bag fall at her feet. "What are you doing here?"

"What are *you* doing here?" he countered.

Rissa fought to recover her breath. "I thought…Frankie called…she said she was…." She stopped.

The stink of rat filled Evan's nostrils, as, evidently, it did Rissa's. They turned to Frankie and demanded, of one accord, *"Frankie?"*

Frankie's triumphant grin split her face, she laughed out loud, looking like a mischievous gremlin. "You should see the look on your faces! Priceless!"

Evan's control was beginning to slip. "Come on, Frankie, what's this about?"

"What do you think it's about? You think it was easy, those last few weeks in Perpignan, having to watch you mope around and sigh and carry on like your life was over? And you, Rissa, for a writer, you write the most depressing e-mails. You sound like a lonely old lady locked away in an attic. It's a wonder you haven't filled your place with cats."

"So?"

"So I think it's high time you two got together and sorted out this mess. You were acting like children, and it was really getting on my nerves. So if I have to be the only grown-up here, and put an end to this stupid standoff, so be it."

"So you made us both come out here?" Rissa asked, aghast.

"Yep."

"What about your situation at school?"

"Fake ID? Buying booze? What, do you think I'm *stupid?* There's no situation at school." She laughed again. "I should almost be offended at how fast you both fell for it!"

Rissa slapped her forehead. "You *lied?*"

"If that's what you want to call it."

"Why?" Evan asked.

"Cause you were taking too long to shake off your funk and come see her yourself. And I got tired of waiting on you to come to your senses, because if you don't see that you need to go after her before you lose her, then you're a big dummy. And you," Frankie pointed an accusing forefinger directly in Rissa's face, "If you think my brother doesn't love you, just because he's too chicken to say it, then you're a bigger dummy than he is. And if you don't do something about it right now, then you both deserve to be miserable."

Having said her piece, she became businesslike, picking up her bag and throwing it over her shoulder. "Anyhow, folks, hate to be leaving you, but I have to get back to school before curfew." Blithely ignoring their stunned faces, she spun around and sauntered jauntily off, leaving a flabbergasted silence in her wake.

When they could no longer see her, Evan sat back down, shaking his head. He didn't know whether to laugh or be thoroughly ticked off. "We were conned," he said finally.

She sat beside him and rubbed her forehead. "Looks like it."

"What'd she tell you?"

"She called me up yesterday and gave me a whole story about getting caught buying alcohol with fake ID."

"Me, too."

"Only she begged me to come out here and sort things out with her principal, because she was afraid of what you'd say if you found out. She said she didn't want to disappoint you, now that the two of you were getting along so well." Then she added dryly, "Looks to me like you should have heeded your own advice."

"What advice?"

"That your sister can be slippery."

The lengths his sister would go to to get her way! He couldn't stop himself from smiling. "Sure looks like it."

Now that that topic had been exhausted, he wondered what he should say next. His head was swimming just from the intoxicating effect of sheer proximity to her, after such a long separation. He stole a sidelong glance at her, taking in the pulled-back hair and make-up free face that made her look almost as young as Frankie. As he examined her, he noticed with a start that *she* was stealing sidelong glances at *him*. That made his entire body flush hot.

What did he say next? His sister had been embarrassingly frank, revealing to Rissa in no uncertain terms that her disappearance had all but gutted him. What interested him all the more was her observation that through her correspondence with Frankie, Rissa, too, had shown that she still missed him. That was a good thing, right?

What should he say? "So, how are you doing?" *Lame, lame.*

"I'm okay." Her response was equally subdued, but she lightened it with a joke. "Haven't started collecting those cats, if that's what you're asking."

He smiled, encouraged by her levity. "And the book?"

"Looks good. I've already gotten two offers. Just waiting to see if anyone else bites, and then I'll make a decision on which way to go."

"Glad to hear that." This was stupid. He was acting like a sixteen-year-old on a first date, not a grown man who had just had a woman walk out of his life, only to discover too late that he loved her. He thought of all the trials he had faced in his life and career, the loss of his parents, growing his business in a competitive field. How had he survived them? By being a man. By seizing control.

That was it: he'd had enough of this nonsense.

He swiveled on the bench so that he could face her. "What was all that about, Rissa?"

She pretended not to understand. "What was what all about?"

"You know exactly what I mean. Walking away from me like that, without any warning. When I thought we were getting somewhere."

She didn't try to fake her way out of it any further. "That was the problem—we weren't getting anywhere. We'd gone as far as we could go."

"Said who?"

"Said you."

"Me?" He was truly perplexed.

"All that talk about you and your storehouse full of junk. Telling me why you would never have any room for me, even if you wanted to."

"Is that what you heard?" he asked softly.

"That's what you *said.*" The shape of her mouth told him that she was far from happy with the memory.

"That's half of what I said," he reminded her. "We were interrupted by Corbin's message, remember? We got up, and rushed over to the park. I didn't get a chance to finish the thought."

Her eyes took on a faraway look as she recalled the event. "You didn't finish the thought?"

"No."

She focused on him again, and her mouth was softer, almost tremulous. "If you had finished it, what would you have said?"

"I'd have explained that it wasn't that there would *never* be any room for you, but that what I needed was time to clear out the space you deserve."

"You were trying to do that?"

"I was, as hard as I could. What I told you about Jeanine that night, and what she did to me, was part of the process. I woke up the next morning feeling that my mind was so clear, finally, after so many years...and then you were gone."

."But she'd done so much to you. Things had been so bad between you, I thought you'd never... Besides, Frankie said you were still in love with her, and that you still wanted her back."

He found the courage to take her hand. She didn't resist. "There are things Frankie knows. For example, she was smart enough to dupe us both into facing each other again, because she knew we probably wouldn't have had the guts to do it on our own. But there are things she can't know, and the details of my marriage are at the top of that list. What I felt for Jeanine died a long time ago, largely at her hands. What has been weighing me down since, what Frankie probably sensed, was hurt and anger and betrayal and fear, but not love. Certainly not love. I don't pine for her. I don't want her back. That's over. The only person I want right now is you."

He watched the emotions pass across her face as she processed that information. He hoped desperately that she believed him. She thought hard, and then asked, "But what about the baby?"

The question threw him, as he had been sure that she had understood exactly how that entire debacle had ended. "There never was a baby, remember?"

"I know that. I meant the baby you've always wanted so badly. You talk about fatherhood all the time."

"I want to be a father, yes."

She pulled her hand away from his grip and waved to emphasize her point. "See? That's what I mean. Even if you think you..." she seemed almost embarrassed to say the next word "...love me—"

"I don't think, I know." He was confident in his assertion. It felt good to have it out in the open.

She halted in what she was about to say, her wide, dark eyes fixed on his. Her mouth moved convulsively, and he half expected her to give in right there. But she persevered, squeezing her eyes closed as though shutting him out would help her be strong. "Evan if you…do, it wouldn't work. Because of the baby."

He was trying hard to understand, but frustration made his answer sharp. "*What* baby?"

"The one I can't have!" She got to her feet and began walking away from him, moving fast, forgetting her bag, her arms wrapped around her chest.

If there were a prize for clumsiness, insensitivity, and sheer stupidity, he certainly would have copped it hands down. That was it! That was the missing piece of the puzzle. How could he not have figured that out? He felt like a complete moron. He snatched up her bag and chased after her, catching up with no effort at all. "Rissa, stop! Stop!"

"Why? Why bother? There's no solution to that little problem, so what's the use? We could get back together, have a nice time, drink wine, share a few laughs, and have *really* great sex…." At that, a few passersby turned to throw them amused grins, but he didn't care. Neither, evidently, did she, as she went on just as loudly, "But sooner or later, it will boil down to that. Sooner or later, months from now, or even a year from now if I'm lucky, you'll start to get restless, and that old hankering for a family will raise its head again. And you know what? You'll be plumb out of luck, because I…can't…help…you!"

He tried to pull her into his arms to quell her agitated pacing, but failed. "Darling, wait…listen."

"Listen to what? There's no cure for what's wrong with me, at least nothing science has come up with yet. I'm damaged goods, and what's missing will be missing forever. There are no miracles waiting in store for me."

"Love is a miracle of its own," he murmured.

She faltered, but not for long. She came back at him with:

"It still can't win out over the biological imperative. The need to procreate."

"Normally, those two go hand in hand," he said reasonably.

Her response was filled with bitterness and anguish. "Not in our case."

"More than one way to skin a cat," he said cryptically.

"What the heck's that supposed to mean?" She was suspicious, but at least she was almost out of steam, and had stopped darting about like a runaway pinball.

Even as the idea took shape in his mind, he was speaking it. "Think of all the babies right here in the States, stuck in institutions, just waiting for someone to come along and love them. I've heard that Black babies are among the hardest to place...."

"What are you...?"

He pushed on ahead, anxious to finish airing his idea before she had the chance to shoot it down. "For that matter, think of the hundreds of thousands of babies all across the most war-torn parts of Africa, who have nothing to look forward to except suffering, unless someone intervenes. Someone who has both the means and the desire to offer them more."

"You're making fun of me," she faltered.

"Why would I do a thing like that? Why would I joke about something so important to both of us? We could start off easy, with one, and then, over the next few years, wind up with a whole brood...."

"Stop it, Evan, that's cruel and you know it!"

"Cruel?" he repeated, perplexed. He was doing his damnedest to find a solution to their problem, one they both could live with, and she was accusing him of being *cruel?*

"I haven't forgotten what you said about all you wanted to pass on to the son you want to have...."

"Knowledge can be passed on to an adopted child as easily

as to a biological child. I'll teach him to sail, you can teach him to write…."

"I wasn't talking about knowledge. I remember how you talked about passing on your parents' genes…."

She had him there. "I know. I remember. That was selfish and arrogant of me, and I neglected to consider the obvious—Frankie has as much of that DNA as I have, and I'm quite sure she'll eventually pass it forward. Hopefully not *soon*," he laughed a little, "but eventually the Maynard family tree will branch out again. It doesn't have to be through me. And I think I'd make a fine uncle." He took a deep breath and held it, waiting for some sign from her that she was understanding what he was saying and, more importantly, warming to his proposition. She had to. His sanity depended on it.

"You'd do that for me?" She was still dubious, still skeptical.

"In a heartbeat." He was as surprised as she was at that assertion. Adoption had never, not once, crossed his mind; he was sure it was something that few healthy males even contemplated. But what was more important? To lay down his own markers in the human gene pool with God alone knew who, or to find what happiness he could with the woman he loved? The decision was an easy one.

"Give up the chance to have children of your own?"

"We're going to have children, lots of them. Just not any that carry our genetic code. But on the scale of everything, when you look at what a wonderful complex creature a child is, that's such an insignificant thing."

"You can say that now, but you'll hate me, eventually, when all the fairy dust you've sprinkled on your idea starts to fade."

"Hate you? That's impossible."

"Why?" Something in her eyes begged him to give the right answer. It was as though she was putting up every obstacle she could think of, but badly needing him to shoot each one down, for her. He had the terrifying feeling that whatever he said next would make or break his case.

His answer came easily, because it was the truth. "Because I love you. I love you now, and I'll love you years from now, when the house is all trashed and grimy and dirty because of our kids. *Our kids,* Rissa. They'll be ours for the best reason of all—because we want them. I just want you to want this as much as I do. The whole package—me, and everything that comes with me. A bunch of squalling brats, an incorrigible kid sister, and a boring lifestyle out in the sticks."

She looked down at the paved walkway beneath their feet, and tiny pearl tears clung to the tips of her lashes. "You aren't boring, Evan. You're…wonderful." She put her hands up to cover her mouth, and her shoulders shook.

This was terrible. The last thing he had meant to do was make her cry! He pressed her against him, and she came willingly. "Sweetheart…please, I'm sorry. Don't cry. I can't stand it."

"I'm not crying," she denied, in the face of all evidence to the contrary.

"When you're done not crying, could you let me know where I stand?"

She took in great gulps of air, and between sobs, tried to say, "The package…sounds…good."

"Does it?" He asked softly, not wanting to whoop in delight in case it scared her.

"Best offer…I've had…all…day."

He had to tilt his head sideways to look at her face. Her tear-streaked smile was like the sun peeking out from behind a gray cloud. "Is it?"

"Uh-huh." The smile broadened, and she managed to take her hands away, leaving her mouth invitingly available.

"And…?"

"And I'm inclined to accept, although maybe…"

"Maybe…?"

"Maybe I should run it by my advisor and see what she has to say about it."

"Your *what?*"

"Frankie."

"Oh, her." He took his teasing gracefully. "I think she'd already said more than her piece. She's a wise one, all right." He let his lips run lightly across hers. "But I think I'll restrict the presence at the negotiating table to just you and me." Exhilaration filled him. He put his arms around her, holding her so close he could feel the reverberation of his own heartbeat against her breasts. She wanted him back! *She wanted him back!*

She squeezed him in return, holding him as tightly as he was holding her, pressing her face against his shirt and letting the tears soak into the fabric. She kissed his chest, sending tiny electric darts tingling through his skin. "Doesn't have to be a table," she pointed out. Her voice was muffled, but light and full of unexpected humor.

He had an inkling as to where she was going with this, but he had to make sure. "What's the alternative?" he asked cautiously.

"I was thinking of a larger, more comfortable piece of furniture. Didn't you say you've got a house nearby?"

"I do."

"How long would it take you to me get there, d'you think?"

"Twenty minutes, maybe—if I don't get pulled over for speeding."

She was beaming at him now, and all he wanted to do was kiss her over and over until she hollered for him to stop. She put her arms up around his neck, her whole face full of love, relief, hope—and a sweet, sexy desire that made a hunger inside him shake itself awake like a sleeping wolf. "You planning on speeding?" Her question was a challenge, a dare, and a plea.

His answer was fervent. "You bet."

KIMANI
ROMANCE

Bestselling author Brenda Jackson introduces the Steele Brothers in a brand-new three-book miniseries

Solid Soul

by Brenda Jackson

COMING IN JULY 2006
FROM KIMANI™ ROMANCE

Love's Ultimate Destination